GRISLY MURDERS,
PEOPLE THAT AREN'T PEOPLE,
THE INSANE, THE MUTILATED,
THE WALKING DEAD . . .

All the deliciously horrifying elements that night-mares are made of.

Nebula award—winning editor Charles L. Grant has assembled a bloodcurdling book—evil offer-ings by some of the most renowned writers of horror: Stephen King, Ray Russell, Chelsea Quinn Yarbro, Ramsey Campbell, Richard Christian Matheson, and many more.

Most of the stories were written especially for this macabre volume. Read them cautiously, and try not to have . . .

NIGHTMARES

EDITED BY
CHARLES L. GRANT

PLAYBOY
PAPERBACKS

Published simultaneously in the United States and Canada by Playboy Paperbacks, New York, New York. Printed in the United States of America. Library of Congress Catalog Card Number: 79-83966.

Books are available at quantity discounts for promotional and industrial use. For further information, write to Premium Sales, Playboy Paperbacks, 747 Third Avenue, New York, New York 10017.

ISBN: 0-872-16868-9

First printing September 1979.
Third printing December 1980.

ACKNOWLEDGMENTS

The editor wishes to thank the following people for their invaluable and most welcome assistance in the production of this volume: Sharon Jarvis, who came to me for this book, bless her evil little heart; Kay McCauley, for introducing me to the works of Chetwynd-Hayes; and Pete and Andrea Pautz, for nagging and for loving a good nightmare just as much as I.

CONTENTS

8 CONTENTS

INTRODUCTION

Analyses of the whys and wherefores of horror stories have been stalking writers and readers of the genre virtually since its inception. With the formal development of psychology, scholars and amateurs were able to unearth even more reasons why we who wrote such material like to write it and we who read such things like to read them. A great many of these studies are reasonable, are logical, and certainly contain truths that abound with indisputable merit.

Unfortunately, they also take away much of the undeniable *fun* in writing and reading horror stories.

And it *is* fun, on both sides of the typewriter.

There is a certain delightfully chilling anticipation when we sit down to read a new tale or take up an old one that has proved itself to us over the years. And I think it is not unlike those blustery winter nights when we were children, when we burrowed under the blankets in a dark room awash with shifting moonlight, knowing full well there was really nothing out there in the corner, over there by the bureau, yet allowing our imaginations to *create something there nevertheless;* or when we sat in the movie theater on Saturday afternoons and, despite the popcorn and candy box throwing, let ourselves be taken by the likes of John Carradine and Lon Chaney, Jr., and Boris Karloff and Lionel Atwill and George Zucco; or when we were brazen enough to walk an empty autumn street . . . at night . . . alone . . . not quite ignoring the sounds that drifted toward us from alleys and gutters and from beneath the porch of that old Victorian, over there on the corner.

We frightened ourselves.

We had nightmares.

And when it was all done, we looked back on it and *we loved it!*

And we went back for more.

It . . . was . . . fun.

Nightmares, then, is a journey. It is a return to those midnights we feared and were drawn to. It is a volume not to be taken at a single sitting, like some monstrous Thanksgiving dinner, nor will every piece within appeal to every taste. There are supernatural horror tales, grisly ones, those that appear to be humorous until one thinks on them, loud ones, quiet ones, a few familiar faces, and many that are not.

Slightly more than half the stories you will read have been written especially for this volume; those that have been seen in other publications were chosen not only for their literary merit but also for their relatively low profiles.

Make yourselves comfortable, then, put the kids to bed, stick the phone under a cushion, and remember what it was like when frightened meant fun.

> Charles L. Grant
> Budd Lake, New Jersey
> 1978

Stephen King—with Carrie, Salem's Lot, *and* The Shining *(which is now being made into a film starring Jack Nicholson)—has thrust himself into the forefront of modern-day spinners of the horror tale. There are few who are able to tell a story as well as he; and while he generally looks upon children as sympathetic or even heroic characters, there are always those exceptions that provide us with nightmares.*

SUFFER THE LITTLE CHILDREN
by Stephen King

Miss Sidley was her name, and teaching was her game.

She was a small woman who had to reach on tiptoes to write on the highest level of the blackboard, which she was doing now. Behind her, none of the children giggled or whispered or munched on secret sweets held in cupped hands. They knew Miss Sidley too well. Miss Sidley knew instinctively who was chewing gum at the back of the room, who had a beanshooter in his pocket, who wanted to go to the bathroom to trade baseball cards rather than use the facilities. Like God, she seemed to know everything all at once.

She was graying, and the brace she wore to support her failing back was lined clearly against her print dress. Small, constantly suffering, gimlet-eyed woman. But they feared her. Her tongue was a school-yard legend. The eyes, when turned on a giggler or a whisperer, could turn the stoutest knees to water.

Now, writing the day's list of spelling words on the slate, she reflected that the success of her long teaching career could be summed and checked and proven by this one

11

everyday action. She could turn her back on her pupils in confidence.

"Vacation," she said, pronouncing the word as she wrote it in her firm, no-nonsense script. "Edward, you will please use the word *vacation* in a sentence."

"I went on a vacation to New York City," Edward piped. Then, as Miss Sidley had taught, he repeated the word carefully. "Vay-cay-shun."

"Very good, Edward." She began on the next word.

She had her little tricks, of course; success, she firmly believed, depended as much upon taking note of little things as it did upon the big ones. She applied the principle constantly in the classroom, and it never failed.

"Jane," she said quietly.

Jane, who had been furtively perusing her Reader, looked up guiltily.

"Close that book right now, please." The book shut; Jane looked with pale, hating eyes at Miss Sidley's back. "And you will stay for fifteen minutes after the final bell."

Jane's lips trembled. "Yes, Miss Sidley."

One of her little tricks was the careful use of her glasses. The whole class was reflected to her in their thick lenses and she had always been thinly amused by their guilty, frightened faces when she caught them at their nasty little games.

Now she saw a phantomish, distorted Robert in the first row wrinkle his nose. She did not speak. Robert would hang himself if given just a little more rope.

"Tomorrow," she pronounced clearly. "Robert, you will please use the word tomorrow in a sentence." Robert frowned over the problem. The classroom was hushed and sleepy in the late September sun. The electric clock over the door buzzed a rumor of three o'clock dismissal just a half-hour away and the only thing that kept young heads from drowsing over their spellers was the silent, ominous threat of Miss Sidley's back.

"I am waiting, Robert."

"Tomorrow a bad thing will happen," Robert said. The words were perfectly innocuous, but Miss Sidley, with the seventh sense that all strict disciplinarians have, could sense a double meaning.

"Too-mor-row," Robert finished. His hands were folded

neatly on the desk, and he wrinkled his nose again. He also smiled a tiny side-of-the-mouth smile. Miss Sidley was suddenly unaccountably sure Robert knew her little trick with the glasses.

Very well.

She began to write the next word with no comment of commendation for Robert, letting her straight body speak its own message. She watched carefully with one eye. Soon Robert would stick out his tongue or make that disgusting finger gesture, just to see if she really knew what he was doing. Then he would be punished.

The reflection was small, ghostly, and distorted. And she had all but the barest corner of her eye on the word she was writing.

Robert changed.

She caught just a corner of it, just a frightening glimpse of Robert's face changing into something . . . different.

She whirled around, face white, barely noticing the protesting stab of pain in her back.

Robert looked at her blandly, questioningly. His hands were neatly folded. The first signs of an afternoon cowlick showed at the back of his head. He did not look frightened.

I have imagined it, she thought. I was looking for something, and when there was nothing, I just made something up. However—

"Robert?" she asked. She had meant to be authoritative; the unspoken demand for confession. It did not come out that way.

"Yes, Miss Sidley?" His eyes were a very dark brown, like the mud at the bottom of a slow-running stream.

"Nothing."

She turned back to the board and a little whisper ran through the class.

"Be *quiet!*" her voice snapped. She turned again and faced them. "Another sound and we will all stay after school with Jane!" She addressed the whole class, but looked particularly at Robert. He looked back with childlike I-didn't-do-it innocence.

She turned to the board and began to write, not looking out of the corners of her glasses. The last half-hour dragged, and it seemed that Robert gave her a strange look on the way out. A look that said, *we have a secret, don't we?*

It wouldn't get out of her mind.

It seemed to be stuck like a tiny string of roast beef between two molars, a small thing, actually, but feeling as big as a cinderblock.

She sat down to her solitary dinner at five, poached eggs on toast, still thinking about it. She knew she was getting older and accepted the knowledge calmly. She was not going to be one of those old lady schoolteachers dragged kicking and screaming from their classrooms at the age of retirement. They reminded her of gamblers emotionally unable to leave the tables while they were losing. But *she* was not losing. She had always been a winner.

She looked down at her poached egg.

Hadn't she?

She thought of the well-scrubbed faces in her third grade classroom, and found Robert's face superimposed over them.

She got up and switched on a light.

Later, just before dropping off to sleep, Robert's face floated in front of her, smiling unpleasantly in the darkness behind her lids. The face began to change—

But before she saw exactly what it was changing into, she dropped off to sleep.

Miss Sidley spent an unrestful night and the next day her temper was short. She waited, almost hoped for a whisperer, a giggler, or perhaps even a note-passer. But the class was quiet—very quiet. They all stared at her unresponsively, and it seemed that she could feel the weight of their eyes on her like blind, crawling ants.

Now stop! she told herself sternly. She paused, controlling an urge to bite her lip. She was acting like a skittish girl just out of Seminary.

Again the day seemed to drag, and she believed she was more relieved than her charges when the dismissal bell rang. The children lined up in orderly rows at the door, boys and girls by height, hands dutifully linked.

"Dismissed," she said, and listened sourly as they shrieked down the hall and into the bright sunlight.

What was it? It was bulbous. It shimmered and it changed and it stared at me, yes, stared and grinned and

it wasn't a child at all. It was old and it was evil and—
"Miss Sidley?"

Her head jerked up; a little *oh!* hiccupped involuntarily from her throat.

It was Mr. Hanning. He smiled apologetically. "Didn't mean to disturb you."

"Quite all right," she said, more curtly than she had intended. What had she been thinking? What was wrong with her?

"Would you mind checking the paper towels in the girls' lavatory?"

"Surely." She got up, placing her hands against the small of her back.

Mr. Hanning looked at her sympathetically. Save it, she thought. The old maid is not amused. Or even interested.

She brushed by Mr. Hanning and started down the hall to the girls' lavatory. A capering group of small boys, carrying scratched and pitted baseball equipment, grew silent at the sight of her and leaked out the door, where their cries began again.

Miss Sidley looked after them resentfully, reflecting that children had been different in her day. Not more polite—children have never had time for that—and not exactly more respectful of their elders; it was a kind of hypocrisy that had never been there before. A smiling quietness around adults that had never been there before. A kind of quiet contempt that was upsetting and unnerving. As if they were . . .

Hiding behind masks.

She pushed the thought away and went into the lavatory.

It was a small, tiled room with frosted glass windows, shaped like an L. The toilets were ranged along one bar, the sinks along both sides of the shorter bar.

As she checked along the paper towel containers, she caught a glimpse of her face in one of the mirrors and was startled into looking at it closely.

God.

There was a look that hadn't been there two days before, a frightened, watching look. With sudden shock she realized that the tiny, blurred reflection in her glasses coupled with Robert's pale, respectful face had gotten inside her and was festering.

The door opened and she heard two girls come in, giggling secretly about something. She was about to turn the corner and walk out past them when she heard her own name. She turned back to the washbowls and began checking the towel holders again.

"And then he—"

Soft giggles.

"She knows, but—"

More giggles, soft and sticky as melting soap.

"Miss Sidley is—"

Stop it! Stop that noise!

By moving slightly she could see their shadows, made fuzzy and ill-defined by the diffuse light filtering through the frosted windows, holding onto each other with girlish glee.

Another thought crawled up out of her mind.

They knew she was there.

Yes, they did, the little bitches. They knew.

She would shake them. Shake them until their teeth rattled and their giggles turned to wails and she would make them admit that they knew, they knew, they—

The shadows changed.

They seemed to elongate, to flow like dripping tallow, taking on strange, hunched shapes that made Miss Sidley cringe back against the porcelain washstands, her heart swelling in her chest.

But they went on giggling.

The voices changed, no longer girlish, now sexless and soulless, and quite, quite evil. A slow, turgid sound of mindless humor that flowed around the corner to her like river mud.

She stared at the hunched shadows and suddenly screamed at them. The scream went on and on, swelling in her head until it attained a pitch of lunacy. And then she fainted. The giggling, like the laughter of demons, followed her down into darkness.

She could not, of course, tell them the truth.

Miss Sidley knew this even as she opened her eyes and looked up at the anxious faces of Mr. Hanning and Mrs. Crossen. Mrs. Crossen was holding a bottle of sharp-smelling stuff under her nose. Mr. Hanning turned around and told the two little girls who were looking curiously at Miss Sidley to go on home now, please.

They both smiled at her, slow, we-have-a-secret smiles, and went out.

Very well. She would keep their secret. For a while. She would not have people thinking her insane. She would not have them thinking that the first feelers of senility had touched her early. She would play their game. Until she could expose their nastiness and rip it out. By the roots.

"I'm afraid I slipped," she said calmly, sitting up and ignoring the excruciating pain in her back. "A patch of wetness."

"This is awful," Mr. Hanning said. "Terrible. Are you—"

"Did the fall hurt your back, Emily?" Mrs. Crossen interrupted. Mr. Hanning looked at her gratefully.

Miss Sidley got up, her spine screaming in her body.

"No," she said. "In fact, something seems to have snapped back into place. It actually feels better."

"We can send for a—" Mr. Hanning began.

"No physician necessary. I'll just go on home." Miss Sidley smiled at him coolly.

"I'll get you a taxi."

"I always take the bus," Miss Sidley said. She walked out.

Mr. Hanning sighed and looked at Mrs. Crossen. "She *does* seem more like herself—"

The next day Miss Sidley kept Robert after school. He did nothing, so she simply accused him falsely. She felt no qualms; he was a monster, not a little boy. And she would make him admit it.

Her back was in agony. She realized Robert knew; he expected that would help him. But it wouldn't. That was another of her little advantages. Her back had been a constant pain to her for the last twelve years, and there had been times when it had been this bad—well, almost as bad —as this.

She closed the door, shutting the two of them in.

For a moment she stood still, training her gaze on Robert. She waited for him to drop his eyes. He didn't. He gazed- back at her, and presently a little smile began to play around the corners of his mouth.

"Why are you smiling, Robert?" she asked softly.

"I don't know." Robert went on smiling.

"Tell me, please, Robert."

Robert said nothing. He went on smiling.

The outside sounds of children at play were far off, distant, dreamy. Only the hypnotic buzz of the wall clock was real.

"There's quite a few of us," Robert said suddenly, as if he were commenting on the weather.

It was Miss Sidley's turn to be silent.

"Eleven right here in this school." Robert went on smiling his small smile.

Quite evil, she thought, amazed. Very, incredibly evil.

"Please don't lie," she said clearly. "Lies only make things worse."

Robert's smile grew wider; it became vulpine. "Do you want to see me change, Miss Sidley?" he asked. "Would you like to see it right out?"

Miss Sidley felt a nameless chill. "Go away," she said curtly. "And bring your mother and father to school with you tomorrow. We'll get this business straightened out." There. On solid ground again. She waited for his face to crumble, waited for the tears and the pleas to relent.

Robert's smile grew wider. He showed his teeth. "It will be just like Show and Tell, won't it, Miss Sidley? Robert— the *other* Robert—he liked Show and Tell. He's still hiding 'way, 'way down in my head." The smile curled at the corners of his mouth like charring paper. "Sometimes he runs around . . . it itches. He wants me to let him out."

"Go away," Miss Sidley said numbly. The buzzing of the clock seemed very loud.

Robert changed.

His face suddenly ran together like melting wax, the eyes flattening and spreading like knife-struck egg yolks, nose widening and yawning, mouth disappearing. The head elongated, and the hair was suddenly not hair but straggling, twitching growths.

Robert began to chuckle.

The slow, cavernous sound came from what had been his nose, but the nose was eating into the lower half of his face, nostrils meeting and merging into a central blackness like a huge, shouting mouth.

Robert got up, still chuckling, and behind it all she could see the last shattered remains of the other Robert, howling in maniac terror, screeching to be let out.

She ran.

She fled screaming down the corridor, and the few late-leaving pupils turned to look at her with large and uncomprehending eyes.

Mr. Hanning jerked open his door and looked out just as Miss Sidley plunged through the wide glass front doors, a wild, waving scarecrow silhouetted against the bright September sky.

He ran after her, Adam's apple bobbing convulsively. "Miss Sidley! *Miss Sidley!*"

Robert came out of the classroom and watched curiously.

Miss Sidley neither heard nor saw. She clattered down the walk and across the sidewalk and into the street with her screams trailing behind her like banners. There was a huge, blatting horn and then the bus was looming over her, the bus driver's face a plaster mask of fear. Air brakes whined and hissed like dragons in flight.

Miss Sidley fell, and the huge wheels shuddered to a smoking stop just eight inches from her frail, brace-armored body. She lay shuddering on the pavement, hearing the crowd gather around her.

She turned over and the children were staring down at her. They were ringed in a tight little circle, like mourners around an open grave. And at the head of the grave was Robert, his little face sober and solemn, ready to read the death rites and shovel the first spade of dirt over her face.

From far away, the bus driver's shaken babble: ". . . crazy or somethin' . . . my God, another half a foot . . ."

Miss Sidley stared numbly at the children. Their shadows covered her and blocked out the sun. Their faces were impassive. Some of them were smiling little secret smiles, and Miss Sidley knew that soon she would begin to scream again.

Then Mr. Hanning broke their tight noose and shooed them away.

Miss Sidley began to sob weakly.

She did not go back to her third grade for a month. She told Mr. Hanning calmly that she had not been feeling herself, and Mr. Hanning suggested that she go to a reputable, ah, doctor, and discuss the matter with him. Miss Sidley agreed that this was the only sensible and rational course. She also said that if the school board wished her resignation she would tender it immediately, although it would hurt her very much. Mr. Hanning, looking uncomfortable, said he doubted if that would be necessary.

The upshot of the matter was that Miss Sidley went back to her class in late October, once again ready to play the game and now knowing how to play it.

For the first week she let things go on as ever. It seemed the whole class now regarded her with hostile, shielded eyes. Robert smiled distantly at her from his first-row seat, and she did not have the courage to take him to task.

Once, while on playground duty, Robert walked over to her, holding a dodgem ball, smiling. "There's more of us now," he said. "Lots, lots more." A girl on the jungle gym looked across the playground at them and smiled, as if she had heard.

Miss Sidley smiled serenely, refusing to remember the face changing, mutating: "Why, Robert, whatever do you mean?"

But Robert only continued smiling and went back to his game. Miss Sidley knew the time had come.

She brought the gun to school in her handbag.

It had been her brother Jim's. He had taken it from a dead German shortly after the Battle of the Bulge. Jim had been gone ten years now. She had not opened the box that held the gun in more years than that, but when she did it was still there, gleaming dully. The four clips of shells were still in the box, too, and she loaded carefully the way Jim had showed her once.,

She smiled pleasantly at her class; at Robert in particular. Robert smiled back and she could see the murky alienness swimming just below his skin, muddy, full of filth.

She never cared wondering just what was impersonating Robert, but she wished she knew if the real Robert was still inside. She did not wish to be a murderess. She decided that the real Robert must have died or gone insane, living inside the dirty, crawling thing that had chuckled at her in the classroom and sent her screaming into the street. So even if he was still alive, putting him out of his misery would be a mercy.

"Today we're going to have a Test," Miss Sidley said.

The class did not groan or shift apprehensively; they merely looked at her. She could feel their eyes, like weights. Heavy, smothering.

"It's a very special Test. I will call you down to the mimeographing room one by one and give you your Test. Then you may have a candy and go home for the day. Won't that be nice?"

They smiled empty smiles and said nothing.

"Robert, will you come first?"

Robert got up, smiling his little smile. He wrinkled his nose quite openly at her. "Yes, Miss Sidley."

Miss Sidley took her bag and they went down the empty, echoing corridor together, past the sleepy buzz of reciting classes coming from behind closed doors.

The mimeograph room was at the far end of the hall, past the lavatories. It had been soundproofed two years ago; the big machine was very old and very noisy.

Miss Sidley closed the door behind them and locked it.

"No one can hear you," she said calmly. She took the gun from her bag. "You or the gun."

Robert smiled innocently. "There are lots of us, though. Lots more than here." He put one small scrubbed hand on the paper-tray of the mimeograph machine. "Would you like to see me change, Miss Sidley?"

Before she could speak, the change began. Robert's face began to melt and shimmer into the grotesqueness beneath, and Miss Sidley shot him. Once. In the head.

He fell back against the paper-lined shelves and slid down to the floor, a little dead boy with a round black hole above the right eye.

He looked very pathetic.

Miss Sidley stood over him, breathing hard. Her scrawny cheeks were livid.

The huddled figure didn't move.

It was human.

It was Robert.

No!

It was all in your mind, Emily. All in your mind.

No! No, no, *no!*

She went back up to the room and began to lead them down, one by one. She killed twelve of them and would have killed them all if Mrs. Crossen hadn't come down for a package of composition paper.

Mrs. Crossen's eyes got very big; one hand crept up and clutched her mouth. She began to scream and she was still screaming when Miss Sidley reached her and put a hand on her shoulder. "It had to be done, Margaret," she said sadly to the screaming Mrs. Crossen. "It's terrible, but it had to. They are all monsters. I found out."

Mrs. Crossen stared at the gay-clothed little bodies scattered around the mimeograph and continued to scream.

The little girl whose hand Miss Sidley was holding began to cry steadily and monotonously.

"Change," Miss Sidley said. "Change for Mrs. Crossen. Show her it had to be done."

The girl continued to weep uncomprehendingly.

"Damn you, *change!*" Miss Sidley screamed. "Dirty bitch, dirty, crawling, filthy, unnatural *bitch!* Change! God damn you, *change!*" She raised the gun. The little girl cringed, and then Mrs. Crossen was on her like a cat, and Miss Sidley's back gave way.

No trial.

The papers screamed for a trial, bereaved parents swore hysterical oaths against Miss Sidley, and the city sat back on its haunches in numb shock—

—Twelve children!

The State Legislature called for more stringent teacher examination tests, Summer Street School closed for a week of mourning, and Miss Sidley went quietly to an antiseptic madhouse in the next state. She was put in deep analysis, given the most modern drugs, introduced into daily work-therapy sessions. A year later, under strictly controlled conditions, Miss Sidley was put in an experimental encounter-therapy situation.

Buddy Jenkins was his name, psychiatry was his game.

He sat behind a one-way glass with a clipboard, looking into a room which had been outfitted as a nursery. On the far wall, the cow was jumping over the moon and the mouse was halfway up the clock. Miss Sidley sat in her wheelchair with a story book, surrounded by a group of soft, trusting, totally mindless retarded children. They smiled at her and drooled and touched her with small wet fingers while attendants at the next window watched for the first sign of an aggressive move.

For a time Buddy thought she responded well. She read aloud, stroked a girl's head, picked up a small boy when he fell over a toy block. Then she seemed to see something which disturbed her; a frown creased her brow and she looked away from the children.

"Take me away, please," Miss Sidley said, softly and tonelessly, to no one in particular.

And so they took her away. Buddy Jenkins watched the children watch her go, their eyes wide and empty, but somehow deep. One smiled, and another put his fingers in his mouth slyly. Two little girls clutched each other and giggled.

That night Miss Sidley cut her throat with a bit of broken mirror-glass, and Buddy Jenkins began to watch the children.

*Bill Pronzini, over the past twelve years, has written eigh-
teen novels and over two hundred pieces of shorter fiction. His newest effort, in collaboration with Barry N.
Malzberg, is* Night Screams *(published by Playboy Press).
And when he isn't writing topnotch suspense stories, he
can be counted on to produce some of the most chilling
bits of horror based on the simplest of notions.*

PEEKABOO
by Bill Pronzini

Roper came awake with the feeling that he wasn't alone
in the house.

He sat up in bed, tense and wary, a crawling sensation
on the back of his scalp. The night was dark, moonless;
warm clotted black surrounded him. He rubbed sleep-
mucus from his eyes, blinking, until he could make out
the vague grayish outlines of the open window in one wall,
the curtains fluttering in the hot summer breeze.

Ears straining, he listened. But there wasn't anything to
hear. The house seemed almost graveyard still, void of
even the faintest of night sounds.

What was it that had waked him up? A noise of some
kind? An intuition of danger? It might only have been a
bad dream, except that he couldn't remember dreaming.
And it might only have been imagination, except that the
feeling of not being alone was strong, urgent.

There's somebody in the house, he thought.

Or some *thing* in the house?

In spite of himself Roper remembered the story the nervous real estate agent in Whitehall had told him about
this place. It had been built in the early 1900s by a local

family, and when the last of them died off a generation later it was sold to a man named Lavolle who had lived in it for forty years. Lavolle had been a recluse whom the locals considered strange and probably evil; they hadn't had anything to do with him. But then he'd died five years ago, of natural causes, and evidence had been found by county officials that he'd been "some kind of devil worshiper" who had "practiced all sorts of dark rites." That was all the real estate agent would say about it.

Word had gotten out about that and a lot of people seemed to believe the house was haunted or cursed or something. For that reason, and because it was isolated and in ramshackle condition, it had stayed empty until a couple of years ago. Then a man called Garber, who was an amateur parapsychologist, leased the place and lived here for ten days. At the end of that time somebody came out from Whitehall to deliver groceries and found Garber dead. Murdered. The real estate agent wouldn't talk about how he'd been killed; nobody else would talk about it either.

Some people thought it was ghosts or demons that had murdered Garber. Others figured it was a lunatic—maybe the same one who'd killed half a dozen people in this part of New England over the past couple of years. Roper didn't believe in ghosts or demons or things that went bump in the night; that kind of supernatural stuff was for rural types like the ones in Whitehall. He believed in psychotic killers, all right, but he wasn't afraid of them; he wasn't afraid of anybody or anything. He'd made his living with a gun too long for that. And the way things were for him now, since the bank job in Boston had gone sour two weeks ago, an isolated back-country place like this was just what he needed for a few months.

So he'd leased the house under a fake name, claiming to be a writer, and he'd been here for eight days. Nothing had happened in that time: no ghosts, no demons, no strange lights or wailings or rattling chains—and no lunatics or burglars or visitors of any kind. Nothing at all.

Until now.

Well, if he *wasn't* alone in the house, it was because somebody human had come in. And he sure as hell knew how to deal with a human intruder. He pushed the blankets aside, swung his feet out of bed, and eased open the nightstand drawer. His fingers groped inside, found his .38 revolver and the flashlight he kept in there with it; he took them out. Then he stood, made his way carefully across to the bedroom door, opened it a crack, and listened again.

The same heavy silence.

Roper pulled the door wide, switched on the flash, and probed the hallway with its beam. No one there. He stepped out, moving on the balls of his bare feet. There were four other doors along the hallway: two more bedrooms, a bathroom, and an upstairs sitting room. He opened each of the doors in turn, swept the rooms with the flash, then put on the overhead lights.

Empty, all of them.

He came back to the stairs. Shadows clung to them, filled the wide foyer below. He threw the light down there from the landing. Bare mahogany walls, the lumpish shapes of furniture, more shadows crouching inside the arched entrances to the parlor and the library. But that was all: no sign of anybody, still no sounds anywhere in the warm dark.

He went down the stairs, swinging the light from side to side. At the bottom he stopped next to the newel post and used the beam to slice into the blackness in the center hall. Deserted. He arced it around into the parlor, followed it with his body turned sideways to within a pace of the archway. More furniture, the big fieldstone fireplace at the far wall, the parlor windows reflecting glints of light from the flash. He glanced back at the heavy darkness inside the library, didn't see or hear any movement over that way, and reached out with his gun hand to flick the switch on the wall inside the parlor.

Nothing happened when the electric bulbs in the old-fashioned chandelier came on; there wasn't anybody lurking in there.

Roper turned and crossed to the library arch and scanned the interior with the flash. Empty bookshelves, empty furniture. He put on the chandelier. Empty room.

He swung the cone of light past the staircase, into the center hall—and then brought it back to the stairs and held it there. The area beneath them had been walled on both sides, as it was in a lot of these old houses, to form a coat or storage closet; he'd found that out then he first moved

in and opened the small door that was set into the staircase on this side. But it was just an empty space now, full
of dust—

The back of his scalp tingled again. And a phrase from
when he was a kid playing hide-and-seek games popped
into his mind.

Peekaboo, I see you. Hiding under the stair.

His finger tightened around the butt of the .38. He
padded forward cautiously, stopped in front of the door.
And reached out with the hand holding the flash, turned
the knob, jerked the door opened, and aimed the light and
the gun inside.

Nothing.

Roper let out a breath, backed away to where he could
look down the hall again. The house was still graveyard
quiet; he couldn't even hear the faint grumblings its old
wooden joints usually made in the night. It was as if the
whole place was wrapped in a breathless waiting hush. As
if there was some kind of unnatural presence at work
here—

Screw that, he told himself angrily. No such things as
ghosts and demons. There seemed to be presence here, all
right—he could feel it just as strongly as before—but it
was a human presence. Maybe a burglar, maybe a tramp,
maybe even a goddamn lunatic. But *human.*

He snapped on the hall lights and went along there to
the archway that led into the downstairs sitting room. First
the flash and then the electric wall lamps told him it was
deserted. The dining room off the parlor next. And the
kitchen. And the rear porch.

Still nothing.

Where was he, damn it? Where was he hiding?

The cellar? Roper thought.

It didn't make sense that whoever it was would have
gone down there. The cellar was a huge room, walled and
floored in stone, that ran under most of the house; there
wasn't anything in it except spiderwebs and stains on the
floor that he didn't like to think about, not after the real
estate agent's story about Lavolle and his dark rites. But
it was the only place left that he hadn't searched.

In the kitchen again, Roper crossed to the cellar door.
The know turned soundlessly under his hand. With the

door open a crack, he peered into the thick darkness below and listened. Still the same heavy silence.

He started to reach inside for the light switch. But then he remembered that there wasn't any bulb in the socket above the stairs; he'd explored the cellar by flashlight before, and he hadn't bothered to buy a bulb. He widened the opening and aimed the flash downward, fanning it slowly from left to right and up and down over the stone walls and floor. Shadowy shapes appeared and disappeared in the bobbing light: furnace, storage shelves, a wooden wine rack, the blackish gleaming stains at the far end, spiderwebs like tattered curtains hanging from the ceiling beams.

Roper hesitated. Nobody down there either, he thought. Nobody in the house after all? The feeling that he wasn't alone kept nagging at him—but it *could* be nothing more than imagination. All that business about devil worshiping and ghosts and demons and Garber being murdered and psychotic killers on the loose might have affected him more than he'd figured. Might have jumbled together in his subconscious all week and finally come out tonight, making him imagine menace where there wasn't any. Sure, maybe that was it.

But he had to make certain. He couldn't see all of the cellar from up here; he had to go down and give it a full search before he'd be satisfied that he really was alone. Otherwise he'd never be able to get back to sleep tonight.

Playing the light again, he descended the stairs in the same wary movements as before. The beam showed him nothing. Except for the faint whisper of his breathing, the creak of the risers when he put his weight on them, the stillness remained unbroken. The odors of dust and decaying wood and subterranean dampness dilated his nostrils; he began to breathe through his mouth.

When he came off the last of the steps he took a half-dozen strides into the middle of the cellar. The stones were cold and clammy against the soles of his bare feet. He turned to his right, then let the beam and his body transcribe a slow circle until he was facing the stairs.

Nothing to see, nothing to hear.

But with the light on the staircase, he realized that part of the wide, dusty area beneath them was invisible from where he stood—a mass of clotted shadow. The vertical boards between the risers kept the beam from reaching all the way under there.

The phrase from when he was a kid repeated itself in his mind: *Peekaboo, I see you. Hiding under the stair.*

With the gun and the flash extended at arms' length, he went diagonally to his right. The light cut away some of the thick gloom under the staircase, letting him see naked stone draped with more gray webs. He moved closer to the stairs, ducked under them, and put the beam full on the far joining of the walls.

Empty.

For the first time Roper began to relax. Imagination, no doubt about it now. No ghosts or demons, no burglars or lunatics hiding under the stair. A thin smile curved the corners of his mouth. Hell, the only one hiding under the stair was himself—

"Peekaboo," a voice behind him said . . .

Dennis Etchison, a World Fantasy Award finalist, is generally noted for his excursions into the more peaceful realms of horror fiction, primarily in the excellent semi-annual magazine Whispers. On occasion, however, Dennis creates more than a bit of thunder for his readers. And when he does, the lightning that strikes is anything but gentle.

DAUGHTER OF THE GOLDEN WEST
by Dennis Etchison

At the school were three boys who were best friends. Together they edited the campus newspaper, wrote or appeared in plays from time to time, and often could be seen huddled together over waxed-paper lunches, over microscopes in the biology lab, sometimes until dark, over desks leafed with papers most Saturdays, elbow to elbow with their English Department advisor, and even over the same clusters of girls gathered like small bouquets of poppies on steps of the cafeteria, joking and conning and in general charming their way through the four long years.

Almost four years.

Don and Bob were on the tennis squad, Don and David pasted up the *Buckskin Bugler* feature pages, Bob and David devised satirical skits for the annual Will & Prophecy Class Assemblies, and together they jockeyed for second, third and fourth positions in their graduating class—the first place was held inexplicably by one of those painted-smile, sprayed-hair secretary types (in fact she was Secretary of the Senior Class) named Arnetta Kuhn, and neither separately nor *en masse* could they dislodge, dissuade, distract, deflower or dethrone that irritating young woman from her destiny as Valedictorian, bent as she had been upon her goal since childhood, long before the boys had met, a target fixed in her mind as a stepping-stone to a greater constellation of goals, which included marrying the most promising young executive in Westside Hills, whoever he might happen to be, and furnishing him and a ranch-style home yet to be built on South American Street with four dishwater-haired children and a parturient drawerful of Blue Chip Stamps. And so it went.

Unitl May, that is: the last lap of the home stretch.

Until Bob disappeared.

In the Formica and acetate interior of the mobile home in Westside Hills Court, Don of the thick black hair and high white forehead, lover of Ambrose Bierce and master of the sweeping backhand, and David, the high shool's first longhair, collector of Marvel comics and articles on black holes, commiserated with Mrs. Witherson over sugar-free cola in cans (it was the only kind she had, now that Bob was gone), staring into their thumbnails and speaking softly in tones like a settling of throttled sighs over an as yet unmarked grave. It was a sad thing, surely, it was mysterious as hell, and most of all, each thought secretly, it was unfair, the most unfair thing he could have done.

The trophies, glassed certificates and commendations Bob had earned reflected around Mrs. Witherson, bending the dim, cold light into an aurora behind her drooped, nodding head.

"Maybe he ran off with a—with some kind of woman. The way his father did."

Instantly regretting it, a strange thing to say, really, Mrs. Witherson closed a shaking hand around the water glass and tipped it to her lips. The sherry wavered and clung, then evaporated, glistening, from the sides; she had taken it up again weeks ago, after the disappearance, and now the two were concerned about her as if by proxy. For Bob had told them, of course, of the way she had been for so long after the loss of his father. He had been too small to remember him, but he had remembered the fuming glasses and shaking hands, he had said, and now his friends remembered them, too, though they did not speak of these things or even look up as she drank.

"I thought—" *Bob's father was killed in the war,* David started to say, but stopped, even without Don's quick glance and furtive headshake.

"He had. So much. Going for him." Bob's mother drained the glass, gazing into it, and David saw the tip of her slow, coated tongue lap after the odor on nonexistent droplets along the lip. "You all know that." And it was a larger statement than it sounded, directed beyond the trailer to include and remind them all, whoever needed to be reminded of the essential truth of it, herself, perhaps, among them.

They jumped, all three of them. The telephone clattered with an unnatural, banshee urgency in the closed rectangle of the trailer. The Melmac dishware ceased vibrating on the plastic shelf as Mrs. Witherson picked up the receiver. She took it unwillingly, distastefully, between the circle of thumb and finger.

David pushed away from the unsteady, floor-bolted table and chewed the inside of his mouth, waiting to catch Don's eyes.

"Mm-hm. Ye-es. I see."

It might have been an invitation to a Tupperware party. A neighbor whose TV set was on the blink. A solicitation for the PTA, which could have accounted for the edge in her voice. But it was not; it was not. They both knew it without looking at each other, and were on their feet by the aluminum screen door seconds before Mrs. Witherson, white-faced, dropped the receiver. It swung from the coiled cord, dipping and brushing the chill linoleum floor.

The lieutenant at the police station wrote out the address of the county morgue and phoned ahead for them. They drove in silence, pretending absorption in traffic lights. It was really not like the movies. An official in a wrinkled white smock showed them 8×10's and there was not much talk, only a lot of nods and carefully avoided eyes and papers to be signed. Don stepped into a locked room and returned so quickly that he must have turned on his heel the instant the sheet was lifted. During that brief moment and through the miles of neon interstices after David did not think of the photographs.

What was left of Bob had been found by a roadside somewhere far out of town.

And it was "just like the other two," the attendant said.

They drove and did not stop when they were back in Westside. Don took corner after corner, lacing the town in smaller and smaller squares until each knew in his own time that there was nowhere to go and nothing to be said. David was aware of the clicking of the turn indicator and the faint green flickering of the light behind the dashboard. Until he heard the hand brake grind up. The motor still running. Without a word he got out and into his own car and they drove off in different directions.

David could not face his room. He hovered through the empty streets around his house for half an hour before his hands took over the wheel for themselves. He found himself in the parking lot of the Village Pizza Parlor. He drifted up next to Don's car and slipped inside, leaving the keys in the ignition.

Don was hunched to the wall, dialing the pay phone. David sidled over to a table in the corner and climbed onto the bench across from Craig Cobb, former star end for the Westside Bucks and student council football lobbyist.

"Hey, listen, Don told me about Bob and, hey, listen, I'm sorry."

David nodded and shuffled his feet in the sawdust.

Craig's lip moved over the edge of the frosted root beer. He probably wanted to pump David for details, but must have dimly perceived the nature of the moment and chose instead to turn his thick neck and scrutinize the player piano in the corner, now mercifully silent.

Don returned to the table.

"My mother's going over to stay with Mrs. Witherson tonight," he said, sliding in next to Craig. Then, meeting David's eyes for the first time in hours, "Craig here tells me we ought to talk to Cathy Sparks."

They looked at each other, saying, *All right, we're in something now, and we're in it together, and we both know it*, and Craig glanced from one to the other and sensed that they were in something together, and that it was about their best friend who was dead and no one knew why, and he said, "R'lly. He went out with her, y'know."

That was wrong. Bob hadn't been going with anybody last semester. If he had, they would have known. Still, the way Don's eyes were fixing him, David knew there was more to hear.

Craig repeated the story. "No, man, it was just that weekend. Saturday." Right, that was the last time they had seen Bob. He had been working on that damned Senior History paper. "I was washing my car, right? And Robert pulls in next to me, the next stall, and starts rollin' up the windows and so I ask him, you know, 'Who're you takin' to the Senior Party?' An' he says he doesn't know yet, and so I say, 'Goin' to any good orgies tonight?' an' he says he's not sure about that yet, either, and then he says, 'What d'you know about the new girl?' I guess, yeah, I think he said he gave her a ride home or something. I got the idea he was goin' over to see her that night. Like she asked him to come over or something. You know."

The new girl. The one nobody had had time to get close to, coming in as she had the last month or six weeks of school. A junior. Nobody knew her. Something about her. Her skin was oiled, almost buttery, and her expression never changed. And her body. Dumpy—no, not exactly; it was just that she acted like she didn't care about how she looked most of the time; she wore things that covered her up, that had no shape. So you didn't try for her. Still, there was something about her. She was the kind of girl nobody ever tried for, but if somebody asked somebody if he'd ever gotten anything off her, you would stop what you were doing and listen real close for the answer.

"So maybe you'll want to talk to her. She's the last one to see him. I guess." The football player, unmoving in his felt jacket, glanced nervously between them.

David stared at Don, and Don continued to stare back. Finally they rose together, scraping the bench noisily against the floor.

"Only thing is, she'll be pretty hard to find, prob'ly."

"Why's that?" asked David.

"I heard she moved away soon as the school year was over."

Later, driving home, taking the long way, thinking,

David remembered the photographs. The way the body was mangled. Cut off almost at the waist. He tried, but this time he could not get it out of his mind.

So they did a little detective work the next day.

Bob's mother had not seen him after that Saturday morning, when he left for the library to work on his research paper. No one else had seen him after that, either. Except Craig. And maybe, just maybe, the girl.

So.

So the family name was in the phone book, but when they got there the apartment was up for rent. The manager said they had moved out the 12th, right after finals.

So they stopped by the school.

The Registrar's office was open for summer school and Mrs. Greenspun greeted them, two of her three favorite pupils, with a warmth undercut by a solicitous sadness of which she seemed afraid to speak. It was like walking into a room a second after someone had finished telling a particularly unpleasant story about you behind your back.

Yes, she had received a call, she said, a call asking that Cathy's grades be sent along to an out-of-town address.

"The young lady lives with her older sister, I take it," confided Mrs. Greenspun.

David explained that he had loaned her a book that she had forgotten to return.

"Of course," said Mrs. Greenspun maternally. And gave them the address.

It was in Sunland, a good hour and a half away.

David volunteered his old Ford. They had to stop once for directions and twice for water and an additive that did not keep its promise to the rusty radiator. In the heat, between low, tanned hills that resembled elephants asleep or dead on their sides under the sun, Don put down the term paper. They had picked it up from Mr. Broadbent, Bob's history teacher, and had put off turning it over to his mother. They had said they were going to read it but had not, sharing a vague unease about parting with the folder.

It was only the preliminary draft, with a lot of the details yet to be put in, but it was an unbelievable story.

"He was really into something strange," muttered Don, pulling moist hair away from the side of his face.

"I guess that means we can talk about it now."

"I guess," said Don. But his tone was flat and he kept watching the heat mirages rising up from the asphalt ahead.

"I've read something about it," pressed David. "It's pretty grim, isn't it." A statement.

"It's got to be the most horrible story I've ever read. Or the most tragic. Depending on how you look at it," said Don. "Both," he decided.

David felt subjects mixing. He was light in the head. He sucked on a bottle of Mountain Dew and tried to shift the conversation. "What did that guy at the coroner's office mean, do you think?"

"You mean—"

"I mean about the 'other two.'" Suddenly David realized he had not changed the subject at all.

"Well, you remember Ronnie Ruiz and—what was the other one's name?"

David remembered, all right. The others had disappeared, one a couple of weeks before Bob, the first a few weeks before that. A month or six weeks before the end of school. He had known what the attendant meant but had been carrying around a peculiar need to hear it confirmed. "Patlian, I think. The younger one, Jimmy Patlian's brother. The junior. But I thought he ran off to join the Reserves."

"I don't know. It must have been him. Give me a swig of that shit, will you? Hey, how can you drink this?"

"I know, I know, my teeth'll fall out," said David, relieved to talk about something else. "But we always had it around the house when I was a kid. I guess you can be raised to like a thing, just like your parents' parents probably gave them the taste. Hard to put down."

"Sure, man, just keep telling yourself that until your stomach starts eating itself. Anyway, I know they found Ronnie Ruiz in some kind of traffic thing. Torn up pretty bad."

"The guy didn't even have a car, did he?"

"I don't—no, now that you bring it up. But they found him by some road somewhere. Maybe he got hit. The way I remember it, no one could identify him for sure for quite a while. Shit, man." He handed back the sweltering bottle. "This is shit."

"It's shit, all right," said David. "A whole lot of it."

"Cathy?"

"I remember you." The girl showed herself at the shadowed edge of the door, out of the blinding sun. "And you. I didn't think you'd bring anyone with you, when you called," she said to David, softly so that it was almost lost in the din of the freeway above the lot.

"This is Don. He—"

"I know. It's all right. My sister will be pleased."

The boys had worked out a scenario to ease her along but never got past side one. She had a quality of bored immobility which seemed to preclude manipulation, and a lack of assertiveness which made it somehow unnecessary.

They sat in three corners of the living room and made conversation.

She was not pretty. As their eyes mellowed to the heavily draped interior, her face began to reflect the warm tones like the smooth skin of a lighted candle: oiled wax. She wore a loose, very old-fashioned dress, high-necked, a ribboned cameo choker. As at school, though now the effect was in keeping with the close, unventilated room studded with fading, vignetted photographs and thin, polished relics of bone china. She moved without grace or style. She all but stood as she walked, all but reclined as she sat, inviting movement from others.

The afternoon passed. She drew them out, and they did not feel it happening.

Finally the ambience was broken momentarily. She left the room to refill their sweating glasses.

Don blinked. "There is something about that girl," he began measuredly, "and this place, that I do not like." He sounded nearly frightened about it, which was odd. "Does any of this remind you of anything?"

David rested his head against lace. His scalp was prickling. "Any of what? Remind me of what?"

When she reappeared with new iced teas, cooled with snowball-clumps of shaved ice, Don had repositioned himself at the mantle. He fingered a discolored piece of an old mirror.

"How well did you know Bob Witherson, Cathy?" he asked, gazing into the glass as if for reflections of faces and events long past, something along the lines of a clue.

She paused a beat, then clinked the refreshments into their coasters. Unruffled, noticed David, trying to get a fix on her.

"I met Bobby at the library," she explained. "I saw the paper he was writing. We talked about it, and he asked me to help him. I invited him over for dinner. At my sister's."

As simple as that.

David had been sitting one way for so long, his eyes picking over the same curios, that he was beginning to experience a false gestalt. When Cathy sat again, he almost saw her sink back into the familiar shimmering outline that was etched on his retinas, the image of her sitting/lying in the overstuffed chair as she had for—how long? Hours? But this time she remained perched on the edge, as if in anticipation. David found himself focusing on details of her face: the full, moistened lips. And her body: the light pressure of her slim belly rising and falling to flutter the thin gingham dress. How much fuller, more satisfied she had looked when he first saw her, right after she came to Westside. Than the last time he had seen her, too, a couple of weeks before graduation. Now she seemed fragile, starved. She was watching him.

"These pieces must be very old," said Don from across the airless room. He lifted a fragment of a teacup. It was decorated in the delicate handiwork of another era, blue and red and purple flowers scrolled into the pure white ground surface of the chinaware.

David, watching Cathy watching him as he waited to make a move, resented the interruption.

"Yes." She spoke easily from another level, undistractible. "My great-great grandmother brought them with her from Springfield. In Illinois."

David inched forward.

"They came West, did they?" continued Don strangely, getting at something. "Would . . . do you mind? I mean, I was wondering," he faltered, atypically, "where did they settle? I mean, where do you come from?"

"Sacramento, originally."

David rose. He crossed the room halfway. He stopped on a worn virgule in the carpet. Cathy's eyes opened wider to him. He was aware in a rush of the power assumed by someone who simply waits and asks no questions. But understanding it made it no less effective.

"Your sister has an interesting house," said David.

"You might like to see the rest," she offered coolly.

But Don was still busy formulating something and he would not let go. David had seen that expression before.

"Why," Don asked carefully, his words hanging like bright bits of dust in the air, "did Bob ask you to help him on his paper?" So he saw what was happening to David, saw it and recognized it and tried to push past it anyway. "Why would he?" he directed at David, as if the obvious reasons were not enough.

For once Cathy ignored a question. She got up and walked into the hallway, drawing it out as long as she could, aware of his eyes on her back. Perhaps she was smiling. She turned. Out of Don's line of sight she said, "The parts you haven't seen yet are in here." And so saying she leaned forward, grasped the hem of her long dress and lifted it to the waist. She was naked underneath. Her eyes never left David.

The moment was unreal. She seemed to tilt before his eyes.

David moved toward the hall.

Don, thinking she was far into another room, launched a volley of words in a frantic stage whisper.

"We've got to get together on this," he said. And, "Think!" And, "I say her people came through Truckee in 18—what. 1846." And, "David, what about it? What does that mean to you?" And, "That's why he wanted her help on the research. It's starting to add up. Does that make sense, Davey? Does it? Does it!" And, "I don't know, it's crazy, but there's something more. What's the matter, you think it scares me? Why should it? You think I'm fucking crazy? *Do you?*"

As David entered the bedroom the roar of the freeway gained tenfold, a charge of white sound in his ears. He thought she was speaking. He could not see her at first. Then a flurry of cloth and a twisting blur of white skin.

Disjointedly he remembered Don as he had left him there in the darkening living room as the sun went down outside. Here in the bedroom it was almost completely dark —the east side of the house, the drapes thicker. Gradually his ears attuned to sounds closer than the churning traffic. Words Don had spoken in that choked whisper: *What about it? What about it?* Over and over like a ticking clock inside him. He felt his body flushed, feverish. People who live like this must be afraid of the cold. His eyes began to clear. He was aware of a slow, tangled movement about the edges of the room. Probably the curtains in the breeze. *Afraid of the cold.* He saw her now faintly like a fish in dark waters, under ice, sliding horizontally under him on the curve of the bed. He felt himself fevered, swelling. Her cold, damp fingers raised his shirt and found the hairs on his chest. She slipped under his belt, thumbed and pulled, straining the buckle. He heard his zipper winding open. Did he? The shapes moving against the walls in the breeze. Hushed, swishing sounds. The freeway? Closer, closer. *There was no breeze.* "Are you hungry?" she asked and then laughed a kind of laugh he had never heard before. She slid back and forth under him, spreading her fishbelly-white legs wider. He moved to her, his body trembling. "No." Her voice. Of course. Of course. "First let me eat you." She said it. All right. All right? In the protracted second as she sat up, as she gripped his waist like a vise, sudden images flashed to mind: words written in the dark and illuminated from within. They came in a surge, crowded in on him. My sister will be pleased, she had said. What sister? He laughed. Almost laughed. Now he was sure of the presence of others in the room. They undulated along the walls. How many? This is crazy. She had sisters, yes, that was it, *sisters,* from Sacramento, descended from Truckee and the great trek to Sutter's Fort. "Oh my God," he said aloud, his voice cracking. And in the next second everything, all of it came at once. As he felt her mouth enfold him he saw Bob with her, and as her lips tightened he saw Bob in the photographs, and as her teeth scraped hungrily over him, drawing him deeper into her, he saw Bob's body, torn, consumed almost to the waist, and as the teeth bit down for the first time, bit down and would not be released, grinding sharply together, it all exploded like a time bomb and he heard his scream off the walls and the freeway's pulse, above her house, the road where young men were tossed afterwards like so much garbage and the sound of the sighing women as he passed into unconsciousness and Don burst confused into the room with the second draft from her desk where he had found it and before he could form an answer or even another question about Bob's paper on the Donner Party and her strange knowledge of it her sisters swooped from the corners where they had been crouched in waiting and then they were upon him, too.

Steven McDonald, who lives and works in Jamaica, the West Indies, has begun to mine Caribbean folklore for some of the most unusual, and terrifying, myths rooted in the West. His stories appear infrequently these days, but there is no question that he will be around for quite some time. Unless, of course, those myths of his . . .

THE DUPPY TREE
by Steven Edward McDonald

It was a long time before your birth (Grandmother Bell said, although in rather more colloquial language); it was even before the birth of your mother and your father—whoever *he* is. Then, Alcan, whose shining mudlake you see, was not even a suspicion, the other bauxite companies a long way from existing. The First World War was over, the Second in the future, Independence not even considered. It was our shame that Marcus Garvey was exiled, and that blacks were low in status—and your dress, daughter, would have shamed everyone, and your hair would have been considered shocking, in truth.

Your overbearing Prime Minister would not have lasted long in those days with his chatter of Imperialism and Socialism and sending armies to South Africa while his own country suffers. His father, Norman Manley, was, in truth, more diplomatic. Bustamante—old Busta—was in his prime, and everybody was very glad for the sugar crops and the banana and the yam, and one lived from the land instead of out of a shopping cart. We sang Tambo and danced the Kumina and worked while we hummed "Missa Potta" or "Rocky Road" or "John Crow"; to that song, the men would make fun of their bosses while the bosses wondered why they broke their backs smiling as if happy. If they only knew!

But, daughter, I see you are fretting; for shame, it isn't this that I should be telling you about.

The man who this story concerns—and if you feel to check, I will tell you how later—was a British colonialist who came to live in the small town that was Mandeville then. Many colonialists came to Mandeville, for it is cool, and the breeze blows most days, and the rains fall often, as they have in these past two months (almost washing me away with them!). It was a good thing that it was cool—the women dressed as if it would freeze suddenly.

This man was named Philip Laird-Hamlyn, and during the Great War of 1914–18 he was a Major in the British army, until he was wounded. It left him with a serious limp and an overbearing attitude toward all, especially "coloreds," as we were then called. He had previously been to Africa, where his wife, poor soul, died of malaria. He had no children. This did not help him to be any more pleasant.

The Major—we always called him the Major, never anything else—came to Mandeville to take charge of the police. In Britain, this could never have happened. In Jamaica, though, it did not matter. Then, there was little crime in Mandeville, perhaps the occasional theft or two, but little of seriousness as there is now. (I trust you will think once more about Kingston after the riots!) People could leave their doors open at night, and the old Greathouses had no burglar bars across their windows. So the Major's job was simply to watch over the police, who were mostly British.

The Major took up residence outside of Mandeville, near where Timber Trails now is, in the Greathouse there. The rent was nominal, as the police department paid for the upkeep. Power came from a noisy old generator, and you could tell when it was working by the smell as you approached.

The Major, of course, needed help. A gardener, a maid or two, a butler, and a cook. In those days there was no minimum wage law, and we were paid very little. We worked often twelve hours a day, and with very little gratitude. But we worked.

The gardener—the Major called him the "garden boy" although the man was almost forty—was called Charlie. He used no power mower to cut all of the grass, but shears or, at the most, a hand mower. He was skilled with the machet, and used very little else, unless digging, when he used a shovel and a fork.

The cook was Miss Imogene, and where she got that foolish name, I do not know. She was under thirty, but with her family, and the hours she worked, she looked much older. The butler was called Johnny, and if I know my men, he was a thief. But he never stole from the Major; at least Johnny had a brain. He was a terror with girls and must have fathered at least half the island! The other maid was named Susan, and she was barely out of her youth. Of course, Johnny was always around her.

I was the other maid. It was a long way to walk to the Major's home, and I would start a little after dawn and walk through the bush. That was the shortest way there. The mist would just be rising from the grass when I started; by the time I reached the house, the grass would be dry. Once there, I would change into my uniform and begin work. I would start by cleaning the verandah of the ground floor—upstairs was Susan's responsibility, poor girl. The Major would have left for work a long time before. Miss Imogene, Charlie, and Johnny lived in.

I had been working there for two months before the trouble came.

There was a huge old cottonwood—more twisted and bent than even this old man you wish to fall on those rude boys who bother you—in the grounds of the Greathouse. It was no harm to anyone, but the Major was haunted by it. It cast its shadow on the window of his room, and, to him, it seemed to move. He had heard the cry of the Rolling Calf a few times, too, although I am sure that he imagined it some of the time.

But one day, before he went out, he told poor Charlie to start cutting down the tree. Charlie was torn between giving up his job, which would not have done him any good, and following the Major's instructions. He did not start cutting right away, however.

Instead he came to me.

"Miz Bell," he said, "me no wan' cut down de tree."

"An' why so?" I said.

He shook his head. "Dat is a duppy tree. Is bed fe me cut it down."

I did not know what to do. I had my own job to hold, and Charlie was weak-souled. If he refused to cut down the tree, he would have pointed at me to back him up, and then we would both have lost our jobs.

So I said, "Mek up you mind youself, sah. Me no wan' get involve'."

He left, shaking his head and muttering bleakly to himself, and I went back to polishing the floor. But from where I worked, I could see that old tree, and, daughter, I could not curse the man for his fright.

Charlie did not cut down the tree that day. When the Major returned from Mandeville, Charlie told him that he needed a strong ax. Charlie could have done it just as well with the machet, but the Major did not know that. He had not been in Jamaica long enough, and being a colonialist, he would not see for a long time the ways of the people.

So, not knowing Charlie's lie, he brought an ax from the town the next day.

The day after that, Charlie was back.

He said, "Miz Bell, me can't cut down dat tree. De duppy dem will 'urt me."

I sighed and leaned on my mop. "Master," I said, "is not fe me to tell you how so you mus' do dese t'ing. Is you who must fe wo'k in de garden, not I."

"But is bad t'ing de Major a say me mus' do," he insisted, rolling his eyes. I have never liked to see anybody doing that.

"Den is bad t'ing you mus' a do," I said.

He clutched his machet and swallowed, fearful. "Is duppy me scare' of. You no a believe in duppy, Miz Bell?"

"Fe shame!" I said. "De duppy dem no' gon' hurt you. Is de Major tell you dat you mus' do dis t'ing." But seeing how frightened he was, I relented a little. "Me tell you den, sah. You mus' a take a lickle white rum an' put it in de corner of de house fe mek de duppy dizzy. Him can't t'ink about you after dat."

He sighed and shook his head. "Yes, Miz Bell, but me still a t'ink you wrong. But me no wan' lose me job."

He turned around and walked out, muttering, "Is bad t'ing, is bad t'ing," until the closing door silenced him.

I stood there thinking about it. I had never had trouble with duppies, and apart from the advice about the white rum—which is to make the duppy drunk so that he will chase the boss—I did not know what to do about them if they got mad. I had told Charlie that the duppy would not hurt him, but I did not know for certain. And there was a powerful presence in that tree.

Still, I had work to do, and I could not lean on my mop all day or the Major would fire me. So I started back to mopping, as Charlie began chopping down the tree. I watched him as I worked.

As I looked out of the window, I saw that he was cutting slowly. Even so, the splinters of wood were flying away from the cut in great chunks.

And you would have sworn, little Eulalee, if you had seen it, that that tree was trying to pull up by the roots and run away from Charlie's ax.

That night, I took one of my chickens—I had very few, but I had to use what I had, and could not afford anything else then—and with it in a sack, went through the bush, under the moonlight and the stars, to where the Obeah man lived.

The Obeah man's home was made from the wood of packing cases and sheets of steel and iron foraged from garbage dumps. It leaned to one side, on the side of a hill much like the one I live on, the water catchment and crude tank the only things holding it in place. That the Obeah man lived in such a place did not surprise me, for Obeah men are simple and require very little besides their powers.

I stopped before the door to the shack, and knocked softly, three times. Only we country folk knew where he was, and we would not tell. None of the colonialists would come down here; their fright-tales of the bush were exaggerated from the old stories of the Maroons and the Land of Look-Behind—the Cockpit Country where the slaves used to run and ambush the soldiers, forcing the soldiers to ride two to an animal, one facing backward.

From inside the shack there was a rustling and bumping, as of someone coming to the door, then the door itself swung open. I could barely see him in what little light I had, but that did not matter. I had come to see him before. The Obeah man then was bush doctor (as I am bush doctor now) and witch and preacher and all.

He was old—you think *I* am old, but *he* was older than you could judge—and stooped; his left hand was gripped around the handle of the door like the claw of John Crow, the vulture. He was stricken with arthritis, although the pain never seemed to bother him; his hands were permanent claws, his back and legs twisted. His clothes were rags. But his eyes were bright and watchful. There was the knowledge of years untold behind them; only one versed in the ways of the Obeah could know what he knew.

In a dark, high voice, he said, "Good night to you, Miz Bell. Mek you come inside, nuh."

He moved aside and let me pass. There was no light inside, as he needed none, but for me he lit an old kerosene lamp. The smoke soon clouded the single room of the shack until he opened one of the board shutters to let it escape. While I sat, he poured some raw rum—foul liquid, let me tell you, daughter—and mixed it with coconut juice in a wooden cup. This he handed to me, and I sipped it. His own drink was the same raw rum mixed with ganja tea, which he poured off from a kettle. There was a smell of old meat inside there, and the shadows flickered and danced with the flame of the lamp; there might be things inside those shadows, but I did not let that bother me. I did not question the Obeah then; I would not do so now.

Eventually, he laid aside his cup of rum and ganja and picked up an old skull, looking at it in the yellow light, turning it toward me. In the eye sockets were set pieces of jade and obsidian, left and right. Many teeth were missing from the jaws, and the top of the skull was cracked and dirty, with little spots of candlewax dripped onto it.

"Dis ya ol' man an' me good frien'," the Obeah said. "Is long time dis ya ol' man a stay wid I an' I. How you stay, Miz Bell?"

The sudden change did not catch me, nor was it meant to. The Obeah man liked to have his guests at ease first; not that he always succeeded, especially when he picked up that skull.

I said, "Me feel fine, sah. How you stay? Is long time me no come fe see you."

He bowed his head slightly. "I man a feel good. But no mek you worry, daughter. Is why you come fe see me? Me can a see by you face dat you a t'ink a somet'ing."

I put aside my cup, glad to be able to do so, and picked up the sack at my feet. The chicken inside squalled, the sound muffled.

I said, "Is duppy me wan' fe know about."

I told him about the Major and the cottonwood he had told Charlie to cut down, and what I had told Charlie.

When I had finished, he shook his head and said, "Is terrible t'ing dat boss-man mek de odder man do. Is bad fe mash down de duppy-mon home."

"Dat is what me a t'ink too," I said. "Is what will happen?"

He sighed. "Is no way we know. De duppy dem funny mon, mebbe not'ing happen, mebbe de house it bu'n down." He spread his hands. "But it gon' be bad-bad if de duppy 'im angry, me a tell you Miz Bell. Is one man me see mek de duppy made, an' he duppy jus' rip 'im arm off an' 'im leg off 'an 'im 'ead as well, an' de mess 'im mek, it terrible. Blood an' bit of dis an' bit of dat all ovah."

The relish with which he said that made me feel ill. And yet the Obeah was speaking only of one encounter with duppies.

"Well," I said, "me not sure dat de tree got a duppy."

He gave me a reproving look. "Is most cottonwood have duppy, daughter."

I sighed. "Is not'ing me can do fe mek de duppy leave I alone?"

The Obeah stood, holding up a hand, and turned to search around his shack among the things piled in corners and on other things, without order. I tell you, daughter, it hurt me, the spirit of tidiness, to see this disorder; but one does not—would!—tell the Obeah these things, or else he might—would!—take offense.

In a few minutes, he had the things he wanted piled on the floor in front of him. There was a big bowl, a jar of small round things, bottles of liquids dark and bright, things that I had no name for, pieces of plants and creatures, a pestle of bone, things to stir with and things to mix with and things to grind and to heat and to pour and to hold.

He sat cross-legged before all this and said, "Me mus' have silence, Miz Bell, so you mus' fe hold you peace while me wo'k."

That wasn't hard to do, although I almost coughed while he worked. The stench from the things he was mixing grew worse with each passing second, gagging me. Many times was I forced to hold my breath against a choking cough. I swear to you, child, that I could have strangled to death there without making a single sound.

He was soon finished with his work, chanting all the time, and he poured off a dark liquid into one bottle, putting it aside as he picked up another. This he made signs over while he chanted in the tongue of the old land, Africa. I am told by those knowledgeable that what he spoke was Xhosa, but I do not care too much about that.

He laid the second bottle, still empty, aside also, and picked up a withered, dried root, putting a hole in the cut end of it with a small punch. Through the hole he put a leather thong, knotting it swiftly, and then laying it before him. Over this he sprinkled herbs and chanted more words, from the sound of them, a blessing. He had not made the sounds of a curse yet.

"You mus' tek dese, Miz Bell," he said. "What is in dis bottle you mus' put on de stump of de tree, fe healin'."

He handed the bottle to me, and I slipped it into the pocket of my skirt. He told me what must be done with the root-necklace and the empty bottle—he made sure that I would remember by making me memorize what he told me, which took most of the night—if necessary.

When he had finished, he took up something else and handed it to me.

"Is good fe de yawnin' you a do," he said, with a smile that had the feeling of a morning bird. "Dat mus' a keep you awake fe de day and you wo'k."

I followed his instruction and chewed it while he stood and walked around, looking out of the shutter.

"Raas!" he said, in surprise. "Me see de dawn risin'." He shook his head and turned back to me. "Is bad t'ing fe me keep you 'ere all a de night, Miz Bell."

I paid that no attention. "Is fe shame me a keep you awake all a de night, Obeah."

He nodded. "But is good t'ing you a come fe see me." He sat down again and looked at the sack holding the chicken. As if it knew, it squalled and struggled. "Is long time me no 'ave chicken fe de pot," he said.

I smiled. "Is no bird fe de pot, Obeah. Is egg-bird dat, an' good egg too, big one."

The Obeah laughed. "Is egg fe fry, egg fe boil, egg fe mash, egg fe dis, egg fe dat. Is egg mek I fart, me a tell you!" But the way he smiled—even without teeth—told me he was pleased. "Me a t'ank you, Miz Bell, fe dat."

"An' me a t'ank *you*, Obeah," I said. "But is good mornin' me mus' a wish you, fe me mus' walk to wo'k, an' dat is a long way."

So we said good-bye, and I left to walk through the bush to the Major's Greathouse.

I reached the Greathouse earlier than usual, for I wanted to complete what the Obeah had told me to do as soon as possible. The stump of the great tree that Charlie had cut down was easy to find, the remains of the tree broken and awkward nearby, and it only took a few minutes to spread the dark liquid over the wood. It soaked quickly in, leaving only a slight darkening of the gray wood.

I put the empty bottle into my pocket and continued on to the house. I would return the bottle to the Obeah man later.

I was still very early for work, and the Major had not yet left. He was dressed, though, and had just finished breakfast when I, in my uniform, went into the house.

"You're rather early, Miss Bell," he said, as he looked up from the magazine he was reading—he had them sent to him from Britain and the United States.

"Yes sah," I said politely. "Me had a terrible night, an' was awake long time before de sun a rise. So me t'ought me would a walk early."

He nodded sharply. "Very good." He seemed about to go back to the magazine but changed his mind, looking up again. "I didn't sleep too well myself, actually." He grunted, a little distant from the morning in his mind. "In fact, I seem to have spent half the night either looking out of windows or prowling around the grounds with the twelve-bore."

"You t'ink dere was somebody out dere, Major?" I said.

His eyebrows rose sharply, and his face reddened a little. "Think? I damn well *know* there was somebody out there!" He tossed the magazine aside. "I even had that stupid garden boy helping me to look, but he kept insisting that it was the wind or nothing at all."

"Mebbe *was* not'ing, sah," I said.

"Damnit woman, *there was someone out there!*" he cried, and I wished I had been silent.

I did not try to push it any further, then. The Major was in a very bad mood, and there was no arguing with him. If the Major had said something was so, then it was so, as if the Obeah man had said it—and you know: when your hand is in a lion's belly, you must take time and draw it out.

"Well, sah, you mus' be right, an' if so, den you mus' tek good care. Mebbe bad things out dere in de night, bad man or duppy or—"

"*Duppy?*" he roared, standing up. "That idiot garden boy said *exactly* the same thing, and frankly I'm more than a little fed up with hearing this nonsense!" He took a deep breath, pushing his chest out. His face was scarlet, and even his heavy mustache seemed to quiver with anger. He wagged a finger at me, snorting between words.

"There was," he said, "a man, or men, outside in the grounds of my house, prowling around for some reason or other. Now, all you lot, African or otherwise, are about the same as far as superstitions go. But let me tell you for once and for all that by God! I don't want to hear any of it." He paused, regaining a little control and taking a deep breath. "And what the devil is this duppy of yours meant to be?"

The force with which he had jumped at me left me quivering a little. He was a forceful man, even with his peculiar limp. So his sudden question caught me while I was unbalanced.

"Well, sah—" I started.

The Major was tapping his foot at my show of fright.

"Well?" he said, booming like a preacher shouting at the Devil. "Come on, woman! I haven't got all day."

I nodded and swallowed, then said, "Well, sah, de duppy is bad t'ing. Like you could say evil spirit, sah."

He raised his left eyebrow and gave me a barely patient look.

I went on. "Is what live in de cottonwood tree, sah, an' is why Charlie no wan' fe cut down de tree."

The Major pursed his lips and nodded slowly, still glowering. "I think," he said, "that I now begin to see what that fool was jabbering about. A confused mixture of ghosts and dryads, eh? What you might call an elemental spirit." He was silent for a moment, waiting for me to say something. I would say nothing. "Well, Miss Bell, it wasn't one of your blasted duppies that was creeping about last night, I'll tell you *that*. It had two legs and it walked upright, and it got frightened as well. Took off like a phantom, true, but I've seen bushmen do the same thing. As for this, I know. I *saw* him." He stretched himself up like a righteous man. "Most definitely a man, and if he hadn't scarpered like a greased eel, he'd have had the contents of two twelve-bore cartridges planted in his arse!"

I sighed. "Well, sah, den you is right, an' you mus' fe tek care. Mebbe de man 'im come back again."

"If he does, he's in trouble. I'll be ready this time." He looked suddenly at his pocket watch. "Damn, I'm going to be late getting down into the town now."

He turned and stalked out of the door, his lame leg dragging a little. It would probably pain him all day now; when he became angry, he stayed angry, and that started his wounds aching.

I was already working when the front door slammed; it was not long before the old Austin in the garage at the end of the drive thundered into life and pulled out. Those old black cars used to put out as much oily smoke and smell as country buses today, and looking after them was difficult; parts were sometimes as hard to get as they are now, and there were very few trained mechanics in the island then.

Within five minutes, both the sight and sound of it had vanished. If I knew the Major, he would be driving as fast as he dared on those roads so that he would reach the police station on time. He would not be back until five o'clock at least.

I laid aside my brush and went to speak to Charlie. The news of this mysterious "prowler" gave me such a feeling of worry so soon after the cottonwood had been cut.

I had to leave by the back door of the Greathouse, going down from the verandah to the lawn, and around by the generator shed and the water pump and tank, to where the quarters for the live-in helpers were. The quarters were built onto the house but were kept around the back, well away from the view of visitors. For a good reason, too, as they were the worst part of the house, drafty and badly made. They were infested with cockroaches and lizards, but the live-in quarters were a place to stay, and at least those who lived in had food to eat and a place to stay out of the rain.

I turned the corner toward Charlie's room and heard a most terrible scream. It was soon followed by another, and then another screaming voice joined with it, and they raced each other for highest pitch and loudest noise. Over it, I could hear Johnny muttering and shouting. What a noise those three made!

As soon as I heard it, I began to run. Miss Imogene and Miss Susan were at Charlie's door, screaming still, their hand fluttering and wringing dry cloth; their faces were faces of horror, Johnny was looking over their heads, his eyes wide and staring, his black color faded to gray-brown, his mouth moving and letting out words. He was praying to the Lord, and even before I looked in, I knew that Charlie must be dead, and steeled my soul to the sight of him.

I pushed Susan out of the way—I was smaller than she and Imogene—and looked in; I was very nearly sick there and then. What I saw was a terrible sight indeed, and I could not blame anyone for screaming. I wanted to scream myself.

Charlie was laid on his bed in his underwear, a branch of the cottonwood tree through his chest, pinning him to the mattress. There was blood everywhere, upon the walls, the ceiling that Charlie's dead eyes stared at, the floor.

You see, daughter, the Major had seen and heard *some-*

thing. But he had been wrong. No man had come in the night.

The duppy had been, and he had been very, very angry with Charlie, and Charlie had died for it.

And I prayed to the Lord for Charlie's soul.

The Major was furious when he returned from Mandeville. We had sent a message to him with a boy, as there was no telephone in the house and no other way to contact him.

"What the devil is going on *now?*" he shouted as he stumped into the house.

I stepped forward and said, "Beggin' you pardon, Major, but dere has been a . . . a mu'der."

His jaw dropped for a moment before he caught himself. "You what?" He looked as if he did not believe me.

"Charlie, sah," I said. "De . . . man you a see las' night, 'im kill Charlie."

"Miss Bell—" He stopped and took a deep breath, controlling himself with an effort. Very quietly, he went on. "If this proves to be simple foolishness, Miss Bell, you will be in serious trouble."

I shook my head. "Is no foolishness, Major sah. Is terrible t'ing happen."

I took him around to Charlie's room and stepped aside as he looked in. He stepped back, his tanned face pale, badly shaken by what he saw.

"My God," he said, in a voice as quiet as the walk of a spider. "Oh my God."

Well, I tell you, child, the police were there soon after, taking photographs with their huge cameras and asking questions and more questions and looking around and dusting this and picking up that and laying down chalk here and tape there and getting in the way of everything. None of it helped poor dead Charlie, except perhaps the preacher. Even I could do nothing, because I did not know where the duppy was.

You see, duppies being spirits, they are unlimited as to where they may travel, or hide. Even the tree, cut down as it was, was still alive, as trees live for days after being cut. The duppy might have been there, but I had seen no sign.

The Major was still shocked by what he had seen. He and his assistants had the theory that Charlie had been killed by somebody who was his enemy. Had he been killed in some other way, I might have thought that too, for men are forever killing other men for little stupidities of one kind or another. But no man takes up a branch of a tree that is almost as thick as my wrist and plunges it into the heart of another man with enough force to impale the poor man on the bed where he sleeps. There is no man who has such strength, unless he is a devil!

No, daughter, I was certain that the duppy had killed Charlie. More: I was certain also that the duppy was not finished. The signs were in the air: The trees were untouched by the breeze, but it was not yet the dog days, and the air was as thick as if there would be a storm soon, yet the skies were clear and blue, with few clouds. And the water pumped to the house was bitter.

By the end of the afternoon, most of the policemen had gone away, with Charlie's body. A few, no more than four, had stayed as a guard and arranged themselves around the house with pistols and shotguns, while the Major kept his twelve-bore weapon near him all of the time. He doubted, he said, that the killer would return. But he wanted to be guarded, just in case.

Miss Imogene gave her notice that afternoon. She would not stay in a house that she said she *knew* to be haunted. She was badly frightened, and by the looks of her would not sleep that night wherever she was. The Major was dubious about letting her leave but did so in the end, after she told him that she would be in Knockpatrick, staying with her sister. She gave him directions to the house, and he wrote them down—she was an illiterate, as most were in those days. The Major sent a policeman with her to go part of the distance.

He told Miss Susan and myself that we should not go home for the night, although he doubted that we had done anything wrong.

"I'd rather you both stayed," he said, looking from Miss Susan to me. "You may be safer here than where you live.

For all I know, this murderous fellow might have it in for both of you as well as Charlie." He paused and looked at Susan, who was wringing her skirt again, her fearfulness betraying her terribly. "At least here we'll be able to keep an eye on you both, in case anybody *does* come sneaking around. I won't stand for having my reputation sullied by murder if there's anything I can do about it."

He twitched his mustache with his right hand and looked at me. "Now that Miss Imogene has left us, Miss Bell, I'm afraid that you and Miss Susan here will have to temporarily adopt her duties. I trust it'll be no bother to you."

One of the policeman staying in the house looked in through the open door. He was a young Englishman, not long out of one of the British colleges, but trained already, and eager.

He said, "Everybody's in position, sir. Packington watching the north, Riggs on the east, Webster taking the south. I'm taking the west watch."

The Major looked around and nodded, shortly, with a grunt. "You'll be relieved at oh six hundred, Gaskin. I'll assign the watches myself."

"Very good, sir," the young policeman said, disappearing from view.

"Gaskin!" the Major called.

Gaskin's head appeared again. "Sir?"

"For Christ's sake, don't shoot at any of our coppers when they get here!"

Gaskin grinned. "Yes sir." And he left again.

The Major turned back to us. "I suggest, Miss Bell, that you handle dinner. Miss Susan—" he turned to her, looking at her reprovingly—"appears rather too distraught to take care of it." He looked back at me. "And while you're at it, please sort out the makings for coffee and tea for the men. They'll appreciate it."

I nodded. "Yes sah." I hesitated before turning away and said, "Where Johnny will be, sah? Me t'ink dat de ... de man might a come look fe 'im."

The Major smiled slightly. "Oh, don't worry about him. He'll be watching your quarters. One of my men will check on him every now and then to keep him awake. I'm sure you'll feel safer for it."

I would not, but I said nothing of it. I thanked him and turned away, taking poor Susan's arm to lead her away. She kept glancing back at the Major fearfully.

In the kitchen, I said, "Stop you worry, gel. No need fe dat."

She shook her head and almost spilled a bag of potatoes. I helped her catch hold again and then took them from her.

"Mek you sit down," I said. "Leave I fe do de cookin'."

She nodded silently and sat in one of the hard wooden chairs around the dining table we helpers had to use. I turned to peeling the potatoes, washing them under the slow flow of water from the tap. It was no work at all to make dinner for the Major; he ate simply. As for Johnny, Susan, and me—well, we had gone hungry all day, but to put anything in our stomachs would simply have turned them over and spilled everything out again.

I soon had everything cooking on the woodstove. I had no need to pay attention to it until it was almost finished, so I sat down at the table, looking across at Susan. She was in misery, tearful, and terribly frightened.

"Fe shame," I said, "is no way fe a young gel fe act, all sorry an' weepy-weepy."

"Me scare' fe duppy," she said. "Me no wan' fe stay in dis 'house."

"Fe shame, *me* no wan' stay, but me no act like dat," I said.

Susan shook her head. "You is old woman, but me is still young gel."

Well, daughter, there was no arguing with *that*.

Poor Charlie's room had been washed clean of his blood and locked off. Miss Susan was given Miss Imogene's room, while I was to sleep in the spare room. Daughter, I tell you, I did not expect to be able to sleep that night, with the whisper of hatred and anger that blew ice winds along my nerves, but I had forgotten that I had not slept the night before and the Obeah man's medicine had only a limited power. So, when I took to my bed at nine-thirty, it was not long before I fell asleep. My body wondered whether *I* would be the next to be impaled, if any were to be impaled, despite the Obeah's actions.

But when I woke, I was untouched.

It was still black as death outside. I lay puzzled for a while, wondering what had waked me. Moonlight touched the window glass with quiet milk-light, and I felt the singing of my nerves. I knew than how a frightened cat must feel, all my muscles tense.

Then I heard an overbearing voice crying a command for someone to halt, angry and frightened. And again: "Halt, blast you, or I'll shoot!"

There was the sound of both barrels of a shotgun being fired off and the sound of running feet.

I got out of bed and put on my uniform, as that was nearest to hand, and opened the door. I could see out onto the rear lawn where the four policemen were running, guns in hand. They had seen something, for certain, but I thought that they would not catch it. I pitied the policemen as they chased illusions.

The Major was not with them; as I turned around, I saw him coming down toward the helpers' rooms. Johnny, rubbing his eyes and yawning, was behind him.

The Major stopped and grinned ferociously at me, almost as if he was a mad dog, one of those starving creatures you see walking hang-head by the side of the road.

"We've got the bastard now," he said, triumphantly. "He can't get away before one of my men bags him; have a job getting up from a twelve-bore blast, he will. Teach him to come committing murder on my property."

I did not say what I thought but instead, "Is good t'ing you a t'ink dis way, Major, sah."

He grunted. "Indeed so, Miss Bell. Never ceases to surprise me how some people can be so damn stupid. Had this sort of thing in Africa—not murder, thievery. Always worked. Back they'd come, and bang."

"Yes, sah. Is what you will do to de man?"

He looked surprised. "By the look of it, I expect the next thing will be to bury what's left of him."

I shrugged, apprehensive. There was still that feeling of thunder in the air. "Well, is good thing you was prepare', sah." The sound of firing was still coming from the bottom of the garden, dozens of yards away. The policemen were shouting directions to each other, chasing moon-shadows now.

"Hmph," the Major said. "Nothing to—"

From Susan's room there was a sudden screaming— long, high wails of horror.

The Major turned, shocked. "What the devil's got into her?"

I did not stop to answer but ran for her room. The screams did not stop, although they were growing more broken-throated, and as I reached the door I heard the sounds of things crashing inside.

I reached for the things the Obeah had given me and realized that I had left them in my other clothes, in my room. There was no time to go for them; if I wasted time, Susan would die.

I fought the door open, crying as I battled the pressure that tried to hold it shut, and slipped inside, shouting for Susan. The door slammed shut behind me.

Susan was pressed back against the wall, screaming still, her eyes wide, her body naked. Her head was bent backward, as though someone was clutching her hair. She was writhing, struggling, attempting to break free, all the while screaming at such a pitch to quake bone.

Her arms and legs were suddenly pinned, making of her body a terrible flesh-and-blood cross. I screamed and threw myself toward her, cursing the spirit that trapped her so, and found myself held back, as though I tried to walk in a night's dream.

Susan's screams died away, and I heard only breathing and what might have been the sounds of a tree, growing. Susan looked down, tears of pain and terror making her face glisten in the moonlight. Something distant moaned, and she answered it with a broken sob.

I shook in anger and horror, hurling myself against the duppy's barrier, willing myself forward. I was released, suddenly; something wooden slid like a lizard between my ankles and twisted. I was thrown to the floor, bruising my face. I struggled to rise, answering Susan's agonized sobs with cries of my own. There was a sudden pain at the back of my head, and I fell again, my limbs paralyzed.

I heard Susan's breathing quicken, rise for another

scream. There was a soft, wet, thud, a terrible gasp, and then, finally, a slow, gentle scraping. I felt wetness suddenly on my hands.

And the darkness came.

There was a wet cloth across my head when I woke and I had a terrible headache. My face was bruised, and the bruises on my body made me groan as I sat up.

The Major came into my view, his face concerned. "How do you feel, Miss Bell?" he asked.

I took the cloth from my forehead. "Me feel like me near dyin'," I said.

He did not smile. "You damn near did. That was a foolish thing to do. You were very lucky to only get knocked out." Then he seemed to remember what he was saying, and said no more.

Behind me, the voice of young Gaskin came. "I don't think she has a concussion, Major. Perhaps we should call Doctor Perry from Mandeville, though."

The Major shook his head. "Not now, Gaskin. In the morning. I want all of you here, and on watch."

"Yes sir." I heard Gaskin move away, and the sound of a door opening and closing.

The Major looked back at me. "What did you see while you were in there, Miss Bell?"

I groaned again, and said, "Not'ing, sah. Not'ing but Miss Susan in de co'ner, screamin' an' shoutin'." I remembered the sound I had last heard, and my heartbeat quickened. "Miss Susan . . . how she stay?"

The Major took a deep breath and shook his head. "Whatever is going on, I don't know." He hesitated a moment, then sighed. "She is dead, Miss Bell. I'm sorry. She was killed the same way as Charlie, a bloody great branch through her heart."

I sank back onto the sofa and stared at the ceiling. If I had thought before leaving my room, I might have saved the poor girl, despite the terror of the attack on her. Her death was my fault.

"You're certain you didn't see anything?" the Major asked.

I nodded. "Not'ing and no one, sah." How could I tell him, daughter?

He grimaced. "It's evil, Miss Bell. The most vicious form of murder I have ever seen. I'd almost believe in . . . in angry ghosts myself, after hearing the sounds from that room." He closed his eyes for a moment, suddenly fighting rage. "How the *hell* did he get *out* of there?" he cried. He turned to me. "This man has murdered two people, and the second time is *trapped*. Utterly and finally trapped. And yet there's no sign!"

"Is duppy doin' dese t'ing, sah," I said.

The Major bared his teeth, almost snarling. "No, Miss Bell. Next time I'll have him. I've matched the best of Africa, and this country is no match." He turned away.

"Major, sah," I said. He looked back. "Me 'ope dis t'ing a man. If it not a man, it jus' gon'——"

A shotgun roared in the garden outside, and the Major swung around, striding to the room's big windows. "What the devil are they shooting at now?" he said. I heard Gaskin shouting commands and directions, and more firing. The Major flung open a side window and leaned out.

The air was suddenly cold and heavy, filled with the strangling wetness that means a hurricane. I sat up and put my feet on the floor, glancing nervously about.

There was a soft whisper, something moving. The light flickered as an ice wind touched the side of my face and left.

The Major leaned back into the room. "Can't see what they're firing at, but they're running around like frightened women. I suppose I'll——"

I said, quickly, "Major, sah, where Johnny is?"

He raised his eyebrows. "I stationed him——"

From the direction of the kitchen, there was a loud, wailing scream, the sound of a frightened man. The Major and I stiffened where we were, scared by its sound. The Major shuddered visibly.

There was the whisper of shuffling footsteps. The light flickered and dimmed, almost leaving us in darkness. Black shadow slipped about the room, and I heard the Major hiss and start forward.

There was a moan. A bent black shape pulled itself into the doorway, pulled itself upright. It staggered forward, reaching, and fell headlong and awkward.

Its landing came with the crash of shotguns outside.

The ice wind fled past my face again. The Major made an animal sound, snarling. "What the hell was that?"

The light sprang back to full brightness. Neither the Major nor I said anything as we stared at the thing that had entered the room. I had known it from the scream, yet I was still struck by the horror of it.

Sprawled and dead upon the carpet was Johnny, a cottonwood branch through him. He had died at that instant, but his corpse, animated by the duppy, had been walked here. Johnny's outstretched hand pointed at the Major.

The Major stared at Johnny's body, then turned his head to look out of the window, toward the place where the men were still shooting. Then, slowly, he turned to look at me. His eyes had emptied of everything that made him a man; he was fearful.

Softly, he said, "There is something evil here." He looked out of the window again. "It has destroyed me."

"Sah?" I said.

He shook his head. "Three deaths in my home, Miss Bell, all murders. Three of them in two days. The scandal will destroy my career, my life." He snorted. "And what do I produce as the killer? Some kind of . . . of . . . perverted dryad." He stood, listening to the firing. "They've been firing those bloody toys of theirs and they haven't hit anything yet, you know. As though they were fighting a bloody bush war."

He turned away from the window, shaking his head, his shoulders bent. He said, "I live for a while in Africa, Miss Bell, in the Congo. I once angered a man I considered a shaman, a witch doctor. He cursed my wife, and within a month, she was dead, of malaria. She died in a hospital, under full medical care; nothing worked for her." He tried straightening his shoulders, and failed. "That evil has followed me here. How does one go about stopping a duppy, then?"

"Me have what me will need, sah. Is jus' a lickle support me need fe get de stuff."

He nodded. "Very well. I hope you can stop this . . . thing."

"Me will try, Major," I said. "You mus' fe pray for me."

* * *

I put on the root-necklace and took up the empty bottle. It was a very good thing that the Obeah had made me memorize what I must say and do so that I needed to think very little. My head ached terribly, and my bones were heavy as I walked. Once or twice the Major had to help me. The policemen were still causing commotion, now at the place where the grounds met the bush.

The stump of the tree was like a gravestone in the darkness. The giant remains of the broken tree, its branches cut and broken, lay near it, like the remains of a battle between giant, malformed spiders.

I felt ice wind around me, a whisper of a question. Quickly, over the stump of the tree, I made gestures with the tip of the root that hung around my neck. The hint of thunder in the air grew, weighing on me. I willed myself to ignore it, although I could feel dismay growing within me. In the dawn side of the sky, the star-sprinkled darkness was becoming purple. I could see the morning star clearly.

I spoke the words of Xhosa that I had been told to say and completed the last gesture. There was no visible sign of success.

I left the stump and stepped toward the broken tree. Ice wind swept around me, and I saw the huge tree shift a little. Branches moved, bent, slid toward me.

Behind me, the Major gasped. I turned my head, to see that he was only shocked by what he saw, and turned back. I stepped forward again, my heart beating, it seemed, like the wings of a Doctor Bird.

The branches lunged, formed a deadly barrier of pointed wood. I gestured, spoke sharply, commanding. The barrier broke, splintering. It was still hard to move, almost as it had been in Susan's room. I strained forward, my will drawn until I could draw it no more. Then I was by the tree, gesturing as swiftly as I dared; if I made a mistake now, I would surely die.

I walked the length of the broken cottonwood, gesturing, speaking, avoiding the few branches that might trip me, walked around the top, and back. I saw the Major, frozen near the stump. His face was contorted as he tried to move toward me. I could still hear firing.

Finished, I moved back to him, gestured over him,

forcing the duppy to release him. I said, "You mus' bu'n de tree, sah. But de stump mus' lef'. De duppy can' come back a de tree now, because de spell lock 'im out. 'Im mus' look new home."

He said, "If the tree was its home, it should have been unable to go back after it was cut down."

I shook my head. "No sah. De tree it still got life, so de duppy 'im don't need anodder place fe hide."

The Major looked at the tree, then at me, and nodded. "What do you do next?"

"We mus' fe catch de duppy 'im. Odderwise, is terrible t'ing 'im a gwan do." I stepped away from the Major, a fluttering in my stomach—where do you look for a tree spirit in a forest? "You mus' fe stay close. 'Im will try fe kill you now."

I took the little empty bottle from my pocket and held it in both of my hands as the Obeah had told me, seeking the presence of the duppy. My heart beat like a Rastaman's drum and I had to catch my breath as a man catches a bird. I willed myself forward, searching, striving to become one with the natural life around me.

The bottle grew warm in my hands and my pace quickened. The sound of firing from the policemen stopped, and there were the sounds of puzzlement. The bottle grew warmer yet.

Ice wind crossed my face and the bottle burned in my hands. I clutched it tightly, turning, following what it told me.

The major fell forward, clutching his chest, his face reddening. He lay on the dark grass, his eyes open and staring, only small twitches to show that he remained alive.

The bottle still burned in my hands. I knelt by the Major, hopeful, and spoke a command to the spirit within. His mouth opened, but no words came.

I said, "You can' command 'uman body, master. Is no good fe you to try." One of the Major's hands lifted toward me. I made a gesture, and the hand fell again. "Is foolish t'ing you a do."

The ice wind fled past my face. The Major groaned and shifted. I left him there and followed the duppy, the Obeah's bottle leading me. I ran down the garden, my feet pounding as hard as my heart, and into the bush, slipping between trees as carefully as a dead man's spirit. Dark fingers of wood felt the morning sky. I heard the whisper of men moving as I moved, and felt pity for them.

I left the bush, the bottle burning my hands once more, and turned.

The young policeman named Gaskin lifted his shotgun and aimed at my face. The bottle was like fire in my hands.

I said, "Is me, sah. Miz Bell, de ol' lady."

There was no answer from the young man. We stared at each other for moments.

Suddenly, the young man lowered his gun and turned. He walked four steps into the main grounds and sank to the ground, sprawling quietly. His weapon slid away from him. I almost fell with relief.

The heat of the bottle in my hands slowly died. I wondered then if I would ever find the duppy again. That old spirit was learning, daughter, and learning more quickly than I could learn how to handle him.

I spoke a spell of power about the spell that the Obeah had laid on the bottle. It warmed a little in my hands, growing warmer as I quested outward. I walked, aware of the changing color of the sky, and the smell and feel of dewing grass. My feet grew wet, and my skin chilled.

The bottle was bright in my hands as I walked into the Greathouse. The door closed quietly behind me. I reached out and touched the wood. It was warm.

I moved quietly through the house, avoiding Johnny's ruined body. His splayed hands seemed to reach for me, though I knew this to be only imagination.

I stopped in the middle of the main room and waited. Ice wind moved around me, and I smelled pain, and fear, and anger. I stayed still, probing the shadows with my ears, clutching what little light there was with my eyes, my skin alive and cringing.

Within shadow, red light glowed and poured, like phantom blood. It crept toward me, moved away as it almost left shadow, and crept to another corner.

The bottle in my hands pulsed. There was a hiss. Ice

wind flowed over my hands, failing to cool the Obeah's bottle. ___

I spoke a final command, and received only a brush of ice wind. Red light grew in another corner, bled through deep shadow.

I took a deep breath and opened the bottle, quickly weaving the Obeah's spell, chanting forcefully, reaching with my mind to compel the duppy to cease. I was surrounded with ice wind, and my skin froze and blotched and burned with cold. Pain touched my nerves. I continued, straining my will and chanting harder, harder, and harder still. My throat burned. I was slowly forced down to my knees. The pain in my head became thunder and fire and all the curses of Hell. Cold hands reached to my soul, closed on it, and tore. I spat curses and tore back, stabbing and striking at my attacker's being, while yet weaving the Obeah's spell.

There was screaming, either or both of us, silently or out loud. I smelled fire and imagined brimstone burning across my skin. We fought now as spirits alone. There was roaring, as of a pack of lions.

I struck again with the power of the Obeah's spells surrounding me, and grasped. There was a rushing and roaring of an ice hurricane and then silence. My spirit reeled in darkness, with nothing left to grasp, reeled and fell and plunged down.

Once more I was aware of my body. I was bruised and weak, even with the power of my spirit, my energy stolen. I still smelled fire and smoke. I clutched the Obeah's bottle tightly, feeling it stirring with the anger and panic of its occupant. Within it, energy swirled and pulsed. The plug of the bottle did not move; the Obeah's spell would contain the duppy despite his anger.

I stirred myself, but could not rise. I heard crackling and roaring, and red light came to me. There was heat around me.

I clutched the bottle and closed my eyes, and sighed. The duppy could not kill me himself; yet he had finally done something that would kill me.

Then I was being dragged upright, lifted, and carried. These old bones of mine were light even then; I still could not spare my voice to thank my rescuer.

Outside, I heard one policeman cursing Gaskin, who was muttering back at him. Another said, "This one's dead; what about the old woman?"

My bearer said, "She'll be all right, mate. Did she set that fire off, Major?"

There was a grunt from the Major; I was relieved to hear that he was all right.

He said, "I very much doubt it, Webster. Good job. I'll see this is on record. As for *you*, Gaskin—"

I heard no more then, daughter, for my hurts won the day, and I fell unconscious.

I see, daughter, that you are impatient to know how it is that the duppy from the Major's house now lives here, when this old man of a cottonwood is obviously older even than I and must have had a duppy of its own.

I stopped first at the Obeah's home to return one of the bottles, and to show him the duppy. He chuckled only and shook his head. There was no more to be said about it.

There was one more spell to cast once I returned home. When that was done—and the casting of it took time and concentration and much of what little energy I had—I opened the bottle. The duppy rushed from it with a roar and a howl, into the weave of my spell. It was compelled thus to plunge into this old man cottonwood.

Such a battle you never saw. For a day and a night, this old man shivered and shook and shuddered like a palsied man as the two duppies fought. I did not dare leave my house for fear of being hurt. They would have no mind for me, however—this battle was between duppies, not between duppies and men.

Finally, there was quiet. There was a final rushing and hissing as ice wind swirled about that old tree. It shook itself once, and the weak duppy, whose home this tree had been, left, seeking a new home. But I did not feel sorry for him—the cottonwood is always springing from the seed, and I had put the healing liquid on the stump of the Major's cottonwood. You see how there is a young cottonwood there now, daughter?

So. It is bad when you play with things, you see. This

twisted old tree and I are good friends, and, I pray to the Lord, I should wish it to stay that way. He is a bad man, true, but I know how to keep him filled with peace; he is not such a rude boy now.

Go make some tea, child. I will give you a little something to make the rude boys leave you alone.

The tree rustled, although there was no breeze, and seemed to bend some of its branches toward Grandmother Bell. In the small concrete house behind the old lady, her young visitor filled an old kettle.

Grandmother Bell smiled and shook her head. "You an' I growin' old together, master. Is silence we want, eh?"

She sighed and turned her head, watching the shining mudlake, and the horizon, listening to Eulalee moving about in the kitchen.

And the rustling and whispering of the old cottonwood tree.

Avram Davidson's career is a most enviable one, and there are few who have such a controlled grasp of craft as he. Winner of the World Fantasy Award for best collection (The Enquiries of Dr. Esterhazy), his flights into science fiction and fantasy are always impatiently awaited; and when he glides most silently into the darker clouds of horror . . .

NAPLES

by Avram Davidson

It is a curious thing, the reason of it being not certainly known to me—though I conjecture it might be poverty —why, when all the other monarchs of Europe were still building palaces in marble and granite, the kings of that anomalous and ill-fated kingdom called Of Naples and the Two Sicilies chose to build theirs in red brick. However, choose it they did: These last of the Italian Bourbons have long since lost their last thrones, no *castrato* singers sing for them from behind screens to lighten their well-deserved melancholy anymore, and their descendants now earn their livings in such occupations as gentlemen-salesclerks in fashionable jewelry stores—not, perhaps, entirely removed from all memory of the glory that once (such as it was) was theirs. But the red-brick *palazzi* are still there, they still line a part of the waterfront of Naples, and—some of them, at least—are still doing duty as seats of governance. (Elsewhere, for reasons equally a mystery to me, unless there is indeed some connection between red bricks and poverty, buildings in the same style and of the same material usually indicate that within them the Little Sisters of the Poor,

69

or some similar religious group, perform their selfless duties on behalf of the sick, the aged, and the otherwise bereft and afflicted; and which is the nobler function and whose the greater reward are questions that will not long detain us.)

Some twenty years ago or so, a man neither young nor old nor ugly nor comely, neither obviously rich nor equally poor, made his way from the docks past the red-brick *palazzi* and into the lower town of ancient and teeming Naples. He observed incuriously that the streets, instead of swarming with the short and swarthy, as foreign legend implies, swarmed instead with the tall and pale. But the expectations of tradition were served in other ways: by multitudes of donkey carts, by women dressed and draped in black, by many many beggars, and by other signs of deep and evident poverty. Almost at once a young man approached him with a murmured offer of service; the young man clutched the upturned collar of his jacket round about his throat, and, as the day was not even cool, let alone cold, it might have been assumed that the reason for the young man's gesture was that he probably did not wish to reveal the absence of a shirt. It was not altogether certain that the young man had no shirt at all, probably he had a shirt and probably this was its day to be washed and probably it was even now hanging from a line stretched across an alley where the sun did not enter in sufficient strength to dry it quickly.

There were many such alleys and many such lines, and, it is to be feared, many such shirts. There were also many such men, not all of them young; and if a count had been made, it might have been found that there were not enough shirts to go around.

Naples.

The traveler continued, with frequent pauses and considerings, to make his way slowly from the port area and slowly up the steep hill. Now and then he frowned slightly and now and then he slightly smiled. Long ago some humble hero or heroine discovered that if the hard wheat of the peninsula, subject to mold and rust and rot if stored in the ear, be ground into flour and mixed with water into a paste and extruded under pressure in the form of long strips, and dried, it would never rot at all and would keep as near forever as the hunger of the people would allow it. And when boiled it formed a food nutritious as bread and far more durable, and, when combined with such elements as oil or tomato or meat or cheese and perhaps the leaves of the bay and the basil, be good food indeed. However, the passage of time failed to bring these added ingredients within the means and reach of all. So, to vary in some measure at least the monotony of the plain pasta, it was made in the widest conceivable variety of shapes: thin strips and thick strips, ribbons broad and narrow, hollow tubes long and hollow tubes bent like elbows, bows and shells and stars and wheels and rosettes and what-have-you. And, if you have nothing, it is anyway some relief to eat your plain pasta in a different design . . . when you have, of course, pasta to eat.

At least every other doorway in the narrow streets and the narrower alleys kept a shop, and many of the shops sold pasta: for the further sake of variety the pasta was not merely stacked up in packages, it was also—the straight kinds—splayed about as though the stalks held flowers at their upper ends. And when the traveler saw these he faintly smiled. The young man who paced him step for step also looked at these modest displays. But he never smiled at them. In fact, although he continued his soft murmurs, he never smiled at all.

Most of these ways seemed hardly wide enough for outside displays, but such there were; there were second-hand clothes and fewer by far displays of some few new clothes; there were whole cheeses, although none hereabouts were seen to buy them whole, and perhaps not very many very often bought them by the slice or crumbling piece. And there were small fish, alive, alive-o, and larger fish in dim slabs that had not been alive in a long time, dry and hard and strong-smelling and salty, redolent of distant and storm-tossed seas. Tomatoes and peppers lay about in baskets. Oil was poured in careful drops into tiny bottles. There were also olives in many colors. Pictures of saints were sold, and the same shops sold, too, odd little emblematic images in coral and silver and—this was surely strange in such a scene of poverty—even gold:

behind the narrow windows of narrow shops, crosses, too, yes, and beads: the universal signia of that religion. . . . But what were these horns? What were these tiny hands, fingers tucked into a fist with the thumb protruding between first and second fingers?'

Best not to ask, you would empty the street in a trice. Everybody in Naples knows, no one in Naples would speak of it above a whisper . . . to a stranger, not at all. Speak not the word, lest it come to pass. Look not overlong at anyone in these streets, particularly not at the children they produce in such numbers of abundance. Who knows if your eye be not evil?

The eye of the traveler passed over the swarming and ragged *bambini* without stopping, and in the same manner he glanced at the scrannel cats and the charcoal braziers fanned by the toiling housewives: When one's home is but one room, one may well prefer the street as a kitchen.

When one has that which to cook, and fuel with which to cook it.

At length the passageway widened into a sort of a *piazza*. At one end was a church, on either side were the blank walls of some *palazzo* a good deal more antique than the brick ones down below: perhaps from the days of Spanish viceroys, perhaps from the days of King Robert. Who knows. There were anyway no more shops, no stalls, no wide-open-to-the-street one-room "houses" . . . and, for once, no masses of people . . . no beggars, even . . . there was even a sort of alley that seemingly went nowhere and that, surprisingly, held no one. And the traveler, who had so far only from time to time looked out from the corners of his eyes at the young man cleaving close to him as a shadow does, and who had made no reply at all to the soft murmurs with which the young man (ever clutching his jacket round about his naked throat) continually offered his services as "guide"; now for the first time, the traveler stopped, gave a direct look fleeting-swift, jerked his head toward the tiny passageway, and stepped inside.

The shirtless one's head went up and he looked at the heavens; his head went down and he looked at the filthy worn stones beneath. His shoulders moved in something too slight for a shrug and his unclothed throat uttered something too soft for a sigh.

He followed.

The traveler turned, without looking into the other's eyes, whispered a few short words into the other's ears.

The face of the young man, which had been stiff, expressionless, now went limp. Surprise showed most briefly. His brows moved once or twice.

—But yes—he said.—Surely—he said.

And he said, with a half bow and a small movement of his arm—I pray, follow. Very near—he said.

Neither one paused at the church.

And now the streets became, all of them, alleys. The alleys became mere slits. The shops grew infrequent, their store ever more meager. The lines of clothes dripping and drying overhead seemed to bear little relation to what human beings wore. What actually dangled and flapped in the occasional gusts of flat, warm, and stinking air may once have been clothing. Might once more, with infinite diligence and infinite skill, with scissors and needle and thread, be reconstituted into clothing once again. But for the present, one must either deny the rags that name, or else assume that behind the walls, the scabby walls, peeling walls, broken walls, filthy damp and dripping-ichorous walls, there dwelled some race of goblins whose limbs required garb of different drape.

The traveler began to lag somewhat behind.

How often, now, how carefully, almost how fearfully, the youngman guide turned his head to make sure the other was still with him. Had not stepped upon some ancient obscenely greasy flagstone fixed upon a pivot and gone silently screaming down into God knows what. Had not been slip-noosed, perhaps, as some giant hare, hoisted swiftly up above the flapping rags . . . Rags? Signal flags? What strange fleet might have its brass-bound spyglasses focused hither? Or perhaps it was fear and caution lest the other's fear and caution might simply cause him to turn and flee. In which case the youngman guide would flee after him, though from no greater fear than loss of the fee.

When one has no shirt, what greater fear?

Turned and into a courtyard entered through a worm-eaten door whose worms had last dined centuries ago, perhaps, and left the rest of the wood as inedible. A courtyard as dim, as dank as the antechamber to an Etruscan Hell. Courtyard as it might be the outer lobby of some tumulus, some tomb, not yet quite filled although long awaiting its last occupant. Shadow. Stench. The tatters hung up here could never be clothing again, should they in this foul damp ever indeed dry. At best they might serve to mop some ugly doorstep, did anyone within the yard have yet pride enough for such. And yet, if not, why were they hanging, wet from washing? Perhaps some last unstifled gesture of respectability. Who knows.

Naples.

Around a corner in the courtyard a door, and through the door a passageway and at the end of that a flight of stairs and at the end of the flight of stairs a doorway that no longer framed a door. A thing, something that was less than a blanket, was hung. The youngman paused and rapped and murmured. Something made a sound within. Something dragged itself across the floor within. Something seemed simultaneously to pull the hanging aside and to wrap itself behind the hanging.

At the opposite side to the door a man sat upon a bed. The man would seemingly have been the better for having been in the bed and not merely on it. On the cracked and riven and flaking, sodden walls some pictures, cut from magazines. Two American Presidents. Two Popes. And one Russian leader. And two saints. Comparisons are odious. Of those whose likenesses were on that filthy fearful wall it might be said they had in common anyway that all were dead.

—Good day—the youngman guide said.

—Good day—the man on the bed said. After a moment. He might, though, have been excused for not having said it at all.

—This gentleman is a foreigner—

The man on the bed said nothing. His sunken eyes merely looked.

—And he would like, ahem, ha, he would like to buy—

—But I have nothing to sell—

How dry, how faint, his voice.

—Some little something. Some certain article. An item—

—But nothing. I have nothing. We have nothing here—

His hand made a brief gesture, fell still.

A very small degree of impatience seemed to come over the face of the older visitor. The younger visitor, observing this, as he observed everything, took another step closer to the bed.—The gentleman is a foreigner—he repeated, as one who speaks to a rather stupid child.

The man on the bed looked around. His stooped shoulders, all dirty bones, shrugged, stooped more.—He may be a foreigner twice over, and what is it to me—he said, low-voiced, seemingly indifferent.

—He is a foreigner. He has, fool, son of a jackal, son of a strumpet, he has money—the youngman turned, abruptly, to the traveler. Said—Show him—

The traveler hesitated, looked all about. His mouth moved. So, too, his nose. His hands, no.

—You will have to show, you know. Can you pay without showing—

The traveler suddenly took a wallet from an inner pocket of his coat, abruptly opened it, and abruptly thrust it in again, placed his back not quite against the noisome wall, crossed his arms over his chest.

Slowly, slowly, the man on the bed slid his feet to the floor.

—Wait outside—he said.—Halfway down—he added.

On the half landing they waited. Listened. Heard.

Dragging, dragging footsteps. A voice they had not heard before.—*No*NO—A voice as it might be from behind the curtain or the blanket or the what-was-it in place of the door. The faint sounds of some faint and grisly struggle. Voices but no further words. Gasps, only.

Something began to wail, in a horrid broken voice. Then, outside the doorframe, at the head of the stairs, the man, tottering against the wall. Extending toward them his hands, together, as though enclosing something within.

—Be quick—he said. Panting.

And, all the while, the dreadful wail went on from behind him.

The youngman sprang up the stairs, his left hand reaching forward. Behind his back his right hand formed a fist with its thumb thrust out between first and second fingers; then both his hands swept up and met both hands of the other. The youngman, face twisted, twisting, darted down the steps to the half landing.

—The money—

Again, hands met. The traveler thrust his deep into his bosom, kept one there, withdrew the other. Withdrew his wallet, fumbled.

—Not here, not here, you know—the youngman warned.—The police, you know—

One look the older man flung about him.—Oh no. Oh God, not here—he said.—On the ship—

The youngman nodded. Roughly divided the money, tossed half of it up and behind without looking back. He did not come close to the older man as they hurried down the stairs.

Above, the wailing ceased. That other voice spoke, in a manner not to be described, voice changing register on every other word, almost.

—Curse the day my daughter's daughter gave you birth. May you burn, son of a *strega* and son of a strumpet, burn one hundred thousand years in Purgatory without remission—

The voice broke, crocked wordlessly a moment. Resumed.

—One dozen times I have been ready to die, and you, witch's bastard, you have stolen my death away and you have sold my death to strangers, may you burst, may you burn—

Again the voice broke, again began to wail.

The two men reached the bottom of the stained stairs, and parted, the younger one outdistancing the other and this time never looking back.

Above, faintly, in a tone very faintly surprised, the man who had been on the bed spoke.

—Die? Why should you die when I must eat?—

Naples.

Chelsea Quinn Yarbro is a Bay Area writer whose previous novels and stories had been primarily in the science
fiction and mystery fields. Nineteen seventy-eight, however, marked the appearance of her first horror novel
(Hotel Transylvania—first in a projected quintology),
whose protagonist you will catch a glimpse of on this
airplane flying across the Atlantic . . . east to west.

SEAT PARTNER
by Chelsea Quinn Yarbro

Jillian had lucked out. TWA had too many passengers
in coach, and so she—she almost giggled as she came
down the aisle of the huge plane—had to ride in first
class, jeans, muslin shirt and all. She found her seat by
the window and shoved her camera bag that doubled as
a purse under the seat, then dropped gratefully into the
wide, padded chair. This was great, she thought as she
fastened her seat belt, and reached down to pull a couple of paperback books out of her bag, then settled back
to read.

She had just got into the the story when a voice spoke
beside her. "Excuse me."

Marking her place with her finger, she looked up and
smiled a little at what she saw. The man was short, dark-
haired, and dark-eyed, with the look of early middle age
about him. His clothes were very simple and obviously
expensive. His black three-piece suit was a wool and
silk blend, superbly tailored to his trim but stocky figure.
His shirt was lustrous white silk against a black silk tie,
just the right width, and secured with an unadorned ruby
stickpin. Jillian noticed with amusement that his shoes

were thick-soled and slightly heeled. "Excuse me," he said again in his pleasant, melodic voice. "I believe that is my seat."

Jillian's face sank. This couldn't happen, not after she had been so lucky. She fumbled in her pockets for her boarding pass. "This is the pass they gave me," she said, holding it out to him.

A stewardess, attracted by the confusion, approached them. "Good morning. Is there some trouble?"

The man turned an attractive, wry smile on the woman. "A minor confusion. Your excellent computer seems to have assigned us the same seat."

The stewardess reached for boarding passes, frowning as she read them. "Just a moment. I'm sure we can correct this." She turned away as she spoke and went toward the galley.

"I'm sorry," Jillian said apologetically. Now that she had had a moment to watch the man, she found him quite awesome.

"No, no. Don't be foolish. Machines are far from perfect, after all. And first class is not wholly filled. We will be accommodated easily." He looked down at her with steady, compelling eyes. "I have no wish to impose on you."

Jillian waved her hands to show that there was no imposition and almost lost the book she was holding. She blushed and felt abashed—here she was, almost twenty-two, and *blushing* for chrissake. A swift glance upward through her fair lashes showed her that the stranger was amused. She wanted to give him a sharp, sophisticated retort, but there was something daunting in his expression, and she kept quiet.

A moment later the stewardess. "I'm sorry, sir," she said to the man. "Apparently there was some difficulty with the print-out on the card. Yours is seat B, on the aisle. If this is inconvenient . . ."

"No, not in the least." He took the boarding passes from her and handed one to Jillian. "I thank you for your trouble. You were most kind." Again the smile flashed and he bent to put his slim black leather case under the seat, saying to Jillian, "I am, in a way, grateful you have the window."

"Oh," Jillian said, surprised, "don't you like the window?"

"I'm afraid that I am not comfortable flying. It is difficult to be so far from the ground." He seated himself and fastened the seat belt.

Jillian started to open her book again, but said, "I think flying's exciting."

"Have you flown often?" the man asked somewhat absent-mindedly.

"Well, not very often," she confided. "Never this far before. I flew to Denver a couple of times to visit my father, and once to Florida, but I haven't been to Europe before."

"And you've spent the summer in Italy? What did you think of it?" He seemed to enjoy her excitement.

"Oh, Italy's okay, but I did a lot of traveling. I decided to fly in and out of Milan because it seemed a good place to start from." She folded down the corner of her page and set the book aside for the moment. "I liked Florence a lot. You've been there, I guess."

"Not for some time. But I had friends there, once." He folded small, beautiful hands over the seat belt. "What else did you see? Paris? Vienna? Rome?"

"Not Paris or Rome. I went to Vienna, though, and Prague and Budapest and Belgrade and Bucharest and Sofia, Sarajevo, Zagreb, Trieste, and Venice." She recited the major cities of her itinerary with a glow of enthusiasm. It had been such a wonderful summer, going through those ancient, ancient countries.

The man's fine brows lifted. "Not the usual student trek, is it? Hungary, Rumania, Bulgaria, Yugoslavia . . . hardly countries one associates with American students."

On the loudspeaker, the stewardess said in three languages that cigarettes must be extinguished and seat belts fastened in preparation for take-off.

Jillian frowned. "Is my being an American student that obvious?"

"Certainly," he said kindly. "Students everywhere have a kind of uniform. Jeans and loose shirts and long, straight blond hair—oh, most surely, an American, and from the way you pronounce your r's, I would say from the Midwest."

Grudgingly, Jillian said, "Des Moines."

"That is in Iowa, is it not?"

Their conversation was interrupted by the sound of engines roaring as the jet started to move away from the terminal.

The stewardess reappeared and gave the customary speech about oxygen masks, flotation pads, and exits in English, French, and Italian. Jillian listened to the talk, trying to appear nonchalant and still feeling the stir of pleasure in flying. The man in the seat beside her closed his eyes.

For five minutes or so they taxied, jockeying for a position on the runway, one of three jets preparing for take-off. Then there was the fierce, lunging roll as the plane raced into the air. The ground dropped away below them, there was the ear-popping climb and the hideous sound of landing gear retracting, and then the stewardess reminded the passengers that smoking was permitted in specified sections only, that they were free to move about the cabin, and that headsets for the movie would be available shortly, before lunch was served.

Jillian looked out the window and saw Milan growing distant and small. Without being aware of it, she sighed.

"You are sad?" asked the man beside her.

"In a way. I'm glad to be going home, but it was such a wonderful summer."

"And what will you do when you get home?" was his next question.

"Oh, teach, I guess. I've got a job at the junior high school. It's my first . . ." She looked out the window again.

"You don't seem much pleased with your job." There was no criticism in his tone. "If it is not what you wish to do, why do you do it?"

"Well," Jillian said in what she hoped was her most reasonable tone, "I have to do something. I'm not planning to get married or anything . . ." She broke off, thinking of how disappointed her mother had been when she had changed her mind about Harold. But it wouldn't have worked, she said to herself, as she had almost every day since the tenth of April when she had returned his ring.

"I'm intruding," said the man compassionately. "Forgive me."

"It's nothing," Jillian responded, wanting to make light of it. "I was just thinking how high up we are."

"Were you." His dark, enigmatic eyes rested on her a moment. "Perhaps you would like to tell me of some of the things you saw in eastern Europe."

"Well," she said, glad to have something to occupy her thoughts other than Harold. "I wanted to see all those strange places. They were really interesting. I was really amazed at how different everything is."

"Different? How?"

"It's not just the way they look, and everything being old," Jillian said with sudden intensity. "It *feels* different here, like all the things they pooh-pooh in schools are real. When I went to Castle Bran, I mean, I really understood how there could be legends about the place. It made sense that people would believe them."

The man's interest increased. "Castle Bran?"

"Yes, you know, it's very famous. It's the castle that Bram Stoker used as a model for Castle Dracula, at least that's what most of the experts are saying now. I wanted to go to the ruins of the real Castle Dracula, but the weather was bad, so I didn't."

"Strange. But why are you interested in such places? Surely the resistance to the Turkish invasions is not your area of study."

"Oh, no," she laughed a little embarrassed. "I like vampires. Books, movies, anything."

"Indeed." There was an ironic note in his voice now.

"Well, they might not be great art, but they're wonderful to . . ."

"Fantasize about?" he suggested gently.

Jillian felt herself flush and wished that she hadn't mentioned the subject. "Sometimes." She tilted her chin up. "Lugosi, Lee, all of them, they're just great. I think they're sexy."

The man very nearly chuckled, but managed to preserve a certain gravity that almost infuriated Jillian. "A novel idea," he said after a moment.

"It isn't," she insisted. "I know lots of people who think vampires are sexy."

"American irreverence, do you think?" He shook his head. "There was a time, not so very long ago, when such an avowal would be absolutely heretical."

"That's silly," she said, a little less sure of herself. In her travels, she had come to realize that heresy was not just an obsolete prejudice.

"Hardly silly," the man said in a somber tone. "Men and women and even children died in agony for believing such things. And there are those who think that the practice should be reinstated."

"But it's just superstition," Jillian burst out, inwardly shocked at her reaction. "Nobody today could possibly believe that vampires really exist . . ."

"Are you so certain they do not?" he inquired mildly.

"Well, how could they?" she retorted. "It's absurd."

He favored her with a nod that was more of a bow. "Of course."

Jillian felt the need to pursue the matter a little more. "If there were such things, they would have been found out by now. There'd be good, solid proof."

"Proof? But how could such a thing be proved? As you said yourself, the idea is absurd."

"There ought to be ways to do it." She hadn't considered the matter before, but she felt challenged by the stranger in the seat beside her. "It wouldn't be the premature burial concerns, because that's a different matter entirely."

"Certainly," he agreed. "If legends are right, burial of a vampire is hardly premature."

She decided to overlook this remark. "The trouble is," she said seriously, "the best way would be to get volunteers, and I don't suppose it would be easy to convince any real vampire that he ought to submit himself to scientific study."

"It would be impossible, I should think," her seat partner interjected.

"And how could it be proven, I mean, without destroying the volunteer? I don't suppose there are any real proofs short of putting a stake through their hearts or severing their heads."

"Burning is also a good method," the man said.

"No one, not even a vampire, is going to agree to that.

And it wouldn't demonstrate anything at all. Anyone would die of it, whether or not they were vampires." Suddenly she giggled. "Christ, this is weird, sitting up here talking about experimenting on vampires." Actually, she was becoming uncomfortable with the subject and was anxious to speak of something else.

The man seemed to read her thoughts, for he said, "Hardly what one would can profitable speculation."

Jillian had the odd feeling that she should be polite and decided to ask him a few questions. "Is this your first trip to America? You speak wonderful English, but . . ."

"But you know I am a foreigner. Naturally." He paused. "I have been to America, but that was some time ago, and then it was to the capital of Mexico. A strange place, that city built on swamps."

His description of Mexico City startled Jillian a little, because though it was true enough that the city had been built on swamps long ago, it seemed an odd aspect of its history to mention. "Yes," she said, to indicate she was listening.

"This is my first visit to your country. It is disquieting to go to so vast a land, and be so far from home."

The stewardess appeared at his elbow. "Pardon me, Count. We're about to serve cocktails, and if you'd like one . . .?"

"No, thank you, but perhaps"—he turned to Jillian—"you would do me the honor of letting me buy one for you."

Jillian was torn between her delight at the invitation and the strictures of her youth that had warned against such temptations. Pleasure won. "Oh, please; I'd like a gin and tonic. Tanqueray gin, if you have it."

"Tanqueray and tonic," the stewardess repeated, then turned to the man again. "If you don't want a cocktail, we have an excellent selection of wines . . ."

"Thank you, no. I do not drink wine." With a slight, imperious nod, he dismissed the stewardess.

"She called you Count," Jillian accused him, a delicious thrill running through her. This charming man in black was an aristocrat! She was really looking forward to telling her friends about the flight when she got home. It would be wonderful to say, as casually as she could, "Oh, yes, on the way back, I had this lovely conversation with a European count," and then watch them stare at her.

"A courtesy title, these days," the man said diffidently. "Things have changed much from the time I was born, and now there are few who would respect my claims."

Jillian knew something of the history of Europe and nodded sympathetically. "How unfortunate for you. Does it make you sad to see the changes in your country?" She realized she didn't know which country he was from and wondered how she could ask without seeming rude.

"It is true that my blood is very old, and I have strong ties to my native soil. But there are always changes, and in time, one grows accustomed, one adapts. The alternative is to die."

Never before had Jillian felt the plight of the exiled as she did looking into that civilized, intelligent face. "How terrible! You must get very lonely."

"Occasionally, very lonely," he said in a distant way.

"But surely, you have family . . ." She bit the words off. She had read of some of the bloodier revolutions, where almost every noble house was wiped out. If his was one of them, the mention of it might be inexcusable.

"Oh, yes. I have blood relatives throughout Europe. There are not so many of us as there once were, but a few of us survive." He looked up as the stewardess approached with a small tray with one glass on it. "Ah. Your cocktail, I believe." He leaned back as the stewardess handed the drink to Jillian. "Which currency would you prefer?" he asked.

"How would you prefer to pay, sir?" the stewardess responded with a blinding smile.

"Dollars, pounds, or francs. Choose." He pulled a large black wallet from his inner coat pocket.

"Dollars, then. It's one-fifty." She held out her hand for the bill, and thanked him as she took it away to make change.

Jillian lifted the glass, which was slightly frosted, and at the clear liquid that had a faint touch of blue in its color. "Well, thanks. To you." She sipped at the cold, surprisingly strong drink.

"You're very kind," he said, an automatic response.

"Tell me," he said in another, lighter tone, "what is it you will teach to your junior high school students?"

"English," she said, and almost added, "of course."

"As a language?" the Count asked, plainly startled.

"Not really. We do some grammar, some literature, some creative writing, a lot of reading." As she said it, it sounded so dull, and a little gloom touched her.

"But surely you don't want to spend your life teaching some grammar, some literature, some creative writing, and a lot of reading to disinterested children." He said this gently, kindly, and watched Jillian very closely as she answered.

"Sometimes I think I don't know what I want," she said and felt alarmed at her own candor.

"I feel you would rather explore castles in Europe than teach English in Des Moines." He regarded her evenly. "Am I correct?"

"I suppose so," she said slowly and took another sip of her cocktail.

"Then why don't you?"

It was a question she had not dared to ask herself and she was angry at him for asking. He had no right, this unnamed former Count in elegant black who watched her with such penetrating dark eyes. He had no right to ask such things of her. She was about to tell him so when he said, "A woman I have long loved very dearly used to think she would not be able to learn everything she wanted to during her life. You must understand, European society has been quite rigid at times. She comes from a distinguished French family, and when I met her, she was nineteen and terrified that she would be forced into the life other women had before she had opportunities to study. Now," he said with a faint, affectionate smile, "she is on a dig, I think it's called, in Iran. She is an accomplished archeologist. You see, she did not allow herself to be limited by the expectations of others."

Jillian listened, ready to fling back sharp answers if he insisted that she turn away from the life she had determined upon. "You changed her mind, I suppose?" She knew she sounded petulant, but she wanted him to know she was displeased.

"Changed her mind, no. It could be said that she

changed mine." His eyes glinted with reminiscence. "She is a remarkable woman, my Madelaine." He turned his attention to Jillian once more. "Forgive me. Occasionally I am reminded of . . . our attachment. I did not mean to be rude. Perhaps I meant to suggest that you, like her, should not permit those around you to make decisions for you that are not what you want."

The stewardess returned with headphones for the movie. It was, she explained, a long feature, a French and English venture, shot predominantly in Spain with an international cast. She held out the headsets to Jillian and to the man beside her.

Though Jillian knew it was unmannerly of her to do so, she accepted the headset with a wide smile and said to her seat partner, "I hate to do this, but I've wanted to see this flick all summer long, and I don't know when I'll have the chance again."

She knew by the sardonic light to his smile that he was not fooled, but he said to her, "By all means. I understand that it is most entertaining."

"Headphones for you, Count?" the stewardess asked solicitously.

"I think not, but thank you." He looked toward Jillian. "If you decide that it is truly worthwhile, tell me, and I will call for headsets."

The stewardess nodded and moved away to the next pair of seats.

"You don't mind, do you?" Jillian asked, suddenly conscience-stricken. The Count had bought her a drink and was being very courteous, she thought, but then again, she did not want him to think that she was interested in him.

"No, I don't mind." He glanced down at his leather case under the seat. "Would it disturb you if I do a little work while the film is running?"

Jillian shook her head and put the thin blue plastic leads to the socket on the arm of her seat. "Go ahead."

He had already pulled the case from under the seat and opened it on his lap. There were three thick, leather-bound notebooks in the case, and he pulled the largest of these out, closed the case, and replaced it. He took a pen from one of his coat pockets and pulled down the table from the seat ahead. He gave Jillian a swift, disturbing smile, then bent his head to his work.

Before the film was half over, Jillian was bored. The plot, which she had thought would be exciting, was tedious, and the filming was unimaginative. Most of the actors looked uncomfortable in their nineteenth-century costumes, and the dialogue was so trite that Jillian could not blame the actors for their poor delivery. She longed to be able to take off the headset and get back to reading, but she was afraid that the Count would engage her in conversation again, and for some reason, this prospect unnerved her. He had a knack for drawing her out. Another half-hour and she would have been telling him about Harold and how he had laughed when she said she wanted to get her master's before they married. Already he had got her to talk about vampires, and she had never done that before, not with a stranger. So she kept her eyes on the little screen and tried to concentrate on the dull extravaganza. Once she caught the Count looking at her, amusement in his dark eyes, but then he turned back to the notebook, and she could not be certain whether or not he had sensed her dilemma.

When at last the film ground to a messy, predictable finish, Jillian was anxious to take off the headset. She made a point of reaching for a book before handing the plastic tubing to the stewardess, and shot a quick look at her seat partner.

"If you do not wish to speak to me," he said without turning his attention from the page on which he wrote, "please say so. I will not be offended."

Jillian was grateful and annoyed at once. "I'm just tired. I think I want to read a while."

He nodded and said nothing more.

It was not until they were nearing Kennedy Airport that Jillian dared to talk to her seat partner. She had been reading the same paragraph for almost twenty minutes, and it made no more sense now than the first time she had looked at it. With a sigh she closed the book and bent to put it in her bag.

"We're nearing New York," the Count said. He had put his notebook away some minutes before and had sat back in his seat, gazing at nothing in particular.

"Yes," she said, not certain now if she was glad to be coming home.

"I suppose you'll be flying on to Des Moines."

"In the morning," she said, thinking for the first time that she would have to ask about motels near the airport, because she knew she could not go into Manhattan for the night. Between the taxi fare and the hotel bill, she could not afford that one last splurge.

"But it is only . . ."—he consulted his watch and paused to calculate the difference in time—"six-thirty. You can't mean that you want to sit in a sterile little room wih a poor television for company all this evening."

That was, in fact, precisely what she had intended to do, but his description made the prospect sound more gloomy than she had thought it could be. "I guess so."

"Would you be offended if I asked you to let me buy you dinner? This is my first time in this city, in this country, and it will feel less strange to me if you'd be kind enough to give me the pleasure of your company."

If this was a line, Jillian thought, it was one of the very smoothest she had ever heard. And she did want to go into Manhattan, and she very much wanted to spend the evening at a nice restaurant. A man like the Count, she thought, wouldn't be the sort to skimp on a night out. He might, of course, impose conditions later.

"I have no designs on your virginity," he said, with that uncanny insight that had bothered her earlier.

"I'm not a virgin," Jillian snapped, without meaning to.

The seatbelt sign and no smoking signs flashed on, one after another, and the stewardess announced that they had begun their descent for landing.

The Count smiled, the whole force of his dark eyes on her. "Shall we say your virtue, then? I will allow that you are a very desirable, very young woman, and it would delight me to have you as my guest for the evening. Well?"

"You don't even know my name," she said with a smile, her mind already made up.

"It's Jillian Walker," he answered promptly, and added as she stared at him, "It was on the envelope your boarding pass is in."

For a moment, Jillian had been filled with a certain awe, almost a dread, but at this simple explanation, she smiled. A niggling image had risen in her mind, an image developed from her reading and the films she loved. A foreign, exiled Count, in black, of aristocratic, almost regal bearing, who had refused wine . . . It was an effort not to laugh. "You know my name, but I don't know yours."

"You may call me Franz, if you like. I am Franz Josef Ragoczy, onetime Count, among other things."

"What's that name again?" Something about it was familiar, but she couldn't place it.

"Ragoczy. *Rah*-go-schkee," he repeated. "It's the German version of the Hungarian variant of the name. As I told you, I come from an ancient line." His expression had softened. "It is agreed, then?"

The plane was descending rapidly, and there was that wrenching clunk as the landing gear was lowered. Ahead the sprawl of Kennedy Airport rose up to meet them.

Whatever reservations that were left in Jillian's mind were banished by the warmth in his eyes. If he wanted more than her company, she decided, she would deal with that as it happened. As the plane jounced onto the runway, she grinned at him. "Count, I'd love to have dinner with you."

He took her hand in his and carried it gallantly, ironically, to his lips. "Dinner with me," he echoed her, "dinner with me." There was secret meaning in the soft words that followed, almost lost in the shrieking of the engines. "I will hold you to that, Jillian Walker. Believe this."

Jack Dann, according to the critics, does not write nearly enough to satisfy either them or his fans. His fantasy tales, in particular, generally appear literally years apart —too infrequently for those who see, as he does, the contemporary world through a glass that is not only dark, it is distorted beyond midnight.

CAMPS
by Jack Dann

As Stephen lies in bed, he can think only of pain.

He imagines it as sharp and blue. After receiving an injection of Demerol, he enters pain's cold regions as an explorer, an objective visitor. It is a country of ice and glass, monochromatic plains and valleys filled with wash-blue shards of ice, crystal pyramids and pinnacles, squares, oblongs, and all manner of polyhedron—block upon block of painted blue pain.

Although it is mid-afternoon, Stephen pretends it is dark. His eyes are tightly closed, but the daylight pouring into the room from two large windows intrudes as a dull red field extending infinitely behind his eyelids.

"Josie," he asks through cottonmouth, "aren't I due for another shot?" Josie is crisp and fresh and large in her starched white uniform. Her peaked nurse's cap is pinned to her mouse-brown hair.

"I've just given you an injection, it will take effect soon." Josie strokes his hand, and he dreams of ice.

"Bring me some ice," he whispers.

"If I bring you a bowl of ice, you'll only spill it again."

"Bring me some ice . . ." By touching the ice cubes, by turning them in his hand like a gambler favoring his dice, he can transport himself into the beautiful blue country. Later, the ice will melt; and he will spill the bowl. The shock of cold and pain will awaken him.

Stephen believes that he is dying, and he has resolved to die properly. Each visit to the cold country brings him closer to death; and death, he has learned, is only a slow walk through icefields. He has come to appreciate the complete lack of warmth and the beautifully etched face of his magical country.

But he is connected to the bright flat world of the hospital by plastic tubes—one breathes cold oxygen into his left nostril, another passes into his right nostril and down his throat to his stomach; one feeds him intravenously, another draws his urine.

"Here's your ice," Josie says. "But mind you, don't spill it." She places the small bowl on his traytable and wheels the table close to him. She has a musky odor of perspiration and perfume; Stephen is remined of old women and college girls.

"Sleep now, sweet boy."

Without opening his eyes, Stephen reaches out and places his hand on the ice.

"Come now, Stephen, wake up. Doctor Volk is here to see you."

Stephen feels the cool touch of Josie's hand, and he opens his eyes to see the doctor standing beside him. The doctor has a gaunt long face and thinning brown hair; he is dressed in a wrinkled green suit.

"Now we'll check the dressing, Stephen," he says as he tears away a gauze bandage on Stephen's abdomen.

Stephen feels the pain, but he is removed from it. His only wish is to return to the blue dreamlands. He watches the doctor peel off the neat crosshatchings of gauze. A terrible stink fills the room.

Josie stands well away from the bed.

"Now we'll check your drains." The doctor pulls a long drainage tube out of Stephen's abdomen, irrigates and disinfects the wound, inserts a new drain, and repeats the process by pulling out another tube just below the rib cage.

Stephen imagines that he is swimming out of the room. He tries to cross the hazy border into cooler regions, but it is difficult to concentrate. He has only a half hour at most before the Demerol will wear off. Already, the pain is coming closer, and he will not be due for another injection until the nightnurse comes on duty. But the nightnurse will not give him an injection without an argument. She will tell him to fight the pain.

But he cannot fight without a shot.

"Tomorrow we'll take that oxygen tube out of your nose," the doctor says, but his voice seems far away and Stephen wonders what he is talking about.

He reaches for the bowl of ice, but cannot find it.

"Josie, you've taken my ice."

"I took the ice away when the doctor came. Why don't you try to watch a bit of television with me, Soupy Sales is on."

"Just bring me some ice," Stephen says. "I want to rest a bit." He can feel the sharp edges of pain breaking through the gauzy wraps of Demerol.

"I love you, Josie," he says sleepily as she places a fresh bowl of ice on his tray.

As Stephen wanders through his ice-blue deamworld, he sees a rectangle of blinding white light. It looks like a doorway into an adjoining world of brightness. He has glimpsed it before on previous Demerol highs. A coal dark doorway stands beside the bright one.

He walks toward the portals, passes through white-blue conefields.

Time is growing short. The drug cannot stretch it much longer. Stephen knows that he has to choose either the bright doorway or the dark, one or the other. He does not even consider turning around, for he has dreamed that the ice and glass and cold blue gemstones have melted behind him.

It makes no difference to Stephen which doorway he chooses. On impulse he steps into blazing, searing whiteness.

Suddenly he is in a cramped world of people and sound.

The boxcar's doors were flung open. Stephen was being pushed out of the cramped boxcar that stank of sweat, feces, and urine. Several people had died in the car and added their stink of death to the already fetid air.

"Carla, stay close to me," shouted a man beside Stephen. He had been separated from his wife by a young woman who pushed between them, as she tried to return to the dark safety of the boxcar.

SS men in black, dirty uniforms were everywhere. They kicked and pummeled everyone within reach. Alsatian guard dogs snapped and barked. Stephen was bitten by one of the snarling dogs. A woman beside him was being kicked by soldiers. And they were all being methodically herded past a high barbed wire fence. Beside the fence was a wall.

Stephen looked around for an escape route, but he was surrounded by other prisoners, who were pressing against him. Soldiers were shooting indiscriminately into the crowd, shooting women and children alike.

The man who had shouted to his wife was shot.

"Sholom, help me, help me," screamed a scrawny young woman whose skin was as yellow and pimpled as chickenflesh.

And Stephen understood that *he* was Sholom. He was a Jew in this burning, stinking world, and this woman, somehow, meant something to him. He felt the yellow star sewn on the breast of his filthy jacket. He grimaced uncontrollably. The strangest thoughts were passing through his mind, remembrances of another childhood: morning prayers with his father and rich uncle, large breakfasts on Saturdays, the sounds of his mother and father quietly making love in the next room, *yortzeit* candles burning in the living room, his brother reciting the "four questions" at the Passover table.

He touched the star again and remembered the Nazi's facetious euphemism for it: *Pour le Semite.*

He wanted to strike out, to kill the Nazis, to fight and die. But he found himself marching with the others, as if he had no will of his own. He felt that he was cut in half. He had two selves now; one watched the other. One self wanted to fight. The other was numbed; it cared only for itself. It was determined to survive.

Stephen looked around for the woman who had called out to him. She was nowhere to be seen.

Behind him were railroad tracks, electrified wire, and the conical tower and main gate of the camp. Ahead was a pitted road littered with corpses and their belongings. Rifles were being fired and a heavy, sickly-sweet odor was everywhere. Stephen gagged, others vomited. It was the overwhelming stench of death, of rotting and burning flesh. Black clouds hung above the camp, and flames spurted from the tall chimneys of ugly buildings, as if from infernal machines.

Setphen walked onward; he was numb, unable to fight or even talk. Everything that happened around him was impossible, the stuff of dreams.

The prisoners were ordered to halt, and the soldiers began to separate those who would be burned from those who would be worked to death. Old men and women and young children were pulled out of the crowd. Some were beaten and killed immediately while the others looked on in disbelief. Stephen looked on, as if it was of no concern to him. Everything was unreal, dreamlike. He did not belong here.

The new prisoners looked like Musselmänner, the walking dead. Those who became ill, or were beaten or starved before they could "wake up" to the reality of the camps became Musselmänner. Musselmänner could not think or feel. They shuffled around, already dead in spirit, until a guard or disease or cold or starvation killed them.

"Keep marching," shouted a guard, as Stephen stopped before an emaciated old man crawling on the ground. "You'll look like him soon enough."

Suddenly, as if waking from one dream and finding himself in another, Stephen remembered that the chicken-skinned girl was his wife. He remembered their life together, their children and crowded flat. He remembered her birthmark on her leg, her scent, her hungry lovemaking. He had once fought another boy over her.

His glands opened up with fear and shame; he had ignored her screams for help.

He stopped and turned, faced the other group. "Fruma," he shouted, then started to run.

A guard struck him in the chest with the butt of his rifle, and Stephen fell into darkness.

He spills the icewater again and awakens with a scream.

"It's my fault," Josie says, as she peels back the sheets. "I should have taken the bowl away from you. But you fight me."

Stephen lives with the pain again. He imagines that a tiny fire is burning in his abdomen, slowly consuming him. He stares at the television high on the wall and watches Soupy Sales.

As Josie changes the plastic sac containing his intravenous saline solution, an orderly pushes a cart into the room and asks Stephen if he wants a print for his wall.

"Would you like me to choose something for you?" Josie asks.

Stephen shakes his head and asks the orderly to show him all the prints. Most of them are familiar still-lifes and pastorals, but one catches his attention. It is a painting of a wheat field. Although the sky looks ominously dark, the wheat is brightly rendered in great broad strokes. A path cuts through the field and crows fly overhead.

"That one," Stephen says. "Put that one up."

After the orderly hangs the print and leaves, Josie asks Stephen why he chose that particular painting.

"I like Van Gogh," he says dreamily, as he tries to detect a rhythm in the surges of abdominal pain. But he is not nauseated, just gaseous.

"Any paricular reason why you like Van Gogh?" asks Josie. "He's my favorite artist, too."

"I didn't say he was my favorite," Stephen says, and Josie pouts, an expression which does not fit her prematurely lined face. Stephen closes his eyes, glimpses the cold country, and says, "I like the painting because it's so bright that it's almost frightening. And the road going through the field"—he opens his eyes—"doesn't go anywhere. It just ends in the field. And the crows are flying around like vultures."

"Most people see it as just a pretty picture," Josie says. "What's it called?"

"Wheatfield with Blackbirds."

"Sensible. My stomach hurts, Josie. Help me turn over on my side." Josie helps him onto his left side, plumps up his pillows, and inserts a short tube into his rectum to relieve the gas. "I also like the painting with the large stars that all look out of focus," Stephen says. "What's it called?"

"*Starry Night.*"

"That's scary, too," Stephen says. Josie takes his blood pressure, makes a notation on his chart, then sits down beside him and holds his hand. "I remember something," he says. "Something just—" He jumps as he remembers, and pain shoots through his distended stomach. Josie shushes him, checks the intravenous needle, and asks him what he remembers.

But the memory of the dream recedes as the pain grows sharper. "I hurt all the fucking time, Josie," he says, changing position. Josie removes the rectal tube before he is on his back.

"Don't use such language, I don't like to hear it. I know you have a lot of pain," she says, her voice softening.

"Time for a shot."

"No, honey, not for some time. You'll just have to bear with it."

Stephen remembers his dream again. He is afraid of it. His breath is short and his heart feels as if it is beating in his throat, but he recounts the entire dream to Josie.

He does not notice that her face has lost its color.

"It's only a dream, Stephen. Probably something you studied in history."

"But it was so real, not like a dream at all."

"That's enough!" Josie says.

"I'm sorry I upset you. Don't be angry."

"I'm *not* angry."

"I'm sorry," he says fighting the pain, squeezing Josie's hand tightly. "Didn't you tell me that you were in the Second World War?"

Josie is composed once again. "Yes, I did, but I'm surprised you remembered. You were very sick. I was a nurse overseas, spent most of the war in England. But I was one of the first service women to go into any of the concentration camps."

Stephen drifts with the pain; he appears to be asleep.

"You must have studied very hard," Josie whispers to him. Her hand is shaking just a bit.

It is twelve o'clock and his room is death-quiet. The

sharp shadows seem to be the hardest objects in the room. The fluorescents burn steadily in the hall outside.

Stephen looks out into the hallway, but he can see only the far white wall. He waits for his nightnurse to appear: it is time for his injection. A young nurse passes by his doorway. Stephen imagines that she is a cardboard ship sailing through the corridors.

He presses the buzzer, which is attached by a clip to his pillow. The nightnurse will take her time, he tells himself. He remembers arguing with her. Angrily, he presses the buzzer again.

Across the hall, a man begins to scream, and there is a shuffle of nurses into his room. The screaming turns into begging and whining. Although Stephen has never seen the man in the opposite room, he has come to hate him. Like Stephen, he has something wrong with his stomach; but he cannot suffer well. He can only beg and cry, try to make deals with the nurses, doctors, God, and angels. Stephen cannot muster any pity for this man.

The nightnurse finally comes into the room, says, "You have to try to get along without this," and gives him an injection of Demerol.

"Why does the man across the hall scream so?" Stephen asks, but the nurse is already edging out of the room.

"Because he's in pain."

"So am I," Stephen says in a loud voice. "But I can keep it to myself."

"Then stop buzzing me constantly for an injection. That man across the hall has had half of his stomach removed. He's got something to scream about."

So have I, Stephen thinks; but the nurse disappears before he can tell her. He tries to imagine what the man across the hall looks like. He thinks of him as being bald and small, an ancient baby. Stephen tries to feel sorry for the man, but his incessant whining disgusts him.

The drug takes effect; the screams recede as he hurtles through the dark corridors of a dream. The cold country is dark, for Stephen cannot persuade his nightnurse to bring him some ice. Once again, he sees two entrances. As the world melts behind him, he steps into the coal-black doorway.

In the darkness he hears an alarm, a bone-jarring clangor.

He could smell the combined stink of men pressed closely together. They were all lying upon two badly constructed wooden shelves. The floor was dirt; the smell of urine never left the barrack.

"Wake up," said a man Stephen knew as Viktor. "If the guard finds you in bed, you'll be beaten again."

Stephen moaned, still wrapped in dreams. "Wake up, wake up," he mumbled to himself. He would have a few more minutes before the guard arrived with the dogs. At the very thought of dogs, Stephen felt revulsion. He had once been bitten in the face by a large dog.

He opened his eyes, yet he was still half-asleep, exhausted. You are in a death camp, he said to himself. You must wake up. You must fight by waking up. Or you will die in your sleep. Shaking uncontrollably, he said, "Do you want to end up in the oven, perhaps you will be lucky today and live."

As he lowered his legs to the floor, he felt the sores open on the soles of his feet. He wondered who would die today and shrugged. It was his third week in the camp. Impossibly, against all odds, he had survived. Most of those he had known in the train had either died or become Musselmänner. If it was not for Viktor, he, too, would have become a Musselmann. He had a breakdown and wanted to die. He babbled in English. But Viktor talked him out of death, shared his portion of food with him, and taught him the new rules of life.

"Like everyone else who survives, I count myself first, second, and third—then I try to do what I can for someone else," Viktor had said.

"I will survive," Stephen repeated to himself, as the guards opened the door, stepped into the room, and began to shout. Their dogs growled and snapped, but heeled beside them. The guards looked sleepy; one did not wear a cap, and his red hair was tousled.

Perhaps he spent the night with one of the whores, Stephen thought. Perhaps today would not be so bad . . .

* * *

And so begins the morning ritual: Josie enters Stephen's room at quarter to eight, fusses with the chart attached to the footboard of his bed, pads about aimlessly, and finally goes to the bathroom. She returns, her stiff uniform making swishing sounds. Stephen can feel her standing over the bed and staring at him. But he does not open his eyes. He waits a beat.

She turns away, then drops the bedpan. Yesterday it was the metal ashtray; day before that, she bumped into the bedstand.

"Good morning, darling, it's a beautiful day," she says, then walks across the room to the windows. She parts the faded orange drapes and opens the blinds.

"How do you feel today?"

"Okay, I guess."

Josie takes his pulse and asks, "Did Mister Gregory stop in to say hello last night?"

"Yes," Stephen says. "He's teaching me how to play gin rummy. What's wrong with him?"

"He's very sick."

"I can see that, has he got cancer?"

"I don't know," says Josie, as she tidies up his night table.

"You're lying again," Stephen says, but she ignores him. After a time, he says, "His girlfriend was in to see me last night, I bet his wife will be in today."

"Shut your mouth about that," Josie says. "Let's get you out of that bed so I can change the sheets."

Stephen sits in the chair all morning. He is getting well, but is still very weak. Just before lunchtime, the orderly wheels his cart into the room and asks Stephen if he would like to replace the print hanging on the wall.

"I've seen them all," Stephen says. "I'll keep the one I have." Stephen does not grow tired of the Van Gogh painting; sometimes, the crows seem to have changed position.

"Maybe you'll like this one," the orderly says as he pulls out a cardboard print of Van Gogh's *Starry Night*. It is a study of a village nestled in the hills, dressed in shadows. But everything seems to be boiling and writhing as in a fever dream. A cypress tree in the foreground looks like a black flame, and the vertiginous sky is filled with great blurry stars. It is a drunkard's dream. The orderly smiles.

"So you did have it," Stephen says.

"No, I traded some other pictures for it. They had a copy in the West Wing."

Stephen watches him hang it, thanks him, and waits for him to leave. Then he gets up and examines the painting carefully. He touches the raised fascimile brush-strokes, and turns toward Josie, feeling an odd sensation in his groin. He looks at her, as if seeing her for the first time. She has an overly full mouth which curves downward at the corners when she smiles. She is not a pretty woman—too fat, he thinks.

"Dance with me," he says, as he waves his arms and takes a step forward, conscious of the pain in his stomach.

"You're too sick to be dancing just yet," but she laughs at him and bends her knees in a mock plié.

She has small breasts for such a large woman, Stephen thinks. Feeling suddenly dizzy, he takes a step toward the bed. He feels himself slip to the floor, feels Josie's hair brushing against his face, dreams that he's all wet from her tongue, feels her arms around him, squeezing, then feels the weight of her body pressing down on him, crushing him . . .

He wakes up in bed, catheterized. He has an intravenous needle in his left wrist, and it is difficult to swallow, for he has a tube down his throat.

He groans, tries to move.

"Quiet, Stephen," Josie says, stroking his hand.

"What happened?" he mumbles. He can only remember being dizzy.

"You've had a slight setback, so just rest. The doctor had to collapse your lung, you must lie very still."

"Josie, I love you," he whispers, but he is too far away to be heard. He wonders how many hours or days have passed. He looks toward the window. It is dark, and there is no one in the room.

He presses the buzzer attached to his pillow and remembers a dream . . .

* * *

"You must fight," Viktor said.

It was dark, all the other men were asleep, and the barrack was filled with snoring and snorting. Stephen wished they could all die, choke on their own breath. It would be an act of mercy.

"Why fight?" Stephen asked, and he pointed toward the greasy window, beyond which were the ovens that smoked day and night. He made a fluttering gesture with his hand—smoke rising.

"You must fight, you must live, living is everything. It is the only thing that makes sense here."

"We're all going to die, anyway," Stephen whispered. "Just like your sister . . . and my wife."

"No, Sholom, we're going to live. The others may die, but we're going to live. You must believe that."

Stephen understood that Viktor was desperately trying to convince himself to live. He felt sorry for Viktor; there could be no sensible rationale for living in a place like this. Everything must die here.

Stephen grinned, tasted blood from the corner of his mouth, and said, "So we'll live through the night, maybe."

And maybe tomorrow, he thought. He would play the game of survival a little longer.

He wondered if Viktor would be alive tomorrow. He smiled and thought, If Viktor dies, then I will have to take his place and convince others to live. For an instant, he hoped Viktor would die so that he could take his place.

The alarm sounded. It was three o'clock in the morning, time to begin the day.

This morning Stephen was on his feet before the guards could unlock the door.

"Wake up," Josie says, gently tapping his arm. "Come on now, wake up."

Stephen hears her voice as an echo. He imagines that he has been flung into a long tunnel; he hears air whistling in his ears, but cannot see anything.

"Whassimatter?" he asks. His mouth feels as if it is stuffed with cotton; his lips are dry and cracked. He is suddenly angry at Josie and the plastic tubes that hold him in his bed as if he was a latter-day Gulliver. He wants to pull out the tubes, smash the bags filled with saline, tear away his bandages.

"You were speaking German," Josie says. "Did you know that?"

"Can I have some ice?"

"No," Josie says impatiently. "You spilled again, you're all wet."

". . . for my mouth, dry . . ."

"Do you remember speaking German, honey, I have to know."

"Don't remember, bring ice, I'll try to think about it."

As Josie leaves to get him some ice, he tries to remember his dream.

"Here now, just suck on the ice." She gives him a little hill of crushed ice on the end of a spoon.

"Why did you wake me up, Josie?" The layers of dream are beginning to slough off. As the Demerol works out of his system, he has to concentrate on fighting the burning ache in his stomach.

"You were speaking German. Where did you learn to speak like that?"

Stephen tries to remember what he said. He cannot speak any German, only a bit of classroom French. He looks down at his legs (he has thrown off the sheet) and notices, for the first time, that his legs are as thin as his arms. "My God, Josie, how could I have lost so much weight?"

"You lost about forty pounds, but don't worry, you'll gain it all back. You're on the road to recovery now. Please, try to remember your dream."

"I can't, Josie! I just can't seem to get ahold of it."

"Try."

"Why is it so important to you?"

"You weren't speaking college German, darling, you were speaking slang. You spoke in a patois that I haven't heard since the forties."

Stephen feels a chill slowly creep up his spine. "What did I say?"

Josie waits a beat, then says, "You talked about dying."

"Josie?"

"Yes," she says, pulling at her fingernail.

"When is the pain going to stop?"

"It will be over soon." She gives him another spoonful of ice. "You kept repeating the name Viktor in your sleep. Can you remember anything about him?"

Viktor, Viktor, deep-set blue eyes, balding head and broken nose, called himself a Galitzianer. Saved my life. "I remember," Stephen says. "His name is - Viktor Shmone. He is in all my dreams now."

Josie exhales sharply.

"Does that mean anything to you?" Stephen asks anxiously.

"I once knew a man from one of the camps." She speaks very slowly and precisely. "His name was Viktor Shmone. I took care of him. He was one of the few people left alive in the camp after the Germans fled." She reaches for her purse, which she keeps on Stephen's night table, and fumbles an old, torn photograph out of a plastic slipcase.

As Stephen examines the photograph, he begins to sob. A thinner and much younger Josie is standing beside Viktor and two other emaciated-looking men. "Then I'm not dreaming," he says, "and I'm going to die. That's what it means." He begins to shake, just as he did in his dream, and, without thinking, he makes the gesture of rising smoke to Josie. He begins to laugh.

"Stop that," Josie says, raising her hand to slap him. Then she embraces him and says, "Don't cry, darling, it's only a dream. Somehow, you're dreaming the past."

"Why?" Stephen asks, still shaking.

"Maybe you're dreaming because of me, because we're so close. In some ways, I think you know me better than anyone else, better than any man, no doubt. You might be dreaming for a reason, maybe I can help you."

"I'm afraid, Josie."

She comforts him and says, "Now tell me everything you can remember about the dreams."

He is exhausted. As he recounts his dreams to her, he sees the bright doorway again. He feels himself being sucked into it. "Josie," he says, "I must stay awake, don't want to sleep, dream . . ."

Josie's face is pulled tight as a mask; she is crying.

Stephen reaches out to her, slips into the bright doorway, into another dream.

It was a cold cloudless morning. Hundreds of prisoners were working in the quarries; each workgang came from a different barrack. Most of the gangs were made up of Musselmänner, the faceless majority of the camp. They moved like automatons, lifting and carrying the great stones to the numbered carts, which would have to be pushed down the tracks.

Stephen was drenched with sweat. He had a fever and was afraid that he had contracted typhus. An epidemic had broken out in the camp last week. Every morning several doctors arrived with the guards. Those who were too sick to stand up were taken away to be gassed or experimented upon in the hospital.

Although Stephen could barely stand, he forced himself to keep moving. He tried to focus all his attention on what he was doing. He made a ritual of bending over, choosing a stone of certain size, lifting it, carrying it to the nearest cart, and then taking the same number of steps back to his dig.

A Musselmann fell to the ground, but Stephen made no effort to help him. When he could help someone in a little way, he would, but he would not stick his neck out for a Musselmann. Yet something niggled at Stephen. He remembered a photograph in which Viktor and this Musselmann were standing with a man and a woman he did not recognize. But Stephen could not remember where he had ever seen such a photograph.

"Hey, you," shouted a guard. "Take the one on the ground to the cart."

Stephen nodded to the guard and began to drag the Musselmann away.

"Who's the new patient down the hall?" Stephen asks as he eats a bit of cereal from the breakfast tray Josie has placed before him. He is feeling much better now; his fever is down and the tubes, catheter, and intravenous needle have been removed. He can even walk around a bit.

"How did you find out about that?" Josie asks.

"You were talking to Mister Gregory's nurse. Do you think I'm dead already? I can still hear."

Josie laughs and takes a sip of Stephen's tea. "You're far from dead! In fact, today is a red letter day, you're going to take your first shower. What do you think about that?"

"I'm not well enough yet," he says, worried that he will have to leave the hospital before he is ready.

"Well, Doctor Volk thinks differently, and his word is law."

"Tell me about the new patient."

"They brought in a man last night who drank two quarts of motor oil, he's on the dialysis machine."

"Will he make it?"

"No, I don't think so, there's too much poison in his system."

We should all die, Stephen thinks. It would be an act of mercy. He glimpses the camp.

"Stephen!"

He jumps, then awakens.

"You've had a good night's sleep, you don't need to nap. Let's get you into that shower and have it done with." Josie pushes the traytable away from the bed. "Come on, I have your bathrobe right here."

Stephen puts on his bathrobe, and they walk down the hall to the showers. There are three empty shower stalls, a bench, and a whirlpool bath. As Stephen takes off his bathrobe, Josie adjusts the water pressure and temperature in the corner stall.

"What's the matter?" Stephen asks, after stepping into the shower. Josie stands in front of the shower stall and holds his towel, but she will not look at him. "Come on," he says, "you've seen me naked before."

"That was different."

"How?" He touches a hard, ugly scab that has formed over one of the wounds on his abdomen.

"When you were very sick, I washed you in bed, as if you were a baby. Now it's different." She looks down at the wet tile floor, as if she is lost in thought.

"Well, I think it's silly," he says. "Come on, it's hard to talk to someone who's looking the other way. I could break my neck in here and you'd be staring down at the fucking floor."

"I've asked you not to use that word," she says in a very low voice.

"Do my eyes still look yellowish?"

She looks directly at his face and says, "No, they look fine."

Stephen suddenly feels faint, then nauseated; he has been standing too long. As he leans against the cold shower wall, he remembers his last dream. He is back in the quarry. He can smell the perspiration of the men around him, feel the sun baking him, draining his strength. It is so bright . . .

He finds himself sitting on the bench and staring at the light on the opposite wall. I've got typhus, he thinks, then realizes that he is in the hospital. Josie is beside him.

"I'm sorry," he says.

"I shouldn't have let you stand so long, it was my fault."

"I remembered another dream." He begins to shake, and Josie puts her arms around him.

"It's all right now, tell Josie about your dream."

She's an old, fat woman, Stephen thinks. As he describes the dream, his shaking subsides.

"Do you know the man's name?" Josie asks. "The one the guard ordered you to drag away."

"No," Stephen says. "He was a Musselmann, yet I thought there was something familiar about him. In my dream I remembered the photograph you showed me. He was in it."

"What will happen to him?"

"The guards will give him to the doctors for experimentation. If they don't want him, he'll be gassed."

"You must not let that happen," Josie says, holding him tightly.

"Why?" asks Stephen, afraid that he will fall into the dreams again.

"If he was one of the men you saw in the photograph, you must not let him die. Your dreams must fit the past."

"I'm afraid."

"It will be all right, baby," Josie says, clinging to him. She is shaking and breathing heavily.

Stephen feels himself getting an erection. He calms her,

presses his face against hers, and touches her breasts. She tells him to stop, but does not push him away.

"I love you," he says as he slips his hand under her starched skirt. He feels awkward and foolish and warm.

"This is wrong," she whispers.

As Stephen kisses her and feels her thick tongue in his mouth, he begins to dream . . .

Stephen stopped to rest for a few seconds. The Musselmann was dead weight. I cannot go on, Stephen thought, but he bent down, grabbed the Musselman by his coat, and dragged him toward the cart. He glimpsed the cart, which was filled with the sick and dead and exhausted; it looked no different than a carload of corpses marked for a mass grave.

A long, grey cloud covered the sun, then passed, drawing shadows across gutted hills.

On impulse, Stephen dragged the Musselmann into a gully behind several chalky rocks. Why am I doing this? he asked himself. If I'm caught, I'll be ash in the ovens, too. He remembered what Viktor had told him: "You must think of yourself all the time or you'll be no help to anyone else."

The Musselmann groaned, then raised his arm. His face was grey with dust and his eyes were glazed.

"You must lie still," Stephen whispered. "Do not make a sound. I've hidden you from the guards, but if they hear you, we'll all be punished. One sound from you and you're dead. You must fight to live, you're in a deathcamp, you must fight so you can tell of this later."

"I have no family, they're all—"

Stephen clapped his hand over the man's mouth and whispered, "Fight, don't talk. Wake up, you cannot survive the death camp by sleeping."

The man nodded, and Stephen climbed out of the gully. He helped two men carry a large stone to a nearby cart.

"What are you doing?" shouted a guard.

"I left my place to help these men with this stone, now I'll go back where I was."

"What the hell are you trying to do?" Viktor asked.

Stephen felt as if he was burning up with fever. He

wiped the sweat from his eyes, but everything was still blurry.

"You're sick, too. You'll be lucky if you last the day."

"I'll last," Stephen said, "but I want you to help me get him back to the camp."

"I won't risk it, not for a Musselmann. He's already dead, leave him."

"Like you left me?"

Before the guards could take notice, they began to work. Although Viktor was older than Stephen, he was stronger. He worked hard every day and never caught the diseases that daily reduced the barrack's numbers. Stephen had a touch of death, as Viktor called it, and was often sick.

They worked until dusk, when the sun's oblique rays caught the dust from the quarries and turned it into veils and scrims. Even the guards sensed that this was a quiet time, for they would congregate together and talk in hushed voices.

"Come, now, help me," Stephen whispered to Viktor.

"I've been doing that all day," Viktor said. "I'll have enough trouble getting you back to the camp, much less carry this Musselmann."

"We can't leave him."

"Why are you so preoccupied with this Musselmann? Even if we can get him back to the camp, his chances are nothing. I know, I've seen enough, I know who has a chance to survive."

"You're wrong this time," Stephen said. He was dizzy and it was difficult to stand. The odds are I won't last the night, and Viktor knows it, he told himself. "I had a dream that if this man dies, I'll die, too. I just feel it."

"Here we learn to trust our dreams," Viktor said. "They make as much sense as this . . ." He made the gesture of rising smoke and gazed toward the ovens, which were spewing fire and black ash.

The western portion of the sky was yellow, but over the ovens it was red and purple and dark blue. Although it horrified Stephen to consider it, there was a macabre beauty here. If he survived, he would never forget these sense impressions, which were stronger than anything he had ever experienced before. Being so close to death, he was, perhaps for the first time, really living. In the camp, one did not even consider suicide. One grasped for every moment, sucked at life like an infant, lived as if there was no future.

The guards shouted at the prisoners to form a column; it was time to march back to the barracks.

While the others milled about, Stephen and Viktor lifted the Musselmann out of the gully. Everyone nearby tried to distract the guards. When the march began, Stephen and Viktor held the Musselmann between them, for he could barely stand.

"Come on, dead one, carry your weight," Viktor said. "Are you so dead that you cannot hear me? Are you as dead as the rest of your family?" The Musselmann groaned and dragged his legs. Viktor kicked him. "You'll walk or we'll leave you here for the guards to find."

"Let him be," Stephen said.

"Are you dead or do you have a name?" Viktor continued.

"Berek," croaked the Musselmann. "I am not dead."

"Then we have a fine bunk for you," Viktor said. "You can smell the stink of the sick for another night before the guards make a selection." Viktor made the gesture of smoke rising.

Stephen stared at the barracks ahead. They seemed to waver as the heat rose from the ground. He counted every step. He would drop soon, he could not go on, could not carry the Musselmann.

He began to mumble in English.

"So you're speaking American again," Viktor said.

Stephen shook himself awake, placed one foot before the other.

"Dreaming of an American lover?"

"I don't know English and I have no American lover."

"Then who is this Josie you keep talking about in your sleep . . . ?"

"Why are you screaming?" Josie asks, as she washes his face with a cold washcloth.

"I don't remember screaming," Stephen says. He discovers a fever blister on his lip. Expecting to find an intravenous needle in his wrist, he raises his arm.

"You don't need an I.V.," Josie says. "You just have a bit of a fever. Doctor Volk has prescribed some new medication for it."

"What time is it?" Stephen stares at the whorls in the ceiling.

"Almost three P.M. I'll be going off soon."

"Then I've slept most of the day away," Stephen says, feeling something crawling inside him. He worries that his dreams still have a hold on him. "Am I having another relapse?"

"You'll do fine," Josie says.

"I should be fine now, I don't want to dream anymore."

"Did you dream again, do you remember anything?"

"I dreamed that I saved the Musselmann," Stephen says.

"What was his name?" asks Josie.

"Berek, I think. Is that the man you knew?"

Josie nods and Stephen smiles at her. "Maybe that's the end of the dreams," he says; but she does not respond. He asks to see the photograph again.

"Not just now," Josie says.

"But I have to see it. I want to see if I can recognize myself . . ."

Stephen dreamed he was dead, but it was only the fever. Viktor sat beside him on the floor and watched the others. The sick were moaning and crying; they slept on the cramped platform, as if proximity to one another could insure a few more hours of life. Wan moonlight seemed to fill the barrack.

Stephen awakened, feverish. "I'm burning up," he whispered to Viktor.

"Well," Viktor said, "you've got your Musselmann. If he lives, you live. That's what you said, isn't it?"

"I don't remember, I just knew that I couldn't let him die."

"You'd better go back to sleep, you'll need your strength. Or we may have to carry you, tomorrow."

Stephen tried to sleep, but the fever was making lights

and spots before his eyes. When he finally fell asleep, he dreamed of a dark country filled with gemstones and great quarries of ice and glass.

"What?" Stephen asked, as he sat up suddenly, awakened from dampblack dreams. He looked around and saw that everyone was watching Berek, who was sitting under the window at the far end of the room.

Berek was singing the *Kol Nidre* very softly. It was the Yom Kippur prayer, which was sung on the most holy of days. He repeated the prayer three times, and then once again in a louder voice. The others responded, intoned the prayer as a recitative. Viktor was crying quietly, and Stephen imagined that the holy spirit animated Berek. Surely, he told himself, that face and those pale unseeing eyes were those of a dead man. He remembered the story of the golem, shuddered, found himself singing and pulsing with fever.

When the prayer was over, Berek fell back into his fever trance. The others became silent, then slept. But there was something new in the barrack with them tonight, a palpable exultation. Stephen looked around at the sleepers and thought, We're surviving, more dead than alive, but surviving . . .

"You were right about that Musselmann," Viktor whispered. "It's good that we saved him."

"Perhaps we should sit with him," Stephen said. "He's alone." But Viktor was already asleep; and Stephen was suddenly afraid that if he sat beside Berek, he would be consumed by his holy fire.

As Stephen fell through sleep and dreams, his face burned with fever.

Again he wakes up screaming.

"Josie," he says, "I can remember the dream, but there's something else, something I can't see, something terrible . . ."

"Not to worry," Josie says, "it's the fever." But she looks worried, and Stephen is sure that she knows something he does not.

"Tell me what happened to Viktor and Berek," Stephen says. He presses his hands together to stop them from shaking.

"They lived, just as you are going to live and have a good life."

Stephen calms down and tells her his dream.

"So you see," she says, "you're even dreaming about surviving."

"I'm burning up."

"Doctor Volk says you're doing very well." Josie sits beside him, and he watches the fever patterns shift behind his closed eyelids.

"Tell me what happens next, Josie."

"You're going to get well."

"There's something else . . ."

"Shush, now, there's nothing else." She pauses, then says, "Mister Gregory is supposed to visit you tonight. He's getting around a bit, he's been back and forth all day in his wheelchair. He tells me that you two have made some sort of a deal about dividing up all the nurses."

Stephen smiles, opens his eyes, and says, "It was Gregory's idea. Tell me what's wrong with him."

"All right, he has cancer, but he doesn't know it and you must keep it a secret. They cut the nerve in his leg because the pain was so bad. He's quite comfortable now, but remember, you can't repeat what I've told you."

"Is he going to live?" Stephen asks. "He's told me about all the new projects he's planning, so I guess he's expecting to get out of here."

"He's not going to live very long, and the doctor didn't want to break his spirit."

"I think he should be told."

"That's not your decision to make, nor mine."

"Am I going to die, Josie?"

"No!" she says, touching his arm to reassure him.

"How do I know that's the truth?"

"Because I say so, and I couldn't look you straight in the eye and tell you if it wasn't true. I should have known it would be a mistake to tell you about Mister Gregory."

"You did right," Stephen says. "I won't mention it again. Now that I know, I feel better." He feels drowsy again.

"Do you think you're up to seeing him tonight?"

Stephen nods, although he is bone tired. As he falls asleep, the fever patterns begin to dissolve, leaving a bright field. With a start, he opens his eyes: he has touched the edge of another dream.

"What happened to the man across the hall, the one who was always screaming?"

"He's left the ward," Josie says. "Mister Gregory had better hurry, if he wants to play cards with you before dinner. They're going to bring the trays up soon."

"You mean he died, don't you."

"Yes, if you must know, he died. But *you're* going to live."

There is a crashing noise in the hallway. Someone shouts, and Josie runs to the door.

Stephen tries to stay awake, but he is being pulled back into the cold country.

"Mister Gregory fell trying to get into his wheelchair by himself," Josie says. "He should have waited for his nurse, but she was out of the room and he wanted to visit you."

But Stephen does not hear a word she says.

There were rumors that the camp was going to be liberated. It was late, but no one was asleep. The shadows in the barrack seemed larger tonight.

"It's better for us if the allies don't come," Viktor said to Stephen.

"Why do you say that?"

"Haven't you noticed that the ovens are going day and night? The Nazis are in a hurry."

"I'm going to try to sleep," Stephen said.

"Look around you, even the Musselmänner are agitated," Viktor said. "Animals become nervous before the slaughter. I've worked with animals. People are not so different."

"Shut up and let me sleep," Stephen said, and he dreamed that he could hear the crackling of distant gunfire.

"Attention," shouted the guards as they stepped into

the barrack. There were more guards than usual, and each one had two Alsatian dogs. "Come on, form a line. Hurry."

"They're going to kill us," Viktor said, "then they'll evacuate the camp and save themselves."

The guards marched the prisoners toward the north section of the camp. Although it was still dark, it was hot and humid, without a trace of the usual morning chill. The ovens belched fire and turned the sky aglow. Everyone was quiet, for there was nothing to be done. The guards were nervous, and would cut down anyone who uttered a sound, as an example for the rest.

The booming of big guns could be heard in the distance.

If I'm going to die, Stephen thought, I might as well go now, and take a Nazi with me. Suddenly, all of his buried fear, aggression, and revulsion surfaced; his face became hot and his heart felt as if it was pumping in his throat. But Stephen argued with himself. There was always a chance. He had once heard of some women who were waiting in line for the ovens; for no apparent reason the guards sent them back to their barracks. Anything could happen. There was always a chance. But to attack a guard would mean certain death.

The guns became louder. Stephen could not be sure, but he thought the noise was coming from the west. The thought passed through his mind that everyone would be better off dead. That would stop all the guns and screaming voices, the clenched fists and wildly beating hearts. The Nazis should kill everyone, and then themselves, as a favor to humanity.

The guards stopped the prisoners in an open field surrounded on three sides by forestland. Sunrise was moments away; purple-black clouds drifted across the sky, touched by grey in the east. It promised to be a hot, gritty day.

Half-step Walter, a Judenrat sympathizer who worked for the guards, handed out shovel heads to everyone.

"He's worse than the Nazis," Viktor said to Stephen.

"The Judenrat thinks he will live," said Berek, "but he will die like a Jew with the rest of us."

"Now, when it's too late, the Musselmann regains consciousness," Viktor said.

"Hurry," shouted the guards, "or you'll die now. As long as you dig, you'll live."

Stephen hunkered down on his knees and began to dig with the shovel head.

"Do you think we might escape?" Berek whined.

"Shut up and dig," Stephen said. "There is no escape, just stay alive as long as you can. Stop whining, are you becoming a Musselmann again?" Stephen noticed that other prisoners were gathering up twigs and branches. So the Nazis plan to cover us up, he thought.

"That's enough," shouted a guard. "Put your shovels down in front of you and stand in a line."

The prisoners stood shoulder to shoulder along the edge of the mass grave. Stephen stood between Viktor and Berek. Someone screamed and ran and was shot immediately.

I don't want to see trees or guards or my friends, Stephen thought as he stared into the sun. I only want to see the sun, let it burn out my eyes, fill my head with light. He was shaking uncontrollably, quaking with fear.

Guns were booming in the background.

Maybe the guards won't kill us, Stephen thought, even as he heard the crack-crack of their rifles. Men were screaming and begging for life. Stephen turned his head, only to see someone's face blown away.

Screaming, tasting vomit in his mouth, Stephen fell backward, pulling Viktor and Berek into the grave with him.

Darkness, Stephen thought. His eyes were open, yet it was dark. I must be dead, this must be death . . .

He could barely move. Corpses can't move, he thought. Something brushed against his face; he stuck out his tongue, felt something spongy. It tasted bitter. Lifting first one arm and then the other, Stephen moved some branches away. Above, he could see a few dim stars; the clouds were lit like lanterns by a quarter moon.

He touched the body beside him; it moved. That must be Viktor, he thought. "Viktor, are you alive, say something if you're alive." Stephen whispered, as if in fear of disturbing the dead.

Viktor groaned and said, "Yes, I'm alive, and so is Berek."

"And the others?"

"All dead. Can't you smell the stink? You, at least, were unconscious all day."

"They can't *all* be dead," Stephen said, then he began to cry.

"Shut up," Viktor said, touching Stephen's face to comfort him. "We're alive, that's something. They could have fired a volley into the pit."

"I thought I was dead," Berek said. He was a shadow among shadows.

"Why are we still here?" Stephen asked.

"We stayed in here because it is safe," Viktor said.

"But they're all dead," Stephen whispered, amazed that there could be speech and reason inside a grave.

"Do you think it's safe to leave now?" Berek asked Viktor.

"Perhaps. I think the killing has stopped. By now the Americans or English or whoever they are have taken over the camp. I heard gunfire and screaming, I think it's best to wait a while longer."

"Here?" asked Stephen. "Among the dead?"

"It's best to be safe."

It was late afternoon when they climbed out of the grave. The air was thick with flies. Stephen could see bodies sprawled in awkward positions beneath the covering of twigs and branches. "How can I live when all the others are dead?" he asked himself aloud.

"You live, that's all," answered Viktor.

They kept close to the forest and worked their way back toward the camp.

"Look there," Viktor said, motioning Stephen and Berek to take cover. Stephen could see trucks moving toward the camp compound.

"Americans," whispered Berek.

"No need to whisper now," Stephen said. "We're safe."

"Guards could be hiding anywhere," Viktor said. "I haven't slept in the grave to be shot now."

They walked into the camp through a large break in the barbed wire fence, which had been hit by an artillery shell. When they reached the compound, they found nurses, doctors, and army personnel bustling about.

"You speak English," Viktor said to Stephen, as they walked past several quonsets. "Maybe you can speak for us."

"I told you, I can't speak English."

"But I've heard you!"

"Wait," shouted an American army nurse. "You fellows are going the wrong way." She was stocky and spoke perfect German. "You must check in at the hospital, it's back that way."

"No," said Berek, shaking his head. "I won't go in there."

"There's no need to be afraid now," she said. "You're free. Come along, I'll take you to the hospital."

Something familiar about her, Stephen thought. He felt dizzy and everything turned grey.

"Josie," he murmured, as he fell to the ground.

"What is it?" Josie asks. "Everything is all right. Josie is here."

"Josie," Stephen mumbles.

"You're all right."

"How can I live when they're all dead?" he asks.

"It was a dream," she says as she wipes the sweat from his forehead. "You see, your fever has broken, you're getting well."

"Did you know about the grave?"

"It's all over now, forget the dream."

"Did you know?"

"Yes," Josie says. "Viktor told me how he survived the grave, but that was so long ago, before you were even born. Doctor Volk tells me you'll be going home soon."

"I don't want to leave, I want to stay with you."

"Stop that talk, you've got a whole life ahead of you. Soon, you'll forget all about this, and you'll forget me, too."

"Josie," Stephen asks, "let me see that old photograph again. Just one last time."

"Remember, this is the last time," she says as she hands him the faded photograph.

He recognizes Viktor and Berek, but the young man standing between them is not Stephen. "That's not me," he says, certain that he will never return to the camp.

Yet the shots still echo in his mind.

Horror tales do not always reach the reader with impact immediately upon completion. There are those that cling like burrs, that will not be shaken off, that have created such unusual images that a bit of puzzling might be necessary to sort out the various horrors one from another. This first publication by Beverly Evans is just such a story —there is more to our heroine's troubles than meets the eye. For now.

THE ANCHORESS
by Beverly Evans

Johnathan came to me in my dreams again last night. He was there in bed with me, teasing and caressing and building the excitement slowly, delectably. He eased himself on top of me, nuzzling his face through my long auburn hair to kiss the side of my neck just below the ear; but when he drew back, it wasn't my husband inside me anymore, it was my son, all grown up, with shock-white hair flailing as if caught in a wind storm, blue eyes burning through their sockets, and a wreath of briars in his hand. His lips were frozen in a demonic grin, but the sound of laughter filled the air and he began to lash his circlet of thorns across my body again and again, spattering bits of skin and blood on the sheets and the walls and his gleaming, naked skin.

I sat up in the darkness, gasping, my sweat-soaked gown clinging to me and making me shiver in the cold air. The pain was fading, but the laughter was real, echoing down the corridor outside my door, slipping boastfully back to the fourth cubicle.

It was near dawn, so I dressed quickly in the chilly

119

room, pausing a moment to glance down at my torso. I saw only a rippling flotilla of goose bumps, their single-haired masts painfully sensitive to the slightest breeze—no lacerations, no blood.

As I came into the kitchen, the first glints of sunrise crept reluctantly through the bubble faults in the window pane. I stood close to the stove while the kettle moved back and forth over the heated burner with a hollow, mocking sound, like a suddenly vacated rocking chair on an uneven floor. I drank my tea slowly, listening to the silences in between the shrilling of birds as they brushed the meadow grasses with their breasts, snatching insects with each dive.

It was time to do the morning chores. Wrapping Johnathan's old sweater around me, I went out to the shed to feed the chickens. I had never liked the chickens, and they, for their part, distrusted me equally. They skittered at my approach, and I felt enough malevolence in their eyes to make me startled at their slightest unexpected movement. We had a goat once, but on the day when Johnathan lay dying, raving with pain and fever, pinned under a poorly felled oak tree up on the ridge, the goat had gotten away. Between the chickens, the goat, and the garden, we were supposed to be totally self-sufficient—at least that was Johnathan's dream, and the reason we were isolated here, a hundred miles from the nearest town.

Back in the kitchen, I pumped water into the tin pitcher and gathered scraps of bread, fruit, and vegetables in the pail. The cubicles were all peaceful, as they usually were as long as I kept coming by at regular intervals. When I had to spend a day food-foraging without coming back to the house, they would set up a terrible howling upon my return, and I always swore I would never stay away too long again. Their cries made me frantic, and they knew it.

I had much to learn in the beginning. I learned how to mix mortar, and how quickly it must be used before it becomes so stiff that the next course cannot be placed on top of it. I learned how to level each course, how to place the stones for maximum wall strength and appearance, and how to leave just a thin, diagonal slit in the wall, about shoulder high, to slip the filled water pouches through, and to pass in the food. The cubicles gave me a measure of peace, making it easier to handle my life without Johnathan.

As our seventy-five-acre homestead had been Johnathan's domain, the old stone farmhouse was mine. It was shaped like two squares partly merged at one corner, giving the corridors odd angles and leaving broad landings on both floors. Open hallways surrounded the curved staircase that led to the second floor. The walls were native stone, weathered and uneven; I used to think of them as strong and protecting like an encircling arm. More and more they seemed to possess the abilities either to caress, or, if they wished, to crush. Without Johnathan here I was no longer certain what held the stones in their places, or kept the night outside.

When I filled cubicle Number One, I called the first one in softly, insistently, inculcating the others with the words that became the ritual for each immurement. In a way, the first one understood how much he was needed, for he came more easily than the rest did later, and waited patiently with huge, solemn eyes while I made my first clumsy stone wall all the way up to the ceiling, enclosing him forever. Like fourth-century nuns driven by fear or holy duty, they were all to be the Anchors, tokens of grace sworn to a vow of silence behind the stone.

Numbers two and three came passively enough, needing only a little coaxing. In the beginning I was more solicitous of the newly immured ones and would always say a little something to them when I came by each morning, but I soon learned that they did better if I maintained a partial vow of silence myself. But the one who helped weave my morning nightmare broke her vow repeatedly, right from the start. She resisted strongly, refusing to be brought in by ritual alone, and set a bad example for the three whose turns were yet to come. Once spent, however, she was limp and quiet, and I had to work the wall up quickly before her strength returned. She was Number Four.

Oh, I'll admit I had my doubts. It was hard for me

to think clearly after Johnathan died. It took that whole day to gather enough stones to cover his body, but the gruesome song of the coyotes that night assured me that we had not protected him properly and that they were feasting on the ridge, snarling and slashing and fighting for the best parts, mingling their own warm blood with the cold dead flesh, giving it a semblance of returned life in the stark moonlight. I thought I could hear Johnathan crying out to me over the growls that came down the hill like distant thunder; although it drove me mad to think that perhaps we had buried him too soon, I could not go up on the ridge into a pack of feeding coyotes. I sat at the front window looking toward the ridge, trying not to hear, yet afraid not to listen for the next whispering cry that might come from whatever was left of my husband.

I was proud of the way I built the cubicles so that all seven blended with the original walls so well. Three were on the first floor: one wedged neatly under the turn of the staircase, one in the corner of the broad hall to the left of the stairs, and another in the back room between the dining room and the hall. Upstairs, the first one was at the end of the long corridor at the top of the steps; the next along the same short wall, flanked by the cast-iron sconces. Another cubicle filled out an alcove just before the balcony, and the last was against an angled corner between two bedrooms on the opposite side. In the half-light of a moving candle, the surfaces of the cubicles turned to brittle lace, as ragged as if they had been tatted in a fiendish frenzy. Dark specters huddled within the cells, reaching to touch me as I passed, and following me with their sightless, milk-glass eyes. The lace would shatter if I looked at it too long, but I could not help glancing through its holes, even though I was afraid.

I tried to space them carefully, but I know that I put Number Four too close to Number Two. Four would call out softly; calling, crooning, cajoling, ordering, inciting. Soon Two would begin to thrash about inside her cell, and Five, a little farther down the hall, would start to whimper. They had always been too closely entwined, all of them, for one to ignore the other now. As Two would howl, Five would begin to cry, and the tension would build among those still silent within their cells. They knew. They knew without being told, for Two and Five spoke for all of them, with their high, grating wails; spoke of the darkness, and the stench, and the isolation —a chorus of tiny midnight sirens lifting and joining and falling with the cadence of their agony.

I tried not to lose control when the crying began, but was never able to stand it for long. I would go from one cubicle to the other and order them to stop, but soon I would be racing from cell to cell, pressing my mouth close to each slit, screaming for them to be quiet. If I ran outside, far from the house, running until I could no longer hear them, until I could no longer imagine I heard them, until my screams no longer matched theirs, the acres of loneliness would start to swallow me, sucking at my feet with every step. The empty sky would press down around me, pinning me to the sharp, dry scrub grass, leaving me exposed and naked in thousands of pairs of compound eyes watching from a thousand weed stalks and rock shadows. When I returned home, I wasn't ever sure if their cries had been real.

This evening after dinner I sat by the fireplace in the living room, as usual, with the field guide to edible wild plants of the Northwest. All the illustrations in the book looked the same to me; the only plants I thought I recognized from my food forays always turned out to be the poisonous ones.

The warmth from the hearth surrounded me like a downy taffeta comforter on a still winter's morning, and I felt time fraying away my edges, not neatly, thread by thread, but as taffeta shreds, in impossible, tangled fluffs. The flame in the glass chimney blew a thick bubble of light around me, and I wished to be as secure as the candle, safe within its isinglass prison.

Glass prison . . . stone prison . . . prison of mica, glistening darkly, peeling away layer by layer, sloughing fragments that floated like sparks of tumbling silver light, splinter-shards piercing the last mirrored surface, fling-

ing crystalline needles through the swirling gray mists
like icy lightning . . .

"Mother, we wish to speak with you."

. . . leaving tortured paths . . .

"Go away . . . go back to your cell . . ."

"Mother, we must speak with you."

We?

"You can't be here, it's impossible. Go back . . ."

"Mother, it is . . ."

"I order you . . ."

"Mother, Number One is dead."

Number One. Dear God, not Number One. This wasn't
supposed to happen; the cubicles were supposed to keep
us all safe. Johnnie's image wavered before my mind,
first too close, then so hard to keep in focus that I fought
through the blur of tears to get it back, to see my son's
tousled blond head again, and his pale blue eyes that
were just like his father's.

Fighting the sudden vertigo that left me dizzy and
weak, I rose from the chair and groped for the table to
steady myself. The glass chimney toppled and shattered
with a faraway popping sound, and the candle sputtered
out against the cold stone floor. I ran from the room,
bumping into the walls and doorways that seemed to
have shifted their positions in the darkness, to be closer
than I remembered. I ran down the corridor that had
lengthened into a nightmare tunnel whose end seemed
no closer until suddenly my outstretched hands slapped
the rough stone of the cubicle and my fingers slipped
inside the slit as far as they would go.

"Johnnie?" I whispered in between the gasping breaths
that seared the back of my throat.

"Johnnie? Johnnie . . . baby?" I pressed my ear to
the slit, cursing the pounding of my own heart and the
maddening noise of my breathing that shut out all other
sounds. I couldn't hear him at all.

Louder, then, and sobbing, I screamed my son's name
over and over, bruising my hands from tearing at the
narrow cleft of stone, and slowly sinking to the floor with
frustration. The hallway around me seemed to melt into
a delicate tracery of mortar-lace, airy and light, until

the spaces began to fill with blind, unblinking eyes where the stones had been before.

"Rebecca? Rebecca, listen to me."

It was a low, husky whisper, a tone he had used only in bed, on those nights when we felt we were the only two people on earth. I froze, holding my breath, trying to tell where it had come from.

"Rebecca . . ."

"Johnathan? Johnathan? Where are you?" I cried.

"I'm right here, Rebecca, on the other side of the wall, and I want you to be here too, with me," my husband's voice whispered with a soft, lulling quality. "We'll be safe, and together, the two of us."

Standing, I tried to see inside the slit, tried to touch him through the stone.

"Johnathan, I need you, what do I do, I want you, oh darling, I don't know what to do anymore . . ." I cried into the black opening in the wall, pressing my forehead against the rough barrier I had built with my own hands.

"Don't worry, Rebecca, just do as I say. Go out to the shed and get the shovel, and the mortar mix, and something to mix it in." His voice was soothing and compelling. Without another word, I turned and raced down the stairs and through the back of the house to the kitchen door. The shed was quiet and faintly illuminated by the quarter moon in the sky, but as I flung open the door, the chickens bolted from their roosts in alarm, and began squawking and flapping inside the small structure, snagging my hair with their gnarled feet and beating against me with their dusty-smelling feathers. I grabbed the shovel and the bag of dry mortar and left as quickly as I could. Going back through the kitchen, I took a bowl from the table, drew a pitcher of water from the sink pump, and made my way back up the stairs, panting and praying under my breath that I would hear his voice again.

But at the cubicle it was silent, and no amount of pleading on my part could make him speak again. I sank to the floor in despair, too tired to cry, too numb to think. And then I knew what he wanted. He had given me the tools; it was up to me to finish. He had never liked to give me the answer to a problem; he wanted me to think things out on my own.

I lit the corner sconce and then began to chip away at the mortar around the slit with the rough edge of the small shovel, working steadily to loosen the stones enough to pry them out with my fingers. It wouldn't take many —just enough so that I could squeeze myself through, and then replace the stones with fresh mortar once I was inside. Inside, safe with Johnathan. Safe. Together.

As the last stone came loose, I sat back on my heels and wiped the sweat from my eyes. It had been harder to tear the wall down than it had been to build it, and my whole body was aching and leaden. Then I heard the soft voice that seemed to be just beside my ear say, "That's right, Rebecca, don't stop now. Come in."

The flame from the sconce was fluttering in a pool of melted tallow, and I squeezed myself into the cubicle by the last wavering light that it gàve. Crouching, with the bowl in my lap, and the pile of stones by my side in the cell, I began to replace the pieces of the wall, as carefully as I had built it the first time. I smoothed the mortar with my hands in the dark, gauging the placement of each stone by feel and memory, working as quickly as I dared, wanting to please Johnathan so he would speak to me again once we were alone. I shoved the trowel through the slit when I was done; the opening was too narrow to fit the bowl through; so I pushed it aside and scraped the mortar from my hands, first onto the sides of the walls, then against the legs of my jeans, and finally wiped the damp strands of hair from my forehead and eyes with the backs of my gritty hands.

It was morning. I could hear the birds faintly through the walls and imagined the chickens clucking and fretting, waiting to be let into the yard. "I did it, Johnathan," I whispered. Tears of fatigue and relief began to sting my eyes, and I reached around the cubicle to find him, eager to touch him and share in the warmth he had promised.

"Johnathan," I said, "I'm here now, I did what you wanted. Johnathan?"

In the corner, in a niche I had forgotten had been

part of the original wall, my hand met the feel of cloth and I touched it joyfully, waiting for his embrace. The cloth began to tear, and I instinctively grabbed his arms to keep him from falling. My hands felt delicate bones beneath dry and wasted flesh, and a small head flopped forward against my chest with a single hollow thump.

Johnathan came to me in my dreams again last night.

Barry N. Malzberg is undoubtedly one of the most controversial figures in contemporary science fiction and fantasy. Yet there can be no denying his artistry with words, whether he is writing about monsters we are all familiar with or those we would rather not meet at all. Especially in a mirror.

TRANSFER
by Barry N. Malzberg

I have met the enemy and he is me. Or me is he. Or me and he are we; I really find it impossible to phrase this or to reach any particular facility of description. The peculiar and embarrassing situation in which I now find myself has lurched quite out of control, ravaging its way toward what I am sure will be a calamitous destiny and, yet, I have always been a man who believed in order, who believed that events no matter how chaotic would remit, would relent, would suffer containment in the pure limpidity of The Word engraved patiently as if upon stone. I must stop this and get hold of myself.

I have met the enemy and he is me.

Staring into the mirror, watching the waves and the ripples of The Change, seeing in the mirror that beast take shape (it is always in the middle of the night; I am waiting for the transference to occur during the morning or worse yet at lunch hour in the middle of a cafeteria, waves may overtake me and I will become something so slimy and horrible even by the standards of midtown Manhattan that I will cause most of the congregants to lose their lunch), I feel a sense of rightness. It must always have been meant to be this way. Did I not feel myself strange as a child, as a youth, as an adolescent? Even as an adult I felt the strangeness within me; on the streets they stared with knowledge which could not have possibly been my own. Women turned away from me with little smiles when I attempted to connect with them, my fellow employees here at the Bureau treated me with that offhandedness and solemnity which always bespeaks private laughter. I know what they think of me.

I know what they think of me.

I have spent a lifetime in solitude gauging these reactions to some purpose, and I know that I am separate from the run of ordinary men as these men are separate from the strange heavings and commotion, ruins and darkness which created them. Staring in the mirror. Staring in the mirror I see.

Staring in the mirror I see the beast I have become, a thing with tentacles and spikes, strange loathsome protuberances down those appendages which my arms have become, limbs sleek and horrible despite all this devastation, limbs to carry me with surging power and constancy through the sleeping city, and now that I accept what I have become, what the night will strike me, I am no longer horrified but accepting. One might even say exalted at this moment because I always knew that it would have to be this way, that in the last of all the nights a mirror would be held up to my face and I would see then what I was and why the mass of men avoided me. I know what I am, those calm, cold eyes staring back at me in the mirror from the center of the monster know too well what I am also and turning them from the mirror, confronting the rubbled but still comfortable spaces of my furnished room, I feel the energy coursing through me in small flashes and ripples of light, an energy which I know, given but that one chance it needs, could redeem the world. The beast does not sleep. In my transmogrification I have cast sleep from me like the cloak of all reason and I spring from these rooms, scuttle the three flights of the brownstone to the street and coming upon it in the dense and sleeping spaces of the city, see no one, confront no one (but I would not, I never have) as I move downtown to enact my dreadful but necessary tasks.

The beast does not sleep, therefore I do not sleep. At

first the change came upon me once a week and then twice . . . but in recent months it has been coming faster and faster, now six or seven times a week, and furthermore I can *will* the change. Involuntary at first, overtaking me like a stray bullet, it now seems to be within my control as my power and facility increase. A *latent* characteristic then, some recessive gene which peeked its way out shyly at the age of twenty-five with humility and then with growing power and finally as I became accustomed to the power, it fell within my control.

I can now become the beast whenever I wish.

Now it is not the beast but I who pokes his way from the covers during the hours of despair and lurches his way to the bathroom; standing before that one mirror, I call the change upon myself, ring the changes, and the beast, then, confronts me, a tentacle raised as if in greeting or repudiation. Shrugging, I sprint down the stairs and into the city. At dawn I return. In between that time—

—I make my travels.

My travels, my errands! Over manhole covers, sprinting as if filled with helium (the beast is powerful; the beast has endless stamina) in and out of the blocks of the west side, vaulting to heights on abandoned stoops, then into the gutter again, cutting a swath through the city, ducking the occasional prowl cars which come through indolently swinging out of sight behind gates to avoid garbage trucks, no discovery ever having been made of the beast in all the months that this has been going on . . . and between the evasions I do my business.

Pardon. Pardon if you will. I do not do *my* business. The beast does *his* business.

I must separate the beast and myself because the one is not the other and I have very little to *do* with the beast although, of course, I am he. And he is me.

And attack them in the darkness.

Seize hapless pedestrians or dawn drunks by the throat, coming up from their rear flank, diving upon them then with facility and ease, sweeping upon them to clap a hand upon throat or groin with a touch as sure and cunning as any I have ever known and then, bringing them to their knees, straddling them in the gutter, I—

Well, I—

—Well, now, is it necessary for me to say what I do? Yes, it is necessary for me to say, I suppose; these recollections are not careless nor are they calculated but merely an attempt, as it were, to set the record straight. The rumors, reports and evasions about the conduct of the beast have reached the status of full-scale lies (there is not a crew of assassins loose in the streets but merely one; there is not a carefully organized plan to terrorize the city but merely one beast, one humble, hard-working animal wreaking his justice) so it is to be said that as I throttle the lives and misery out of them, I often *turn them over* so that they can confront the beast, see what it is doing to them, and that I see in their eyes past the horror the heartbreak, the beating farewell signal of their mortality.

But beyond that I see something else.

Let me tell you of this, it is crucial: I see an acceptance so enormous as almost to defy in all of its acceptance because it is religious. The peace that passeth all understanding darts through their eyes and finally passes through them, exiting in the last breath of life as with a crumpling sigh they die against me. I must have killed hundreds, no, I do not want to exaggerate, it is not right, I must have killed in the high seventies. At first I kept a chart of my travels and accomplishments but when it verged into the high twenties I realized that this was insane, leaving physical evidence of any sort of my accomplishments that is, and furthermore, past that ninth murder or the nineteenth there is no longer a feeling of victory but only *necessity*. It is purely business.

All of it has been purely business.

Business in any event for the beast. He needs to kill as I need to breathe, that creature within me who I was always in the process of becoming (all the strangeness I felt as a child I now attribute to the embryonic form of the beast, beating and huddling its growing way within) takes the lives of humans as casually as I take my midday sandwich and drink in the local cafeteria before passing on to my dismal and clerkly affairs at the Bureau, accumulating time toward the pension credits that will be mine after twenty or thirty years. The beast needs to kill; he draws his strength from murder as I do mine from food and since I am merely his tenant during these struggles, a helpless (but alertly interested) altar which dwells within the beast watching all that goes on, I can take no responsibility myself for what has happened but put it squarely on him where it belongs.

Perhaps I should have turned myself in for treatment or seen a psychiatrist of some kind when all this began, but what would have been the point of it? What? They would not have believed that I was possessed; they would have thought me harmlessly crazy and the alternative, if they did believe me, would have been much worse: implication, imprisonment, fury. I could have convinced them. I know that now, when I became strong enough to will myself into the becoming of the beast I could have, in their very chambers, turned myself into the monster and then they would have believed, would have taken my fears for certainty . . . but the beast, manic in his goals, would have fallen upon those hapless psychiatrists, interns or social workers as he fell upon all of his nighttime victims and what then?

What then? He murders as casually and skillfully as I annotate my filings at the Bureau. He is impossible to dissuade. No, I could not have done that. The beast and I, sentenced to dwell throughout eternity or at least through the length of my projected life span: there may be another judgment on this someday of some weight but I cannot be concerned with that now. Why should I confess? What is there to confess? Built so deeply into the culture—I am a thoughtful man and have pondered this long despite my lack of formal education credits—as to be part of the madness is the belief that confession is in itself expiation, but I do not believe this. The admission of dreadful acts is merely to compound them through multiple refraction and lies are thus more necessary than the truth in order to make the world work.

Oh, how I believe this. How I do believe it.

I have attempted discussions with the beast. This is not easy but at the moment of transfer there is a slow, stunning instant when the mask of his features has not settled upon him fully and it is possible for me, however, weakly, to speak. "Why must you do this?" I ask him. "This is murder, mass murder. These are human beings, you know, it really is quite dreadful." My little voice pipes weakly as my own force diminishes and the beast, transmogrified, stands before the mirror, waving his tentacles, flexing his powerful limbs, and says then (he speaks a perfect English when he desires although largely he does not desire to speak), "Don't be a fool, this is my destiny and besides *I* am not human so this is not my problem."

This is unanswerable; it is already muted by transfer. I burrow within and the beast takes to the streets singing and crouching, ready once again for his tasks. Why does he need to murder? I understand that his lust for this is as gross and simple as my own for less dreadful events; it is an urge as much a part of him as that toward respiration. The beast is an innocent creature, immaculately conceived. He goes to do murder as his victim goes to drink. He sees no shades of moral inference or dismay even in the bloodiest and most terrible of the strangulations but simply does what must be done with the necessary force. Never more. Some nights he has killed ten. The streets of the city scatter north and south with his victims.

But his victims! Ah, they have, so many of them, been waiting for murder so long, dreaming of it, touching it in the night (as I touch the selfsame beast), that this must be the basis of that acceptance which passes through them at the moment of impact. They have been looking, these victims, for an event so climactic that they will be able to cede responsibility for their lives and here, in the act of murder, have they at last that confirmation. Some of them embraced the beast with passion as he made his last strike. Others have opened themselves to him on the pavement and pointed at their vitals. For the city, the very energy of that city or so I believe this now through my musings, is based upon the omnipresence of death and to die is to become at last completely at one with the darkened heart of a city constructed for death. I become too philosophical. I will not attempt to justify myself further.

For there *is* no justification. What happens, happens. The beast has taught me at least this much (along with so much else). Tonight we come upon the city with undue haste; the beast has not been out for two nights previous, having burrowed within with a disinclination for pursuit, unavailabe even to summons, but now at four in the morning of this coldest of all the nights of winter he has pounded within me, screaming for release, and I have allowed him his way with some eagerness because (I admit this truly) I too have on his behalf missed the thrill of the hunt.

Now the beast races down the pavements, his breath a plume of fire against the ice. At the first intersection we see a young woman paused for the light, a valise clutched against her, one hand upraised for a taxi that will not come. (I know it will not come.) An early dawn evacuee from the city or so I murmur to the beast. Perhaps it would be best to leave this one alone since she looks spare and there must be tastier meat in the alleys beyond . . . but the creature does not listen. He listens to nothing I have to say. This is the core of his strength and my own repudiation is nothing as to his.

For listen, listen now: he sweeps into his own purposes in a way which can only make me filled with admiration. He comes upon the girl then. He comes upon her. He takes her from behind.

He takes her from behind.

She struggles in his grasp like an insect caught within a huge, indifferent hand, all legs and activity, grasping and groping, and he casually kicks the valise from her hand, pulls her into an alley for a more sweeping inspection, the woman's skull pinned against his flat, oily chest, her little hands and feet waving, and she is screaming in a way so dismal and hopeless that I know she will never be heard and she must know this as well. The scream stops. Small moans and pleas which had pieced out the spaces amid the sound stop too and with an explosion of strength she twists within his grasp, then hurls herself against his chest and looks upward toward his face to see at last the face of the assassin about which she must surely have dreamed, the bitch, in so many nights. She sees the beast. He sees her.

I too know her.

She works at the Bureau. She is a fellow clerk two aisles down and three over, a pretty woman, not indifferent in her gestures but rather, as so few of these bitches at the Bureau are, kind and lively, kind even to *me*. Her eyes are never droll but sad as she looks upon me. I have never spoken to her other than pleasantries but I feel,

feel that if I were ever to seek her out she would not humiliate me.

"Oh," I say within the spaces of the beast, trapped and helpless as I look upon her, "oh, oh."

"No!" she says, looking upon us. "Oh no, not you, it can't be you!" and the beast's grasp tighten upon her then. "It can't be you! Don't say that it's *you* doing this to me!" and I look upon her then with tenderness and infinite understanding knowing that I am helpless to save her and thus relieved of the responsibility but saddened too. Saddened because the beast has never caught a victim known to me before. I say in a small voice which she will never hear (because I am trapped inside), "I'm sorry but it's got to be done, you see. How much of this can I take anymore?" and her eyes, I know this, her eyes lighten with understanding, darken too, lighten and darken with the knowledge I have imparted.

And as the pressure begins then, the pressure that in ten seconds will snap her throat and leave her dead, as the freezing colors of the city descend, we confront one another in isolation, our eyes meeting, touch meeting and absolutely nothing to be done about it. Her neck breaks, and in many many many ways I must admit—I will admit everything—this has been the most satisfying victim of them all. Of them all.

Richard Christian Matheson may have inherited his delightful sense of the macabre from his well-known father, but he has, over the years, developed a literary voice uniquely his own—especially when he takes the commonplace and gives it that one necessary twist into the realm of horror . . . and distinct plausibility.

UNKNOWN DRIVES

by Richard Christian Matheson

Ahead, the truck pulled onto the road. It cut off Don's Mustang.

"Damn!" said Don.

The truck was going no more than twenty-five miles an hour. Don's wife, Kerry, shook her head in disbelief.

"These local farmers must think they own the road," she began. "The speed limit is fifty-five."

Don looked at the rear of the truck. In faded letters on the wooden cage that surrounded the bed was written something.

"Field's Produce," Don read aloud, ". . . great, he's probably delivering to the next county."

Kerry smiled.

"Well, there goes the vacation," she said lightly.

"Let's just see," replied Don under his breath.

He leaned his body to the left and gradually pulled the Mustang out into the opposing lane. As he accelerated, he quickly snapped the steering wheel to the right, and the Mustang swerved sharply back into the right lane.

"What's the matter?" asked Kerry, startled.

Don sighed loudly.

"Road work," he explained, pointing to the left side of the road.

At that moment, the Mustang passed a row of hinged yellow barricades, all crowned with blinking orange lights. The barricades completely blocked off the opposing lane.

Ahead, the truck was still going twenty-five. There was no way for Don to get around it and it went no faster. Just a slow, never-changing, aggravating twenty-five.

Don looked at the other lane. It was still blocked. He edged the Mustang slightly to the left and looked down the road as far as he could see, then pulled back into his lane.

"Those barricades look like they go on for a couple of miles," he said, with controlled frustration. "They're repaving the other lane."

Kerry nodded understanding and patted her husband's leg calmingly. She reached to a styrofoam picnic container on the floor and removed a coke.

"Sip?" she asked, opening it.

"No," said Don, his eyes glued to the truck. "Not now. I want to pass this guy. He's beginning to bug the hell out of me."

Don could see the back of the farmer's head. The man seemed completely at ease. His right hand brought a thinly smoking pipe to his mouth every few moments.

Don made an impatient face and honked several times, holding the horn down for several long blasts.

"Pull over, you sonofabitch!" he hissed.

The farmer ignored the honking. He puffed easily on his pipe and the smoke furled in the truck cab.

"That smug bastard," said Don, looking at the Mustang's speedometer incredulously, "I think he's going slower."

Kerry could see Don getting angrier.

"He's just an old man, Don. I'm sure his slow driving is just habit. I didn't notice him slowing down."

"Like hell he didn't," insisted Don. "I could see it on the speedometer."

Kerry tried to take Don's right hand and he pulled away from her nervously. He glanced at her, his mood brittle.

"He's hogging the road," said Don, "I've got to get around him. This could go on all day."

He quickly looked to his left.

The yellow barricades had ended. The other lane was open again.

"Finally," said Don with tentative relief.

Without hesitating, he pulled the Mustang out and tried to pass the truck. He was just about ready to floor the engine when his pulse doubled. Both he and Kerry screamed at what was coming as they swayed fully into the opposing lane.

A one-lane bridge was ahead by only a few yards.

As the truck lethargically rolled across the bridge, behind, Don slammed on his brakes. He put all his weight on the pedal, his eyes widening.

The Mustang skidded loudly and almost slid over a muddy embankment into the slime-thick marshwater beneath the bridge.

There was a last cloud of exhaust as the engine stalled. All was still for a moment. No sounds.

"Are you all right?" Don asked Kerry in a throaty whisper. He was leaned over the steering wheel, breathing heavily.

Kerry looked over at him, the shock still on her face. Her mouth moved almost spasmodically as the perspiration ran from her upper lip to her mouth.

"I wasn't expecting that," she said, her mouth dry.

Don reached over and hugged her.

"There wasn't even a sign," he whispered.

"I'm beginning to hate this route," said Kerry, reaching to the glove compartment and pulling out a box of Kleenex.

"I'm in no rush, Don," she said, wiping his face and then her own of perspiration. "Can't we just drive slower . . ."

"No," said Don, tensely, "this is the only route through the county and I'll be damned if I'm going to let some old man make me late."

"Your brother won't mind if we're a few minutes late," she said. "Please, Don."

Don ignored her and put the Mustang in reverse. He pulled free from the muddy embankment and pushed the transmission into DRIVE. He floored the pedal and the Mustang bolted back onto the road.

"I'm going to pass him," said Don. "All I need is a clear stretch."

He looked over at Kerry as they sped along the highway. She was sipping at her Coke.

"Just let me try a couple more times," he said, reassuringly. "I'll quit if it's no good. I promise."

Kerry looked at him and smiled weakly.

"Good," said Don, coming up behind the truck. "Then let's leave this bastard in the dust and get on with it. We'll show him."

The truck was rocking slightly in front of them. It still didn't waver from twenty-five.

Don watched the truck with scorning fascination.

"He must have something in that rig to keep it going one speed," he said, tapping his fingers on the steering wheel.

In the truck, the farmer was still smoking his pipe. He adjusted his hat as he drove and shrugged his shoulders a bit.

Sensing that the timing was right to pass, Don pulled the Mustang out into the other lane.

It was no good.

There was a truck coming from the other direction. Don pulled back into the lane and waited again.

"Almost," he said to Kerry. "Next one."

He edged every few seconds to the left so he could see the oncoming traffic. It seemed to be thickening.

"Goddamn this," muttered Don, as several enormous trucks passed on his left.

"Look!" interrupted Kerry.

Don smiled unbelievingly as he watched the truck brake and signal for a right-hand turn. It began to veer slowly to the right.

"Patience," said Don with an ironic smile, "that's all it took."

Not missing his chance, he shoved the pedal to the floor with his right foot and the Mustang roared around to the side of the truck. It streaked along the opposing lane and Don gripped the wheel firmly. He began to roll down his window.

"I'll take that Coke, now," he said, smiling at Kerry.

It was too late. The Coke had spilled all over the Mustang. The window was rolled only halfway. No further.

From the right side of the farmer's truck, off a side road, in Don's blind spot, came another enormous foundry truck. He and Kerry ran directly into it and were thrust bloodily through the Mustang windshield. Their bodies landed on the road and pools of deep-red blood formed hideous perimeters around their asphalt-torn flesh.

Don's face was etched horribly by the sharp glass of the windshield and his hair was matted with sweat and oozing blood.

The Mustang suddenly caught fire, and explosions of searing hot metal ransacked the silence of the countryside. Flaming colors of orange, red, and blue were everywhere.

Several pasture animals looked on, chewing and kicking their hooves. The fire began to go out and the Mustang sizzled and groaned on the highway.

The animals lost interest.

The truck pulled up in front of the farmhouse and the farmer got out and knocked his pipe against the muddy running board. Chunks of burned tobacco tumbled out and he walked to the kitchen door of the farmhouse.

He entered, and his wife was standing at the stove, stirring a boiling stew. She continued to stir and as he filled his pipe with new tobacco, she sniffed and ran a finger beneath one nostril.

"How was your day?" she asked.

He held a match to his pipe bowl.

"Good day," he said. "I got me one."

Geo. W. Proctor is no stranger to fantasy fiction. His name (and various pseudonyms) has appeared on dozens of stories and novels in the field, as well as on some of the finest illustrations to appear in the last few years. J. C. Green, his collaborator, is an accomplished poet whose work here marks her first story publication. Both authors are Texans, and it is no coincidence that their effort here deals with a myth unique to the Lone Star State, though not to our nightmares . . .

THE NIGHT OF THE PIASA
by J. C. Green and Geo. W. Proctor

Susan Avery gripped the sides of the toilet bowl and emptied her stomach until she wracked with dry heaves. Legs liquid and arms rubbery, she stood there, doubled over, cramping, eyes clamped tightly, trying to blot out what she had seen.

Minutes grinding like hours passed before she regained the strength to reach out and flush away what remained of her evening meal. Then she stood.

Shaking and weak, she pushed open the stall door. Somehow she managed to walk across the restroom to a row of sinks lining the opposite wall. Within her quivering insides, she felt a bit of relief. She was alone. The last thing she needed now was one of her students walking into the restroom to find her like this.

She twisted one of the faucets, cupped her hands under the water, and splashed the coldness over her flushed face. The harsh chill brought her to life, penetrating the numbness that filled body and brain.

"You were right to run," she said aloud, assuring herself.

She *was* right. She had no doubt about it now, not even a twinge of guilt. Justice had been served. A man had killed and had died in return. That she left the scene was of no consequence.

She could picture tomorrow's headlines exalting the valor of a young officer who risked his life to rid the city of a butcher—a crazy Indian gone berserk on wine or drugs.

More importantly, there would be no investigation, no questions to disturb a past she had no wish to unveil. She had been right; she ran.

Washing the bitterness of her own bile from her mouth, Susan stood and gazed into the cracked mirror above the sink. She smiled. The traces of her queasy stomach were fading. The face that smiled back at her was more than attractive, perhaps not beautiful, but more than just attractive.

Despite an almost Eurasian cast to her features, she appeared every inch "Anglo." Her own careful planning was aided by the atavistic genes of some forgotten Spanish lord who had taken an interest in the "immortal soul" of one of his forced converts. Later, he sent a pregnant squaw back to her family hogan to bear his bastard. Susan's face held no hint of that Indian blood running in her veins.

Her smile widened. Su-Ni-Ta Aguilar took ten years to bury. But the black-braided, dirty-faced girl who once chased goats through the reservation was dead. Susan Avery was alive and well.

She had earned the White Seal of Approval.

And she damn well intended to see that she kept it.

Why not? She had paid her dues. At fourteen, tribal funds sent her to an Indian school to learn the ways of the white man's world. She learned them, but not at the school with its black uniforms and scratchy muslin underwear.

She learned them on her back, held spread-eagle while five of the town's white studs repeatedly raped her.

The judge had tutored her, too. He handed down six-month probated sentences for statutory rape to each of her assailants after they testified they had bought her virginal body at five dollars a head. They went free, and she bore the lable of a young Indian whore.

The name of the lesson—survival.

She learned it well. She graduated at the top of her class, which opened the way to government grants for the underprivileged, and college. But not before she spent a week's salary as a waitress in a local dive to pay the price of legally obtaining a white man's name. All it took was a court order and seventy-five dollars, and Susan Avery was born.

She learned the lesson, learned it so well that she was now in her second year of teaching at the most white, antiminority school in the Southwest. She didn't pass for white—she *was* white. Her clothes were white. Her hair style was white. She talked white. She laughed white. Her bed was for white lovers, men of her own choosing; men manipulated so subtly that few ever really realized she was the agressor. And should any of them feel dependent or a bit possessive, she gracefully and amicably broke the relationship.

Susan kept but one possession of the dead Indian girl that was her past. Her eyes drifted to the silver medallion hanging around her neck, a gift from her grandfather that last day on the reservation. The jade-green stone inset at its center gave the pendant an obscurely oriental appearance. But closer inspection revealed the designs of the rabbit, crow, wolf, and thunderbird surrounding the stone. The medallion could never hint at her own heritage, so she wore it occasionally to remind her of the buried Su-Ni-Ta Aguilar, and how far she had come since that Indian girl had died.

Her only other tie to Su-Ni-Ta was these Wednesday-night classes. Each week she left the security of her suburban apartment for the ghetto dubbed the Little Reservation by the city fathers. At the turn of the century, the district had been reserved for the rich and the elite. Time brought the blacks, then the Indians and a few Chicanos. Her class, basic American history for the adult education program, was composed of ninety percent Amerindian.

She had never understood what prompted her to accept a position in the program, guilt or a wish to share her fortune with the people she had spent half her life trying to forget. For whatever reason, she did not want to be here tonight, not after what had happened less than an hour ago.

The door to the restroom swung inward. Two round-jowled women, fat and well past their prime, entered. Both were engrossed in a detailed discussion of the sexual attractiveness of a young English instructor. Susan caught the dark glance of their eyes in the mirror. She smiled. Immediately the two fell silent and moved to two stalls, closing the doors behind them.

Susan ran her hands over her pants suit, pressing out imagined wrinkles. Then she stood straight and stiff before the mirror. Satisfied with her appearance, she nodded to the reflection. Despite the jumbled mass of confusion still plaguing her mind and stomach, she could force herself to endure one hour in the classroom.

Just walk in and proceed as though nothing happened, she told herself.

Sucking in a deep breath, she turned, pushed open the door, and stepped into the deserted hallway.

Bells tore through the relative silence of the school. The hall filled as classrooms emptied. Bodies swarmed around her, shoving, pressing. A familiar face here and there smiled and nodded a greeting. She ignored them all. Her stomach churned violently, threatening to upheave its emptiness. In desperation, she pushed through the flowing river of people, seeking the refuge of her classroom.

Without a glance at the faces that peered at her when she entered, Susan slipped behind her desk, a barrier of authority to insulate her from the all-too-real world swarming around her. She jerked the file drawer open and ducked down, huddling there to thumb through meaningless folders that postponed facing her thirty adult students.

It didn't help. They were staring at her. Even through the desk's wood, she could feel their dark eyes coursing over her, drilling, probing, exploring, exposing the frayed edges of her sanity.

She could leave—feign sickness.

No! It's only guilt, she reprimanded herself, *guilt be-*

cause I survived. The admission brought no relief. She was sick. She *was*. And she had to escape, save herself before she was engulfed.

Another bell rang. She jerked upright, startled. The trap closed. Every eye in the room turned to her. Panic gripped her. Her stomach refused to stop its churning. *Too late,* she realized, *too late to run.*

Susan stared out, her gaze moving above their heads, trying to avoid eye contact. She swallowed, cleared her throat, but could not force a word up through the dryness of her mouth.

Then she found her voice. "A paper . . ."

She mumbled off, unable to remember the lesson for the night. Frantically, her eyes dropped to the top of the desk, searching for her textbook. It wasn't there. She had left it in the car during her mad rush to the restroom.

"A paper," she forced herself to begin again, "I want you to write a paper applying tonight's assignment to your own life. How history has affected you personally . . . both socially and economically."

There were no groans of protest. These students were not the pampered children of the white elite she taught during the day. These were frustrated adults, fighting to better themselves in a world that really didn't give a damn whether they did or not. She had not been fair in the assignment. But it took their eyes off her, letting her retreat back into her thoughts. Her gaze moved over their slumped heads and shoulders.

A face stared at her.

One lone head was turned toward her. A single young man stared up. Susan glanced away, shuffling a pile of papers stacked to one side of the desk. When her eyes chanced to rise, the young man was still there. His gaze was intimate. His black, gleaming eyes coursed over her. She could feel him mentally peeling away her clothing, leaving her naked to his caressing gaze.

She shivered, unsure whether disgust or excitement stirred her. Finding the seating chart in the top drawer of the desk, she quickly scanned it and found his name —Cully Ghant. How could she have forgotten?

She looked up again, her eyes meeting his with an iciness she had perfected to quell the most rebellious student. "Mr. Ghant, don't you think you'd best begin the assignment?"

Several heads turned to the young man. His eyes lowered to the blank paper atop his desk.

Stupid Indian! She cursed to herself, calmly sitting behind the desk. He was pure-blood and wore his red skin like a badge. His every move spoke, "I'm Indian . . . red is beautiful!" Cully Ghant was chief of the dead-end tribe and the stupid bastard didn't even know it.

There was no trace of the filth and squalor of the reservation about him. His was the look of the Little Reservation—city-bred Indian, streetwise, a prowler, a scavenger. Cully Ghant would never be found at a Wounded Knee. He had learned his survival lessons too. But he didn't have the courage to become white. He hid behind false racial pride while he hungered for white power and all its material trappings. He stalked the streets, accepting the scraps thrown his way.

She felt his eyes on her again but ignored them, refusing him the satisfaction of disturbing her again. Instead, she sat there, counting the minutes and trying to forget the classroom, Cully Ghant, and the flashing blade.

The bell rang. Still she sat there, accepting the papers the students placed on her desk as they left.

Cully Ghant waited until the room emptied, then rose. He didn't walk toward her, but sauntered around the desk to invade her barrier of security. He pressed close, intimately. His eyes roved over her.

She felt naked. She shivered, unable to restrain a strange mixture of attraction and revulsion. She wanted to run . . . run before he moved even closer.

His hand rose.

She winced, then smiled nervously. He held a sheet of paper to her. She took it, glancing down at a sketch of the pendant she wore.

"Mr. Ghant . . . what is this?" she managed to ask.

"Your medallion," he said, then added, "little red sister."

"I'm not your sister, Mr. Ghant!" She crumpled the paper and tossed it into the waste paper can. "And this is not an art class!"

"Brujo," he said, ignoring her anger. "You wear the stone of a *brujo."*

She suppressed an uneasy tremble that threatened to destroy what remained of her composure. "Indian jewelry is very popular and stylish . . ."

"Not this," he said, cutting short her explanation. He reached out to lift the disk in his hand. The hard ripple of his knuckles brushed over the contours of her breast. Susan shivered, even more unsure of herself. She pulled away from him.

He made no attempt to veil a smile of amusement. The encounter was no accident. He let the medallion fall back.

"A trinket . . . I bought it in Albuquerque . . ." she said in a murmur, trying to ignore the warm glow where his hand had touched her, ". . . not even turquoise."

"Don't give me that!" He grasped her shoulders. His fingers were demanding, yet gentle, as though he could feel the trembling of her flesh beneath her blouse. "The blood of the *diablero* runs in your veins, little sister. Not even the whiteness of your skin can hide that. Only a *brujo* wears the stone of the shape-changer. The heart of the *Piasa* is passed from generation to generation—never pawned away into white hands! Never!"

She shook her head, trying to form an answer with her lips, but could not find the lies. Abruptly, he pulled her to him. She stiffened, then his hands were gone, and he stepped back.

"When you tire of your white way," he said, "I'll be waiting, little sister."

She didn't answer. She broke and ran. An echoing laughter rose within her, mocking her flight.

The alley was empty, then it wasn't. A garbage truck loomed out of the darkness, wheeling onto the street.

Susan's foot slammed the brake. Tires cried out in protest as asphalt bit into rubber. The Volkswagen lurched, shuddering to a halt. The truck rumbled by, fender missing fender by mere inches.

Unable to curse or give thanks, Susan collapsed onto the steering wheel. Her body shook uncontrollably and she sobbed. Her knuckles stood out a tortured white as she clung to the wheel in desperation. The night was too much for her. Bit by bit, it was stripping away the fabric of her sanity. It gathered around her. She felt it, a predator stalking its prey. It surrounded her, pressing closer and closer—the Little Reservation, the faces of her students, Cully Ghant, the silvery flash of the knife, the . . .

No! Damnit, no!

Fear and guilt gave way to anger. She shoved away from the steering wheel and sat straight in the seat. There was no room within her for fear and guilt or self-pity. She was alive; she was surviving, that was all that mattered, nothing else.

She froze. The laughter, the mocking voice was there, moving within her once again. It echoed up from the core of something dark and hidden, resounding against the wobbly foundations of her composure.

"Old man. Hey, old man, give us a drink."

"Yeah, share that bottle with us, old man."

Susan's head jerked, startled by the voices intruding from outside. Across the street two young boys, no more than thirteen or fourteen, taunted a wino squatted on the curb. With one hand, the man clutched a bottle of cheap booze to his chest. His free arm flailed the air, swatting away the hands trying to liberate his precious treasure.

"Go away, leave me alone." The man's words were slurred, thick with alcohol. "Get out of here."

The two boys laughed. The old man's protests only seemed to increase the vigor of their attack.

Susan felt it before the shadow passed over the Volkswagen. Like a cold finger, it pressed at the base of her spine, and she knew it.

It was there, that shifting, mistlike presence she had seen once before this night. Black even against the night sky, it floated over the street to hover above the man and the boys. As before, Susan could not take her eyes from the sifting form. She wanted to cry out, to warn the three, but the writhing cloud mesmerized her.

She was an observer again, removed and distant from the scene she gaze upon. The mist was different, changed. It seemed larger and dense, as though it was solidifying. In two hours could it have changed?

The cloud writhed, swirled, churned. A single tendril coiled down from its belly. It touched the boys, then the man, as if feeling, probing.

The mist dropped, cloaking itself to the wino.

A growl rumbling from the depths of his throat, the old man sprang to his feet. He gripped the neck of the bottle, holding it like a club. "Here, take your drink."

Arm and bottle lashed out. There was a fleshy thud, then the shattering of glass. One of the boys reeled back and fell to the pavement, his hand clutching his temple.

The old man spun, the broken bottle extended before him like a jagged-edged knife. In one swipe, he raked it across the throat of the remaining youth. The boy stumbled away a step or two, as if in a daze, unable to comprehend what had happened. He stared at the wino turned killer, the object of a harmless prank but a moment ago. Then the boy crumpled to the sidewalk, life flowing from the slash opening his throat.

As Susan stared, the presence lifted from the old man. Floating upward, it drifted above the buildings, soaring, and for the second time that night she heard its laughter, a sound that found resonance with the mocking voice deep within her.

The breaking of glass drew attention back to the wino. The remains of his deadly bottle glittered around his feet, silvery shards reflecting the street lamps. The old man's mouth opened. His quivering lips formed a whimpering sob that rose higher and higher to a whining cry of terror. His shaking head turned to one boy, then the other. Stumbling back a few steps, he looked up, seeing the Volkswagen. Then he ran. Screaming at the night, he ran.

Susan watched until he disappeared around a corner. It happened again. Like a woman coming out of a dream, she realized it had happened again!

Panic twisted within her. She couldn't stay here. She couldn't be caught at the scene. The police meant questions, inquiries that might unearth Su-Ni-Ta Aguilar. She wouldn't let that happen, not after all she had done to bury the Indian girl, not after all the time it had taken.

She glanced around. Except for two still bodies on the sidewalk, the street was empty. She was safe.

A piteous gasp escaped her throat.

In the rear-view mirror, she saw a man. His features were hidden in the shadows, but she saw his smile. She shuddered. It was the same smile, the same man who had shared the . . .

It can't be! It just can't be him, not again! But she knew she lied to herself. It was the same man who had stood in the alley outside the drive-in grocery earlier that night, watching her. *God! Oh god, he's coming toward me!*

The man behind her moved closer. She could almost see his face. His hand stretched out, beckoning her.

Susan reached out, twisting the ignition key. The Volkswagen coughed, the motor catching. Her foot floored the gas pedal as she slammed the gear shift into first. Tires squealed against the pavement. Susan Avery ran, fleeing toward the security of her suburban apartment, away from the Little Reservation, Su-Ni-Ta Aguilar, and the night.

He sat cross-legged in the dirt, huddled over a small fire of piñon pine. The day was sweltering, but he hugged a brightly colored blanket around his lean frame. His coarse gray hair was pulled back in a knot held by a silver clasp set with a huge chunk of male, blue turquoise. His face was as sun-baked and sand-blasted as the barren arroyo he stared down into.

His spoken name was Beasos Dihi, Dark Feather—his secret name was known only to himself. To his face, he was called Hasteen Chi, a term of respect. But whispers of fear behind his back named him *brujo* or *diablero,* a man who carried the secrets of forgotten days.

He was not a chanter men sought for the healing ceremonies of the soothing Night Chant, or to cleanse themselves of outside contact with the Enemy Way. Those who consulted Beasos Dihi did so only in secret and never revealed what transpired. The only ceremony he performed for the tribe was the burial rite; death was the greatest taboo of the People. Even the name of the dead could not be uttered, and the hogan that held death was always destroyed.

It was to this man Su-Ni-Ta had come, seeking his blessings before her journey into the white man's world.

Unlike the others, she carried no fear of Beasos Dihi. In the days before the reservation school, he had taught her the stories of the Changing Woman and the Hero Twins. She had learned the ways of the desert, the plant and animal lore of her people. His teachings had been given with the love and humor that befit a grandfather.

The old man held out his hand, indicating Su-Ni-Ta was to sit at his left. She did. In the old way, neither spoke for a long time, and neither looked directly at the other. Instead they gazed north, out across the desert. Here stunted juniper and greasewood fanned out to be replaced by sage and sandstone.

"You will leave the *Dinetah*," Beasos Dihi broke the silence. He used the ancient name, Land of the People, refusing to accede to the name given by the Spanish invaders.

"You have talked with my mother," she answered with a nod.

"I have spoken with those who know more than your mother."

"Have they told you I will go to the white man's school?"

"It is not the first time," he said, turning to her, "our women have been taken to the Place of Bells."

"I will not be taken to Albuquerque." Su-Ni-Ta repeated what had been said a hundred times before. "I want to go, to learn."

"To leave the old ways."

"The old ways are dying . . . our poeple are dying." She did not argue, she pleaded. "I want to live, *Tschai*, Grandfather."

"The old ways die, but the new are no better," Beasos Dihi said, staring off into the horizon. "You will go, but I will not see you return. Like the ways of the *Dineh*, my time is over. This I have seen."

Su-Ni-Ta was silent for several minutes in respect for his vision of death. Then she asked, "What do you see for me?"

"I see what is not old or new." The old man shook his head. "I see what I cannot understand, both pain and pleasure. I see what must go unspoken. Look, daughter, look at the horizon and tell me what you see."

Su-Ni-Ta gazed over the desert. Unlike her grandfather, her sight was limited to her eyes. To the left, the sun was fast sinking behind the rolling sandstone, tinting it coral and crimson. Before her, to the north, the direction of death, she could see the gathering darkness of night. But as she watched, she saw a deeper blackness boiling near the ground.

"The night brews a sandstorm for tomorrow," she said. "We will have desert grit for breakfast."

Beasos Dihi said nothing but slipped an amulet from his neck and held it out to Su-Ni-Ta. She took it, staring at the symbols of the rabbit, crow, wolf, and thunderbird cut into its shining surface. As its center was the polished jadelike stone—the heart of the *Piasa*—the soul of the thunderbird. She started a choked protest, but the old man stopped her short.

"No!" His voice was stern, containing a ferocity she had never heard before. "I have no need anymore. But your need will be great. Wear it always. The time will come when it will open a path . . ."

His words trailed off into silence.

No more would be said, she realized. Pushing herself up from the dirt, she placed the medallion around her neck, then started back down the trail to the village.

"Now you go on your way alone.
What you are now, we know not.
To what clan you now belong, we know not.
From now on, you are not of this Earth."

Beasos Dihi chanted in the quavering drone of a tribal singer. It was the Death Song of the People, but she did not know if he was singing it for himself or her.

There was no trace of sand or wind the next morning when she left for the white man's school.

His hand shifted into the frayed pocket of his jeans. It rummaged there a moment, then withdrew. His copper-brown fingers caressed the imitation mother-of-pearl handle of an oversized pocket knife. A broad-knuckled thumb tapped the spring-loaded insert near the end of the handle.

A razored blade flashed out.

Hidden at the rear of the store, Susan Avery saw the man approach the check-out counter. She hugged the shelves, clinging there like a trembling rabbit. She wanted to scream and warn the clerk. She wanted to free the terror ripping through her throat.

But her own hand clamped over her mouth, muting her cry to an inaudiable sob. Unable to move, to scream, Susan stood there and stared down the aisle at the clerk and—the man with the knife.

"Hey!" The clerk's head twisted from the portable television that held her attention. Rough-hewed features marked the man edging toward the cash register as Amerindian, wino. "What the hell ya think you're doing, chief?"

The woman froze.

Her eyes dropped to the gleaming sliver of steel he gripped. Total incomprehension filled her face, a blankness erasing the lines of vanished youth that caked make-up failed to conceal.

Disconnected, removed from the small drive-in store in which she stood, Susan gazed on the scene with a sudden coolness that frightened her far more than the knife brandished by the man. Idly she found herself studying the clerk's features. The woman was in her mid-thirties, never beautiful, never even attractive.

Animation crept back into the clerk's face. Her eyes widened, dilating with fear. Her head moved from side to side in uncertain jerks, her hair trembling as if stirred by a chilling breeze. Her mouth opened. Her lips moved but produced no sound, not even a little whimper.

The man smiled and stepped behind the counter. The clerk shrank before his imposing hulk, no more than a fragile Dresden doll in the shadow of a descending sledge hammer. The man's smile broadened to a yellow, tobacco-stained grin.

About him was a presence, a sifting, shifting presence. Susan saw it—felt it—instinctively warned by the ancient blood coursing beneath the veneer of her civilized skin. Here was something familar yet totally alien, something that linked her to the man with a bond stronger than their common heritage.

The man's arm jerked into the air—then fell!

"God . . . oh, God . . ." the clerk moaned, her eyes locked to the blade buried in her breast. "No . . . no . . . please don't . . ."

He wrenched the knife free. The woman winced and staggered back, her retreat barred by the counter. She slumped there.

The knife, a silver fang, lashed out, rending, cutting. Again. Again. The clerk found the full strength of her vocal cords and screamed.

Susan pushed against the shelves, trying to melt into the aspirin, laxative, and toothpaste that packed the aisle. Terror gripped every fiber of her body. But beneath the fear lay an even greater horror. At the core of her being was a glowing pleasure, an orgasmic release of something carefully confined behind the walls of social restraint. It laughed within her. It taunted, mocking her fascination with the bestial slaughter being staged for her benefit alone.

Again and again, the man's arm jerked up and fell, jerked up and fell, like a disjointed marionette, dancing a macabre fling. A roar of canned laughter blared from the flickering television behind the two, forming a grotesque choral.

The clerk's screams gave way to mindless sobs, and finally silence. In limp resignation, her arms fell to her side. Her eyes rolled to the ceiling. She was still.

The man thrust the lifeless body from him.

He staggered back. His chest heaved as he gulped down breaths in exhaustion. Trembling with excitement, he hovered over the dead woman, seeking some trace of movement. There was none. He twisted, vaulted over the counter, and ran into the night.

Without so much as a glance to the dead woman or the untouched cash register, Susan ran down the aisle after him. Outside, in the mercury vapor glow of the street lights, she saw him stumble across the street. Around him swirled a dark mass, boiling like a swarm of blow flies. It lifted from him and drifted upward.

The fleeing man stiffened for an instant. His head jerked around. Confusion contorted his face. He held the knife and his bloodied hands out before him. Shaking his head in disbelief, his fingers touched the blood-sodden front of his shirt. He cried out hysterically, slinging the knife to the street. It shattered the unnatural silence of the night when it struck the pavement and careened across the asphalt into the gutter.

The man sank to his knees and doubled over. With great wracking heaves, he retched.

Susan barely noticed the convulsively shuddering man. Her gaze riveted to the writhing mist above the street. Illuminated by the frosty light of the vapor lamps, it churned in upon itself. She shivered. It made no sound, yet she knew it laughed, a laughter that chorused the taunting pleasure moving within her.

The moment no longer belonged solely to her. She could feel eyes staring at her. She shivered again. Her gaze ran up and down the empty block several times before locating the source of her uneasiness.

There, in the shadow of an alley directly across from her, stood a man. She could see the glint of his eyes, but his face remained in darkness. She felt rather than saw his smile. A thin smile twisted over her own lips. The man in the alley gave credence to the events unfolding this night.

"My God! I didn't mean it!" the man in the street cried out, pushing to his feet. He held his hands toward Susan. "Sweet Jesus, I didn't . . ."

The enormity of what had happened was too heavy. He gave a choked groan of despair, then turned to run down the street.

Rubber squealed against asphalt. A black-and-white squad car fishtailed around a corner. Like a spectator to a surrealistic movie, Susan watched.

The dark mist shimmered and dipped to touch the police car.

The officer within jerked, slamming the brake to the floorboard. There was no way the officer could know what had happened in the store, Susan realized, as he flung himself from the car and drew his service revolver.

An exploding cannon rent the night.

The fleeing man shuddered. His ankles collapsed under him. He fell, rolling. His twitching fingertips brushed the knife he had tossed to the gutter but moments before.

Twice more the gun fired, spitting lead into a dead body. The revolver extended before him, the officer cautiously crept up to his victim.

Susan's gaze rose back to the black mist. It was no longer there. Her eyes darted along the street and found it crouched beside a fire hydrant like some feline licking the filth from its fur. Then it rose, drifting upward, melting into the night.

She glanced to the man in the alley for assurance that what she had seen was real. He was gone.

The full realization of what she had witnessed struck her. She came alive, no longer the spectator. She ran . . . ran.

Susan bolted upright in bed. She shivered; her whole body was drenched with sweat. Her eyes darted around for a few moments before she realized she was in her bedroom, in the safety of her own apartment. She sighed and shook her head.

Real, the dream had been so real, perhaps even more vivid than the scene she witnessed in the grocery earlier that night. She sighed again, remembering the flashing knife, the gunshots, the shattering bottle.

For an instant she considered lying down again, but she knew it would be useless. The dream would come again, haunting her.

A drink, she thought. *I need a drink.*

Grabbing her robe from the foot of the bed, she walked into the living room of the apartment. She found a bottle and a glass and poured three fingers. Huddling on the couch, hugging her knees, she downed half the drink.

She smiled. The bourbon was smooth. It warmed her stomach and flowed into her veins, soothing her frayed edges. Another drink, or three, would help bring the oblivion she sought. Tomorrow, the whole night would be no more than a faded memory, like some half-forgotten nightmare.

A knock came at the door.

She jumped. Bourbon splashed down the front of her robe. Her head twisted to the wall clock. Midnight. She expected no visitors. Her friends were not in the habit of dropping in unannounced during the middle of the night. She decided to let the door go unanswered.

The knock was louder, more demanding the second time.

She couldn't ignore it. Whoever it was might wake the whole building. Placing her drink on the coffee table, she crossed the room to flick off the lights. Only a soft glow penetrated the room from outside. She opened the door just enough to peer out. A startled gasp whimpered from her throat.

The man from the alley!

She recognized the silhouette of his body, the relaxed flex of his shoulders. He had followed her; he had followed her all the way from the Little Reservation where she left him in the street beside the two dead boys. His eyes glinted in the darkness. She gasped again, staggering back into the room.

The door swung in and the looming figure invaded the sanctuary of her apartment.

"I decided not to wait, little sister." The voice was unmistakably Cully Ghant's.

"You!" Her voice was a mere whisper. She watched him lock the door behind him. "You were . . . tonight . . . you saw!"

"All of it," he said, moving to her. "And I knew."

"Knew?" She shook her head, confused and frightened. He gave no answer, except to draw her to him. She came without protest, trembling when his mouth covered hers. Then she returned his kiss, willingly accepted his rough embrace. If sex was what he wanted, she would give it—anything to survive.

Abruptly, his arms left her. The light flared on overhead. Cully moved to the couch and sat there a few moments just staring at her. A pleased smile played over his lips. Finally he said, "Something to drink. I need something to drink."

Unquestioning, she walked to the kitchen. She passed by a six-pack of beer in favor of a bottle of wine neatly tucked away on the bottom shelf of the refrigerator. The wine was an expensive gift from an appreciative lover, and she had been saving it for a special occasion. Mindless of what she was doing, she pulled out the bottle. Instead of a crystal champagne glass, she took a large tumbler from the cupboard and filled it.

"So this is the hogan of my little *bruja*," Cully said as she handed him the glass. He drank deeply, draining away most the wine in one gulp. He glanced up to her. His black eyes ran over her body. "Not bad."

She stared at him, attempting to attain a superior air, yet uncertain whether he meant the apartment, the wine, or her.

"The little *bruja* is bewildered, perhaps a bit disappointed. She thinks I'm here for her body . . . to rape her." He grinned, amused. "Has she forgotten so much of her people? A brave will force himself on a woman taken from an enemy, but never a woman of the People."

He called himself a "brave," a man warring against an enemy. Cully Ghant would think of himself at war, Susan thought. It fit his image of the city-bred Indian, a lone brave against a world of Anglos. But if he hadn't come for her, then what did he want? Money? Blackmail?

His gaze slowly moved around the apartment. "No one would suspect to find one of the People here, let alone a *diablera*. Very expensive, very white. The perfect place for you to hide and wait."

"Hide?" What was he talking about? She was confused. Did he know something, more than what they had witnessed this night? It had to be blackmail.

"At the heart of the enemy camp, that's where I sit, at the arm of a *bruja*," he said, either not hearing her or ignoring her question. He was taking his time about getting to the point, playing with her.

Cully sipped at his wine, then said, "My parents were an ordinary man and woman, without the sight, or *brujo* blood running in their veins. But they believed in the ways of the People. On the night I was born, my father had a dream, a vision. He saw his son sitting safely in the heart of the enemy camp beside a woman, yet that woman was a *diablera*."

"What in hell are you talking about?" What was he doing? Why was he dragging this out? She didn't understand.

"A vision a man held for his son is all I'm trying to tell you about," he said. "The same vision that has guided that son for twenty-five years. My father believed his dream foretold of greatness for his son, a brave who would serve the People at the arm of a powerful *bruja*. I've shared that belief. My whole life has been spent on the streets. I've learned them and their ways, because with that knowledge I'd be strong and ready to serve. And I've searched for that *bruja* in the face of every woman I've met, waiting to be called."

"Streetwise Cully Ghant ruled by the vision of another man." Her tone was thick with contempt. He was crazy or on drugs to ramble on like this. "Get off it. It doesn't suit you, chief. You're not that stupid. No one is. The magic in visions died when the first Spaniard set foot in the New World. That's reality, not some dream."

He glanced up at her. There was no trace of anger in his expression. "You're bruised."

She followed his gaze to the pendant around her neck and the purpling flesh beneath it. She winced, suddenly aware of the throbbing pain. Cully's embrace had been rougher than she realized. She twisted away from him, ashamed of letting him see that he had hurt her.

"I saw the look on your face after what happened in the store," he said. "I saw you watching it up there, then again on the street after class. You enjoyed it! You felt it, and you enjoyed it!"

"Saw what?" Susan pivoted back to face him, glaring challenge. Now he got to it. He wouldn't win. She wouldn't admit anything.

"The power, little sister." Cully casually took another sip of the wine. "I've been watching it. It was bred out there in the Little Reservation, conceived in the tenements. I've seen it. Anybody could have. It's been out there stalking the sewers, prowling the alleys—seeking. It found nourishment in the streets, sucking up the hate, the frustration, the guilt, the desires. I've watched it grow. I've watched it flex its muscles, test its strength. Tonight it singled us out—touched us. It revealed its full power to you and me. It chose us from all the People in the Little Reservation."

"The People, the old ways—they're dead! There's nothing left of the People except dirty blankets and tourists traps. They traded their ways for a bottle of cheap muscatel!"

"Nothing dies, little sister," he said. "It just changes, alters shapes. The power flows up from the land to its people. The whites, the blacks, the browns, they forgot the land. They never recognized its force. They thought they had killed it. But from the ashes of a charred body, the spirit escaped and took a new form. We saw it. Tonight it chose us!"

"You've been chewing too many peyote buttons," Susan said with no attempt to veil her contempt. "Your mind's gone."

"My father and mother gave me the name Ishacolly. Tonight, the Wandering Wolf found his *bruja*—a *diablera* to open the door to the power." He was ignoring her sarcasm. "All you have to do is accept it, little sister, allow its strength to enter you. I will follow. I'm here to serve."

Despite herself, she shivered, remembering the man with the knife, the glowing pleasure he had released within her soul, the wino and his bottle, and her fascination as he killed the two boys.

"Just you and me, little sister. That's all it will take," Cully said. "You have the blood of a *bruja*, and you carry the stone, the heart of the *Piasa*. You're the focal point. All you have to do . . ."

"Oh, no! Not so fast, chief! There's no you and me. Just *me!*" Her coolness and ferocity frightened her. But her fear of this man had turned to anger. "You came here to scare me. You did it. But now it's over—one cheap thrill to a customer. That's all there is to it. I'm not on your trip, chief. I didn't see anything tonight, and there's no way you can prove I did. Now, get out, you two-bit, half-breed hustler!"

She walked across the room in quick, stiff strides, flung the door open, and stood there, trying to contain her anger.

Cully took a lingering last swig of his drink. He stretched with aggravating languor, then stood and sauntered to the door. He stopped a few inches from her, looking her up and down. There was no expression on his face, but she could feel his disgust.

"You saw it. It's still in your eyes, little sister. When you're ready, I'll be there, waiting." He stepped through the doorway and was gone.

Susan could not sleep. She tried but only stared at the ceiling. Even the bourbon wasn't helping. Cully Ghant refused to leave her mind. He had invaded the sanctuary of her apartment, and his presence lingered, taunting her.

Who did he think he was, trying to drag her back, trying to destroy what had taken so long to build? Su-Ni-Ta was buried. She would stay that way. Cully Ghant could keep the Little Reservation all to himself. She didn't need it.

Still she could not sleep. Pushing from the bed, she found jeans and a blouse in a closet. Quickly dressing, she left the apartment to escape into the night.

The air was clear and unseasonably warm. Caring little about her direction, she walked, leaving the lingering ghost of Cully Ghant and his dead-end tribe to slowly die behind her.

She should never have allowed him in the apartment. She should have screamed. It had been a mistake, now she had to forget it.

Turning at the end of the block, she strolled across the street to a small neighborhood park. When she first came to the city, the park had been her refuge. She came here often, hiding behind the wall of trees and shrubs, letting them blot out the buildings and streets that closed in around her. Tonight it would hide her from Cully Ghant.

The park refused to shelter her. Autumn had stripped the branches, leaving them barren. Their skeletal forms did nothing to close off the city. There was no privacy, only isolation; no smell of summer grasses and flowers, just the pungent stench of automobile exhaust. The park was a mistake. The walk was a mistake. Susan turned to retrace her steps back to the apartment.

"Hey, *chica*."

There were four of them. They moved from the shadows of the trees.

"Hey, *guapa, guapita*."

For a moment she froze, uncertain of what to do. That

moment was all they needed. They closed around her, moving in with each beat of her heart.

They were Chicano. Even without their voices, she could tell that. Anglo, Spanish, Indian all bred within them; almost blood brothers. She recognized their common heritage, but they didn't. To them, she was white. White had cast them in the roles that they now intended to act out.

"Bonita, venga aqui," the youth closest to her said with a leer. In his hand a silver blade glinted. "Easy, take it easy and everything will be all right. We won't hurt you."

A malicious chuckle came from behind her. She twisted around to stare into another leering face and a slowly swaying knife.

Suddenly hands gripped her shoulders, forcing her to her knees, to her stomach. They pulled at her, rolling her to her back. The fabric of her blouse rent under the rough grasp of their fingers.

"God, please don't, please." She begged, her arms desperately trying to hide her vulnerable, exposed body. "Money! I'll give you money!"

An open palm slapped sharply against the side of her face. Their faces blurred above her. Her temples pounded, threatening to explode.

"Afterwards, *bonita*." One of them laughed, his hands sliding over her bare stomach to fumble with the buttons of her jeans. "Afterwards, we'll take your money."

The feel of his hands—their hands—was too much to endure. She panicked. She kicked out, her knee connecting solidly with his groin. The man howled, staggering back.

This time, a fist slammed into her cheek. Dazed and hurting, her arms flailed the air to fight off any further blows. It was useless. The next fist struck her jaw, driving her toward unconsciousness.

"Another stunt like that, pretty one," one of them said, spittle splattering over her face, "and my knife will ruin your beauty."

Helplessly, her hands dropped back to her chest. Her fingertips brushed something, something warm and hard and smooth. The crystal of her amulet—the heart of the *Piasa*—it vibrated with strength, pulsed with power.

Again the voice moved within her. No longer did it mock her. It called to her in the voice of Beasos Dihi. It opened the path. It opened its arms to her—the arms of Cully Ghant. It was the door.

"Yes!" She screamed out, accepting it when there was nothing else to accept.

Darkness flowed over her. She felt it massing around her, blotting out the faces of her assailants. It touched her, then entered her body, permeating the very core of her soul.

"Little sister!" A voice called to her.

She looked up. Cully was there. He came out of the night like his namesake. Recklessly, he pushed through her four attackers before they realized what was happening. Then he was there, lifting her to her feet, his arm around her waist for support.

The four rushed them. But it didn't matter. She stood there, no longer a part of the threatening scene. She prayed as she had never prayed in her life. She opened herself to the power that flowed within and without her.

A talon with great recurved claws ripped out from the night. It raked across one of the faces that moved toward her. The man screamed and fell back. But not before the talon opened his chest.

She heard the growls and the snapping jaws. She saw the torn throats of two men, life flowing crimson from them. Again there were the talons, the flapping of wings. The last of her assailants screamed, his voice drowned in a terrible cry of triumph. The man collapsed to the winter-brown grass. A mass of red stared up at her where his face had once been.

A warm glow of pleasure suffused her body as she surveyed the butchered corpses strewn at her feet. It was a fitting beginning. Her head twisted to the black wolf sitting on its haunches beside her. Its darkly gleaming eyes rolled to her, reflecting the same satisfaction.

Her own golden eyes glittered with newfound pride. She unfolded the expanse of her great wings, then rose into the air.

The night was hers—the first of many to come. She rose, soaring and swooping. The currents caressed her. It was glorious. It would have been enough just to float there on the winds. But there was much that had to be done this night. Tribute to be taken.

She turned her attention to the heart of the city. Its lights glared red in anticipation of the reign of carnage brought on the night winds. She lifted her fire-plumed head and again screamed a cry of triumph.

Below her, on the pavement, ran a dark, living shadow —a wolf that no longer wandered.

A horror story need not be supernatural to produce a chilling effect. Ray Russell, from his classic "Sardonicus" to the story you are about to read, has proved it often enough to have him stand out among his peers as the master of the tale that is not nearly so quiet as you may think.

THE RUNAWAY LOVERS
by Ray Russell

The runaway lovers were captured just before they reached the border of the duchy.

They were dragged immediately before His Grace, the Duke, whose noble mien and halo of snowy curls lent him the aspect of a painted angel; and his face was sad as he looked reproachfully at his errant young wife, then at her troubadour lover, and then, with a great sigh and tears brimming in his soft old eyes, paid their captors in gold and turned the two prisoners over to his warder.

The Duke's curt instructions to the warder were surprising, for he enjoyed a reputation far and wide as a clement and a pious lord:

The lovers were to be taken to the dungeons and severely punished for a total of seven days—one day for each of the cardinal sins—finally to be irrevocably demised upon the seventh. During this time, they were to be prohibited, by the most direct of means, from looking upon or speaking to each other, from proffering solace by either words of courage or glances of love.

"The most direct of means," chattered the genial warder as, keys jangling, he led the unhappy pair down into the subterranean dungeons. "Aye, that would be to remove

165

your eyes and tongues." They howled in outraged protest, but he laughed merrily and assured them it was a simple operation, done with pincers and hot irons in a few seconds.

Still, all the world loves lovers, and the warder was a merciful man. He chose to postpone removing their eyes and tongues until the morrow, allowing them the night in which to see and speak to each other. See and speak, but not touch or fondle, for after stripping them he stuffed them into separage cages, tiny cages designed for minimum ease. Leaving one smoky torch flickering in a wall sconce, the warder took his leave of them. The lovers, squatting on bare haunches, their toes gripping the hard iron of the cages' floors, were free to console each other as best they could with words and looks.

The woman was the first to speak. "See to what a sorry state we have come," she said through tears. "And all because of you."

"Of *me?*" the youth replied. "It was I who insisted you remain with your husband the Duke, for we could easily take our pleasure of each other under his sanctimonious old nose and he be none the wiser. But no—you had to run away."

"Any other course would have been ignoble. Running away was the only decent thing to do."

"You speak of decency? *You?*" he cried. "All hot and hungry mouth you were from head to foot, burning with thirst, parched from an old husband's neglect, bold, unquenchable, depraved—"

"Shut your vile lips! *You* are to blame for our foul fortune. I would not be crouching here naked, like a plucked peacock in a parrot cage, awaiting seven days of torture, if you had not made advances to me in the first place."

"Your memory is as tarnished as your virtue! It was *you* made the first sign toward me!"

"You are a liar!"

"You are a trollop!"

She wept. Repenting a little of his words, he grumbled, "It well may be it is no fault of ours but of your hoary hymn-singer of a husband . . ."

"Whorey? No, that is the very rub, he did not—"

"You misrender me. His fault, I mean, to wed a wife

whose years are but a third his threescore span. His fault
to let her languish unslaked. His fault to throw the two of
us so much together, telling me how much you loved my
songs, telling you how much I loved your singing of them.
His fault for living in such purblind holiness, such ignorance of fleshly wants, such idiot innocence that he could
not foresee the natural outcome of it all. Yes, *his* the
fault! All his! Ah, damn him for a prating prig!"

She murmured tonelessly, "It was of latter days the
Duke eschewed my bed. When first we wed, my youthful
flesh so kindled him that his silver locks and holy ways
were quite forgot, and he was less like monk and more
like monkey, or, as one might say, like goat or bull or stal-
lion, what you will. Then, for reasons never understood
but which I took for sad depletion of his aged energies, he
grew mild and no more than a brother to me . . ."

"Brother?" the troubadour scoffed. "Grandsire!"

A dank draft of air tinkled the bones of an old skeleton
that hung by dry wrists from rusted ceiling chains. It drew
their eyes and their unvoiced wonderings: who had it
been and how long ago and was it a man or a woman?
For what had it died and how had it died—strung up with
grim simplicity to starve, or had there been other things,
less simple? The man shuddered and the woman wept
afresh and both were silent for a while.

Then he said, "Let us think clearly. In all his long life,
has the Duke ever been feared for harshness? Has he condemned to torture even the most black-hearted malefac-
tors? Has he so much as flogged the lowest churl? Is he
not laughed at by lackeys for his softness? Sneered at as a
weak and womanish wight? Is not his meekness the mock
and marvel of the land? Is he not praised by priests and
prelates for his piety, his charity, his unending orisons, his
saintliness? Well? Do I speak true?"

A stifled "Yes" escaped the crouched woman in the
neighboring cage.

He resumed: "How, then, can it be that such a man
could visit hideous torments upon two human creatures,
and one of them his comely wife?"

She sniffled, her head crammed between her knees, her
tears running in rivulets down her bare legs to glisten on

her toenails. "You grasp at straws," she moaned. "You heard him. Seven days of torture—"

"Of *punishment!*" he crowed. "And what, pray, does *he* deem punishment, that lily-livered nun of a man? Fasting and kneeling and praying and mortifying the flesh? Hair shirts for seven days? Stern sermons, righteous rhetoric?" He laughed. "A little discomfort, a humble show of repentance and a deal of yawning boredom! *That* is the 'torture' you fear!" He laughed again, rocking back on his heels as far as the cage would permit.

The woman delivered herself of a despondent sigh. "You are a fool," she said without rancor, as a plain statement of fact. "On the seventh day, we die. That was his command."

"*Demised!*" he said. "We are to be *demised* upon the seventh day!"

"The selfsame thing . . ."

"Not so! A word of many meanings! Chief among them: to be *released!*" He laughed louder. "Released! Can corpses be released? Can cold cadavers be granted freedom? No! We will but genuflect and beg forgiveness for seven short days—one day for each of the cardinal sins, you heard the pious dotard—and then we will be set free. Free! 'Irrevocably demised'—released without revoke! Our worries are for naught!"

Her eyelids, puffed and pink from weeping, opened slowly and her eyes sought his, scornfully, piteously. "Do you so soon forget? Is that thing within your skull of no more substance than a fishnet? Has fear so much unmanned you that your mind does not recall what else was said? A thing about our *eyes and tongues?*"

He opened his mouth to speak, but closed it. Sick horror shadowed his face once more.

She sneered, "Equivocate your way out of that!"

Soon, he smiled. "For your unkindness and unpleasant words, I should allow you to continue thinking we will lose those necessary and delightful organs. Why should I comfort you, when for my pains I reap but snide rebukes?" He chuckled. "And so I will be mum."

A long silent moment passed. At length, she cried out, "Speak, wretch!"

He laughed triumphantly. "Because I love you, sweetmeat, I will speak. And you will hearken. Call back to mind those dreadul words about our eyes and tongues. Recall who spoke them. Was it your saintly husband? Or was it a somewhat lesser lord, a slavering menial, none other than our lackwit turnkey?"

She gave it thought. "My husband said . . ."

"Your husband said we must not look upon or speak to one another. This is to be done, said he, by the most direct of means. Well, then. Gags and blindfolds! Are they not more direct than pincers and hot irons? Our stupid jailer was but wool-gathering, unlawfully elaborating upon your husband's orders. Those orders, when they are carried out, will be no more stringent than the rapping of a child's knuckles. Believe this, my saucy chuck—fear is a phantasm born out of air; it has not dam nor sire. Fret no further, dry your tears. A week of sackcloth and ashes, and we will be absolved, forgiven, and most magnanimously *demised*."

His words contained a certain logic. She began to be assured. "I pray you are right," she said.

"Trust in me," he replied. "Your husband would not allow us to be either tortured or slain."

A little later, the warder, that kindly man, returned and greeted them with a cheery smile and sat down near them to eat a bowl of gruel, his meagre supper. Between slurpings and smackings, he spoke:

"His Grace, the Duke, he says as how 'twould be unjust for you to dwell in ignorance of what is soon to come. Fair's fair, he says, being no cruel man, no tyrant like some I've served, no fiend who would allow poor gentles like yourselves to fear that worst of all bad fates—that is to say, things unknown. Far better, says he, for them to know what lies in store for them, and certain it is there's truth and wisdom in that, by bloody Christ's own hooks, if my lady will forgive the language. So go, good man, he says to me, go back to them and tell them both each single thing that will be done to them, the seven things in seven days, and not be chary of detail, he says, for it is good they know the most, that they may fear the least and in serenity consign their souls to Heaven. Aye, he's a fine man, a Godly man, is His Grace."

Wiping his lips and setting aside his empty bowl, the

jolly fellow said, "Well, now, tomorrow is the first day of the seven, is it not, so at the brink of dawn, after the good night's sleep I hope you'll have, this is what will be done upon the pair of you . . ."

When he told them of the First Day, they paled. When he told them of the Second Day, they groaned. When he told them of the Third Day, they cursed. When he told them of the Fourth Day, they wept. When he told them of the Fifth Day, they screamed. When he told them of the Sixth Day, they retched. When he told them of the Seventh and Final Day, a day that took almost a score of minutes in the telling, they fainted in the middle of it and he had to douse them into wakefulness with cold water, in order to finish it out. "And that be the whole of it," he smiled, "after which there will be no vile heathen disrespect for the remains but decent burial and Christian obsequies for both. So said His Grace. Good night to you, then, my lady, young sir. Sleep well." Humming a tune, he left the dungeon, closing the metal door with a dismal clang.

The youth, maddened by despair, rattled the bars of his cage, beat his fists against them, clawed at the lock until his fingers bled. At length, he collapsed into a lump of quivering, whimpering flesh.

She, her eyes blank with shock, mouthed disjoined words in a voice no stronger than a whisper. "Obscene . . . disgusting . . . more loathsome than I could ever dream . . . more horrible than all the agonies of Hell! *Seven days!* Each day unending! Oh God! To suffer thus? To undergo such foul abominations for a few moments of pleasure? No! No! . . ."

Her lover looked up at her with a slackened face. He blubbered: "You must beg him, plead with him, entreat him! Tell him it was *you* who tempted me, and I, poor human clay, was sucked inexorably to the lodestone of your lust. Tell him that! Why should we *both* die so horribly? Why should I suffer for your unfaithfulness?"

She shrieked at him: "Coward! Serpent! You would see me ripped and broken, to save your own skin? *You* must seek his mercy, tell him you snared my soul with devilish tricks and necromatic arts, rendering me a helpless slave to your cravings!"

"I? Scream my throat to shreds for seven unthinkable days and nights—all for a wench? A pair of lips, and eyes, and—and—and—"

His stammering tongue was impaled by something he saw outside his cage. He blinked. He licked dry lips. "Look," he said, pointing with an unsteady hand.

She looked. There on the stone floor, near the empty bowl, not far from the cages in which they were bent double, lay a heartlifting circle of hope: the warder's keyring.

"The k—" she began to shout, but "Shhh!" her lover cautioned, his finger to his lips. He whispered hoarsely: "Not a word. Not a sound. This is the Hand of Providence itself."

Also in a whisper, she said, "Stop prating holy hogwash like my husband and *get it.*"

He stretched his arm out between the bars of his cage, but his reach fell far too short. He squeezed his naked shoulder painfully between the bars, extending his reach, but still his fingertips raked empty air, inches away from the ring of keys. Finally, exhausted, he went limp.

Now she, from her cage, reached between the cold black iron of the bars, her tapering slim fingers writhing like little snakes in the attempt to grasp the keyring. Grunting indelicately, cursing vulgarly, she stretched her pretty arm still further, one round ripe fruit of a breast crushed cruelly against the bars. A sheen of sweat covered her whole body, despite the dungeon's chill. But still her fingers did not touch the taunting keys.

He, watching her efforts, whined, "No use . . . no use . . ."

She was loath to give up so easily. Hissing an unladylike oath, she now unbent her shapely long legs and, wincing at the pins of pain that shot through them after the hours of squatting restraint, she forced them between the bars, toward the metal circle of keys that lay between them and escape. Her toes flexed and curled, reaching for the keys. Her legs stretched still further, as her full thighs now were scraped and squashed by the cage bars. Biting her lip, she gripped the bars with her hands and pressed her belly and loins relentlessly against the unyielding iron, almost splitting herself in two on the bar that separated her thighs, gasping in pain, her toes clenching and unclenching, the sweat streaming from her flesh, until, at length, with a moan of thanksgiving, her efforts were rewarded, her feet closed upon the ring, she felt the welcome cold shafts of the keys between her toes, and slowly, carefully, she drew her feet back toward the cage, reached out and seized the keyring in her hand, then fell back, slimed with sweat and the blood of scraped skin, panting, sobbing, victorious.

Her lover in the other cage, eyeing the keys almost lasciviously, croaked, "The locks! Open the locks!"

She inserted one of the dozen keys into the lock of her cage door. It did not fit. She tried the next. And the next. Both lovers cursed, despair flooding them again and filling the great space hope had excavated in their hearts, as she tried key after key.

The tenth key worked. She swung open the creaking door of her cage and crawled out upon the stone floor of the dungeon. Slowly, agonizingly, she pulled herself to her feet and stood at her full height, magnificently, nudely beautiful.

Then, walking past his cage, she went straight to the dungeon door.

"Wait!" he cried. "Would you leave me here?"

"Who travels light travels best," she said, and unlocked the dungeon door.

"Strumpet! Open this cage!"

She laughed softly and blew him a mocking kiss.

"You need me!" he screamed. "You need me to overpower the guards, to steal horses, food, clothing. If you leave without me, I will bellow my lungs out, awaken the entire castle, the warder and the guards will apprehend you before you reach the first wall!"

She looked at him thoughtfully. Then, smiling, she walked back to his cage. "I was but teasing you," she said, and released him.

"I choose to believe you," he growled, "bitch!"

The two of them swung open the heavy dungeon door. Quiet and swift, hardly daring to breathe, they padded on bare feet up a narrow corkscrew of stone stairs to the armory.

There, serried ranks of soldiers stood in wait!

No: thus they appeared to be at first glimpse, but were revealed to be no more than empty suits of armor, the eyeslits as devoid of life as the sockets in the grinning skull below.

Up more stairs they climbed, and skittered spiderishly along a pitch black, airless corridor so constructed that it seemed to grow narrower as they penetrated it, the ceiling built gradually lower and lower until they were obliged to crouch, the walls themselves so close together at one point they had to go in single file and then to crawl on their bellies through the foul air and impenetrable dark.

It seemed upward of an hour before they felt cool air and, shortly after, crawled out and stood upright in a place no less dark but which felt to be a species of tunnel. They ran blindly through what proved to be a vexing, labyrinthine network of such tunnels, often colliding painfully with hard stone walls, until they heard a liquid sound and knew the maze to be a system of drains or conduits or somewhat, for soon they were splashing in filthy, stinking water up to their ankles, then to their knees, then feeling panic seize them as the icy wetness lapped their naked backsides.

An eternity of headlong splashing flight they suffered, hearing the chattering of rats and seeing their red eyes in the dark, before a pinpoint of light in the far distance brought hoarse sobs of triumph from their throats and they ran toward it pell-mell, splashing, sliding, falling, scrambling to their feet again and plunging on toward the blessed beckoning spot of light, out of the noisome water that now fell to below their knees, then to their ankles, until they were running in dryness again, the light growing brighter and bigger until, with aching limbs and flaming lungs, they burst out of the tunnel and into—

The dungeon. The selfsame dungeon whence they had escaped. For there were the cages, with the doors standing open, and there was the dangling skeleton, and there was their amiable warder, a truncheon in his hand, greeting them with a gap-toothed smile.

"A trick," the troubadour groaned, collapsing to his knees.

"Aye, lad," the warder nodded. "A trick to pass the time and take your minds off your troubles."

The woman shrieked, "A fiendish trick! A trick to raise our hopes and dash them down again! A gloating demon's trick!"

"Now, now," the warder chided, "into your little cages, the pair of you, and quick about it or I'll be obliged to break a bone or two with this . . ." He riased the truncheon meaningfully. Taking the keyring from her hand, he locked them in the cages again.

"All wet, are you, all wet and bare and blue with cold?" the warder said, solicitously. "Take heart, there will be heat enough at dawn." And, significantly, with broad winks, he opened a cabinet and took down a pair of branding irons which he placed upon a bench. "Aye, fire enough and heat enough," he grinned. From the cabinet he also took two long sharp blades, like gigantic paring knives. "Fire and heat and other things as well," he added, placing the awful knives next to the branding irons. He then closed the cabinet, squinted at the hideous equipment on the bench, and said, "That be enough. For the First Day, at least, it be enough." Then, deliberately shaking the keyring and filling the air with its sour jangle, he walked toward the dungeon door, saying, "This time I'll not be forgetting my keys, like a naughty knave. Good night, my lady, young sir, or rather, good morning, for dawn will break in less than an hour."

The door clanged shut.

The Duke's face wore an expression of shock. "Dead, you say? Both of them?"

"Aye, that they be, Your Grace," replied the warder, "and by their own hands. Behind my back, they reached out from their cages and took the blades Your Grace bade my put upon the bench for them to look at. The Lord have mercy on their souls."

The Duke crossed himself, dismissed the warder, and turned to the tonsured clergyman at his side. "You heard, Monsignor? Smitten by remorse, consumed by guilt, they took their own lives."

"And, as suicides," solemnly said the priest, "plummeted straight to the fires of Perdition—there to suffer chastisement infinitely more severe than if they had died by your command."

"True, true, poor burning souls," said the Duke. "I never, as you know, intended bodily harm to come to them."

"Of course not. Such cruelty would have marred the good repute you bear among all men."

"Those grisly tales I bade the warder tell them, those skeletons and other things, were but to harrow and humble their spirits for a night. Oh, I do repent me—"

"Of those harmless tales and bones?"

"Not they so much, Monsignor, as I repent my overtrusting nature that placed those two young people in temptation's path. Is mine the blame? Is mine the hand that led them to depravity, discovery, and death?"

The priest spoke firmly. "No! Your Grace's guileless goodness cannot bear the blame for the sins of others!"

"It is good of you to say it."

"You never could foresee or wish the death of your young wife!"

"Oh, no."

"You never could desire to yet *again* become a widower!"

"Heaven forbid."

"And dwell in mournful loneliness once more!"

"O doleful day!"

"No man in all the realm can blame you."

"I pray not."

"The hearts of all your friends, your faithful courtiers, the meanest churls, the highest lords, His Majesty, the Church itself—all these mourn with you in this heavy hour!"

"Thank you, Reverend Father."

"But if I may, without offense, speak of your sudden sad unmarried state, I would remind Your Grace that a certain advantageous alliance is now possible with a family whose name is so illustrious I need not give it breath . . ."

"At such a time as this," the Duke replied, "one cannot think of marriage. But when I have composed myself, then we may have some words anent that prince to whom you have alluded, and whose sister is, I do believe, of fifteen summers now and therefore ripe for wedding. To you, Monsignor, I leave all small details of the nuptial ceremony, which must take place, I need not say, only after what is called a decent interval."

"A decent interval, of course," replied the priest.

Peter D. Pautz is a psychologist and Executive Secretary of the Science Fiction Writers of America and is currently completing his first novel, The Cicatrix. *He is a most gentle man, though not necessarily when it comes to considering summer afternoons and what children do when nightmares come true.*

FISHERMAN'S LOG
by Peter D. Pautz

The new sunlight shone only on the upper tips of the bright green trees. Elms, oaks; barely touching the maples. The waterbound willows still hunched in darkness, bent, shaggy gnomes frozen in their desperate divings back to the earth. The deep throatings of the bullfrogs began to disappear, leaving only the persistent chirruping of the snowy-tree crickets vibrating over the pond.

Paul and Chris Johnson stood like small and bulbous tree stumps in their dew-spotted slickers, their ears pinpointed to the lone insect they had finally managed to locate among the tussocks of thick reedy weeds at the water's edge. Paul had his wrist cocked to a single beam of light breaching the high branches, gleaming off the tiny sweep hand of his Timex. His younger brother craned his neck around his arm, silently counting off the seconds.

"Okay, fifteen, Pauley," he said, straightening. "How many?"

"Twenty-two," the twelve-year-old replied. "They'll be moving around soon. Let's get going, shrimp."

Chris made a face his brother could not see as he bent over and picked up his gear. You're *only* three years

177

older, he thought, slapping his hipboots over his shoulder. But he knew better than to say it out loud. Paul had been on his side, prodding his parents into letting him go fishing despite the damp morning air. Even with only two years of interest in the sport himself, Paul had been enough in tune with their rules of reasons to hit the right note.

"Mom, you can't always baby him. Do you want him to go back to kindergarten? Let him try. Please, Mom. I'll be there."

She had begun to waver then. Nobody, least of all she, wanted him to go back to wheezing, sputtering at every little thing, just as he had done all through his first year at school. They still would not believe him when he began to choke, to gasp for air that somehow would not pass his throat. His earliest memory of his mother was her yelling at him, "Stop it, Chris. Right now."

He had never found a way to tell her that he could not, did not even know what he was doing that he was supposed to stop. Breathing? He just didn't know.

It was difficult moving through the tall grass and snagging bushes that surrounded the water. They had to swish their poles back and forth like lion tamers' whips to keep them from catching dangling foliage. The graphite flexed easily, swaying wildly, but kept in perfect control by their practiced hands. Chris had practiced for hours alone in the back room of the basement, flailing and swishing the rod until he could imitate anyone from Captain Blood to Lawrence Welk. He wasn't about to let Pauley show him up. Lure baskets, fly-speckled fisherman's hats, nets. They were really decked out. And they knew it.

By the time they reached their spot, the only place along the entire shore of the pond where bare bank met the algae-crusted rim of the water, the sun was already glaring its warmth off the surface. Setting their equipment down with exaggerated noiselessness, they sat and began luring up their lines.

Paul grimaced and shook his head when he saw the shiny, yellow-spotted plug that his brother had pulled from his gearbox. Chris noticed the gesture out of the side of his eye and, acting as if he had not, replaced the bait and took instead a duplicate of the one Paul was attaching to his own line.

They fished for hours, not saying a word. Except for once when Chris's line began to jump off of his reel, the ratchet clicking like some madly racing stopwatch.

"Play him, dummy," Paul had yelled when Chris started to jerkily pull the fish in. The small silvery creature rose to the water's surface twice early on, fighting like something a dozen times what his size said he was. Chris watched his line zigzag through the waterglare for over ten minutes, reeling in about ten inches every half-minute. When Paul clucked his tongue and moaned low in his throat, he figured it had been long enough and wound the device in earnest.

When the fish was safely on land, Paul returned to his own pole and Chris took the canvas bucket from his pile of gear, filling it, plopping the still squirming sunny inside. Then, he went back to his rod and sat beside his brother, grinning at the score. One to nothing.

After a minute, Paul stood and yanked in his line. "I'm going up the stream a little. There's no fish in the pond today," he said, smirking. "Except the *stupid* ones."

Pulling on his hipboots, he reached for his short-net and a box of flies. "Be back in about an hour, shrimp," he called over his shoulder and trudged off into the thick brush toward the stream at the far end of the pond.

Chris sat quietly on the bank, staring blankly at the easy ripples that marked some underwater obstruction in the slowly moving current. Laying his rod on the ground, he removed his heavy raincoat, only now conscious of the heated air beginning its daily climb toward a full dog day. He would wait for Pauley to come back and then they'd take their swim. He'd go in now except they had promised mother never to stick to the buddy system they used to use at camp. When he was a kid.

At the beginning of the summer, he had helped Pauley build a plank ladder up the side of an old oak tree several feet from the shore. About twenty feet up, they had constructed a small landing. A rope dangled to it, attached to it by a thirty-five-foot piece of string to pull the thick hemp back after each swing. It had taken him over a dozen attempts to learn to let go of the rope at its apex, carrying him far out over the dizzying water after streaking a bare three feet over the bank's edge. His mind quickly moved away from those memories. Jumping from the tree. Rushing toward the ground. The air ramming back into his mouth like a typhoon chopping the breath from between his lips. He shuddered and twisted his mind from even its small backward glance.

He picked up his rod again and stared at the rippling mirror of the pond's surface. He thought of all the cartoons he had seen of some guy fishing and some prankster under the water, out of sight, placing all kinds of weird stuff on the fisherman's hook. Old boots, cans, tires. Or a gigantic fish leaping out of the water, breaking the pole and jumping back into the lake. The images made him laugh, though he felt he had outgrown them.

A breeze high in the trees began shaking the leaves gently, scattering the light. And the dark. Shadows bounded into each other, sharp borders cutting themselves into strange, hovering shapes. Shades that never touched the earth, wafting overhead. The steamy moisture around the boles of the harsh old timber hung on him like a sodden blanket. A light bubbling could be heard in his breath.

Birds fluttered in the branches, shrilling, not singing. Insects popped, whined, buzzed through the dank atmosphere. Then Chris realized why he had laughed. He was scared. They all belonged here, lived and bred here. But he was intruding, out of place. Something inside of him —maybe outside, hidden in the trees, under the water; he couldn't tell—warned him to get out, whole, while he could.

He felt a slight pull on his fishing line. A large ripple broke where it disappeared beneath the surface and it smoothed again. Behind him, at a short distance, wood creaked, low and grating. And there was no wind now. Something ruffled in the leaves above his head, unplaceable and unnatural. He did not bother to breathe, straining to hear through the numbing batting smothering his body where his flesh tried to crawl away from its surroundings.

He slowly knuckled the ground, began to stand, when a terrifying shriek broke through the air. Something dove through the sky, from the left, behind him. Toward him.

He froze, trying to scream, half crouched off the ground. But his lungs hadn't the air.

The reverberating Tarzan yell peaked as Pauley swung past him on the rope, missing him by inches, reaching the top of his flight over the water and dropping. Forever.

Falling.

It was not until his body broke the surface that Chris was able to breathe again, dispelling that much of his icy terror. But only that much and no more.

Then Pauley's head broke the top of the water, laughing. "Boo, shrimp." He rocked back and forth howling, treading water, until he caught a mouthful of liquid from his own splashings. He choked, coughing out the algae-tinged water.

"Swallow a fish?" the younger boy jeered, relaxing at the sight of his big brother enacting his own malady in all seriousness. But he knew Pauley would recover too quickly to worry about giving it any real concern. Yeah, Pauley would, he thought.

Slowly, then, Chris stripped off his own clothes and slid over the mossy bank into the reedy shallows. The water barely covered his belly, but it was plenty deep for him. He forced himself to keep his head level, away from the smothering water and the leafy enshadowed branches that hung several feet over the entire rim of the pond.

Paul swam over to him, keeping his body under the cooling fluid. He knew what it took for his brother to even get into the water, to go near anything that might cut off his air a second from now.

"You okay?" he whispered, not wanting to make the point too loudly. The kidding had stopped. No way was he going to move more than a single arm's length from his brother. Chris was sure of that and he breathed a little easier.

"Yeah. It's just a little cold." Chris always shivered when he was in the water, the excuse always ready. But this time, something else added to his tremblings. The choking, smothering oppression had moved from around him, as if it had congealed somewhere off in the distance, solidifying itself into action.

A spray of dull, sweaty drops whipped off Chris's body as he spun around at the bellowing croak from the open bank.

"What are you boys doing here?" The voice was harshly cracked, biting off the air in harsh chunks. It seemed as if bellowing was its only possible manner of speech. "Get away from my property!"

The boys could not move, stunned as they were from the sudden vituperation. They hung in the water and stared at the old man. He was short and wide, front to back, swaying slightly in the hot air. His bald head gleamed with a sweaty, natural oil that even slicked his deep, evenly wrinkled face. Nondescrpit as his clothes were, they fell in gray-green folds from his almost non-existent shoulders. Some coarse material with the life long washed out of it. Large black eyes caught glints of sunlight, scintillating wildly like the surface of the pond.

It was very hard for the boys to look directly at the stranger. As if he somehow should not be there, was deathly out of place. Only a long, handmade net hanging from one sharply clutched hand seemed appropriate, complementing his nature.

"Get!" he screamed, thrashing his arms violently. The froggy bellow was horrible coming from that wide slash of a mouth.

The boys bolted toward the shore and began scrambling to their gear on the bank and behind the old oak. Quickly, almost trying to rotate on his feet, the man blocked their flight.

"Leave the equipment," he cried. "Just get!"

He took a single step menacingly in their direction, reaching across his body and spreading the net in front of him. They turned and ran into the woods, Paul stopping only once when he was still just barely in sight to yell, "We don't know you. We've never seen you before. This isn't your land."

"It's mine," he exclaimed, taking another step. "Get away!"

And as Chris ran after his brother he heard a loud splash far behind him in the pond. He halted for a moment, his fists clenched. Our equipment, he thought. Paul stopped next to him before he could start running again and he heard him mumble, "Damn you, you old bastard."

Then Paul raced after him and did not stop until he caught up with him. Clamping his brother's arms, he yanked him to a halt. Chris's lungs pumped desperately, forcing air into their phlegm-laden pores. He couldn't have gone much farther.

"Relax," Paul said, "he's not coming. Didn't leave the pond."

Not able to respond, he let himself be pulled to the ground and Paul straightened him out on his back. It was not until then that he realized that they had not been able to retrieve their clothes either. They were naked and it was starting to get cold. The midafternoon wind rustled through the trees, scratching leaves together into a sound almost too soft to hear. Clouds scudded before the sun to reinforce the chill.

After his brother had resumed normal breathing, Paul looked back icily the way they had come. "The dirty old bastard threw our stuff into the pond," he whispered, forcing the words between clenched teeth. His eyes remained fixed, the lips squeezing them tightly above and below.

"Pauley, it's cold," Chris complained, sitting up. "Let's go home."

"Not me," Paul snapped. "I'm going back for my gear. And that old bastard better leave me alone."

Chris had never heard him so angry. He was afraid to go back there, but he did not want to stay here alone either. He knew he would go, too, even if just to stay with Pauley.

"Okay." He swallowed tightly and stood to show his readiness. "Let's go."

"Not you, shrimp."

"He's got my stuff, too, Pauley."

"No. If I have to run again, I don't want to have to pull you after me." Paul turned and gazed at him carefully. "You're still having trouble breathing now."

"I'm going," Chris demanded, pulling back his shoulders. "I can run all right. I beat you here, didn't I?"

Paul shook his head slightly, jumped to his feet, and waved him to come along. Chris could tell what he was thinking. Little brothers could be a real pain. But they had talked enough; they were going back for their equipment.

The clouds had moved away from the sun and light slanted through the trees again, undercutting the higher branches. The greens muted behind the glare. Only the dark brown trunks stood out, pinioned to fuzzy bright grays from above.

Paul moved lithely through the woods, Chris close at his back. Nearing the pond, they slowed and stepped lightly over the brittle carpet of last year's leaves. They skulked silently to the small clearing by the bank and peered through the tall, thin branches of the last sumac bush.

The ground was empty; no equipment, no clothes. And no old man. The only movement was the sparkling ripple of the water's surface, energized by the rising afternoon wind. They were both beginning to shiver.

"Come on," Paul urged as he rounded the bush, headed toward the pond. His eyes scanned back and forth across the trees, looking for the least sign of movement.

"Pauley, I—"

He turned his head and noticed that his brother had not moved at all. Chris was anxiously biting his lower lip, staring at the water.

"Okay. You stay here." He knew his brother was too agitated to go near the water again. "Keep a lookout for Mr. Crab."

With another few quick steps he was off the bank and diving toward the water—before Chris could tell him that it was not the water that had immoblized him. Not the wind that made him shiver.

He saw their gear, crushed and shattered, lying behind a fallen log on the other side of the pond. Only the end of a pole and shredded foot of a hipboot rose above its rotting top, but he could tell that the rest of their gear must lie beneath it, supporting it.

As he turned to yell to Pauley, to warn him that their gear was not under water, he saw that the surface was unbroken. He must have been diving, searching for their gear. But it wasn't there. Something else had splashed into the pond.

Then suddenly his brother rose to the surface, pulling in deep gasps of air. He looked toward the bush where Chris was hiding and began to shout, telling him that he could not find anything, that the slow current must have pulled it off somewhere. But he stopped in the middle of a word, jerking his head around toward the stream across the water and his eyes bulged as he saw the spidery thing come flying out of the trees, directly at him.

The net. The old bastard's net.

Before Pauley could bring his legs up to move out of its way, the expertly thrown net was already around him. Chris saw his brother trying to pull it off of him, to swim out from underneath it. But the tough, stringly line only tightened more around his arms and head, cocooning them to his torso.

Chris ran quickly, desperately from behind the bush, toward the water. He had to get to his brother. In the water.

In the water?

Something jammed through his body, grinding him to a halt barely inches from the fluid's enticing glimmer. Like a cobra's eyes. He began to shiver again, but this time it was not the fear of the water engulfing him, smothering him. It was something that was already around him. *All* around him.

Then Pauley broke the surface again and a terrified gurgling scream shattered in his ears. Without another chance to think, Chris jumped in. His feet hit bottom and sank into the mud for several inches, but he leaped forward, swimming to Pauley, and they came free.

Huge drops splashed onto his face, into his mouth from his own frantic stroking. He felt as if he had swum for miles before his hand finally nudged something beneath the surface. He grasped it tightly and tried to lug it back to the air, but it was too heavy, and still. The words *dead weight* broke in his mind.

He fought to hold on to the net, to lift Pauley's body to the surface, but it was too much. His face kept getting yanked down into the water. He tried one more desperate pull, and his mouth and nose filled with waterdeath. Loud splashes sounded all around him. Currents and waves shifted, bounding in large, expanding circles.

He was under.

As the fluid clogged his throat, he searched fiercely for the surface. Suddenly cold and slimy hands grabbed him at the neck and arm, lifting him clear of the water. The sun shone brightly in his face and he felt the arms cock back in a wide arc.

The hands jerked and left him, flinging him through the air. His body rose in a high curve and landed roughly far back into the woods. Several twigs pierced his skin, and his buttocks and right thigh ached horribly from where he had fallen. But his attention was on his feet. They were running. Away.

As far away as he could get. But he would come back for Pauley. With help. Sometime after he had stopped running.

Back at the pond the old man was standing in the shallows glaring into the woods. He reached into an inner fold of his dull gray-green clothing and extracted a small folder. Taking the pencil from its sleeve, he turned to the date in his log.

July 28th.

He began to write.

One large sonny today.

Let a smaller one go. Too sickly, small. Needs growing. But not much.

Replacing the pencil, he returned the folder to its silvery, natural pocket. Then he slowly moved deeper into the pond. Until, once again, he was beneath it.

In the spring of 1978, your editor came across this story in the March issue of Ellery Queen's Mystery Magazine. As soon as I finished it, I knew that somehow I would use it in an anthology the first chance I had. And I am not ashamed to say that it is one of the most touching, and chilling, pieces I have read in years. Ms. Mackenzie is a citizen of Rhodesia, which is all any of us know about her—except that she definitely knows what true horror is . . .

I CAN'T HELP SAYING GOODBYE
by Ann Mackenzie

My name is Karen Anders I'm nine years old I'm little and dark and near-sighted I live with Max and Libby I have no friends

Max is my brother he's 20 years older than me he has close-together eyes and a worried look we Anders always were a homely lot he has asthma too

Libby used to be pretty but she's put on weight she looks like a wrestler in her new bikini I wish I had a bikini Lib won't buy me one I guess I'd stop being so scared of going in the water if I had a yellow bikini to wear on the beach

Once when I was seven my father and mother went shopping they never came home there was a holdup in the bank like on television Lib said this crazy guy just mowed them down

Before they went out I knew I had to say goodbye I said it slow and clear goodbye Mommy first then goodbye Daddy but no one took any notice of it much seeing they were going shopping anyway but afterwards Max remem-

187

bered he said to Libby the way that kid said goodbye you'd think she knew

Libby said for gosh sakes how could she know be reasonable honey but I guess this means we're responsible for her now have you thought of that

She didn't sound exactly pleased about it

Well after I came to live with Max and Libby I knew I had to say goodbye to Lib's brother Dick he was playing cards with them in the living room and when Lib yelled Karen get to bed can't you I went to him and stood as straight as I could with my hands clasped loose in front like Miss Jones tells us when we have choir in school

I said very slow and clear well goodbye Dick and Libby gave me a kind of funny look

Dick didn't look up from his cards he said goodnight kid

Next evening before any of us saw him again he was dead of a disease called peritonitis it explodes in your stomach and busts it full of holes

Lib said Max did you hear how she said goodbye to Dick and Max started wheezing and gasping and carrying on he said I told you there was something didn't I it's weird that's what it is it scares me sick who'll she say goodbye to next I'd like to know and Lib said there honey there baby try to calm yourself

I came out from behind the door where I was listening I said don't worry Max you'll be okay

His face was blotchy and his mouth was blue he said in a scratchy whisper how do you know

What a dumb question as though I'd tell him even if I did know

Libby bent down and pushed her face close to mine I could smell her breath cigarettes and bourbon and garlic salad

She said only it came out like a hiss don't you ever say goodbye to anyone again don't you ever say it

The trouble is I can't help saying goodbye

After that things went okay for a while and I thought maybe they'd forgotten all about it but Libby still wouldn't buy me a new bikini

Then one day in school I knew I had to say goodbye to Kimberley and Charlene and Brett and Susie

Well I clasped my hands in front of me and I said it to each of them slow and careful one by one

Miss Jones said goodness Karen why so solemn dear and I said well you see they're going to die

She said Karen you're a cruel wicked child you shouldn't say things like that it isn't funny see how you made poor little Susie cry and she said come Susie dear get in the car you'll soon be home and then you'll be all right

So Susie dried her tears and ran after Kimberley and Charlene and Brett and climbed in the car right next to Charlene's mom because Charlene's mom was doing the car pool that week

And that was the last we saw of any of them because the car skidded off the road to Mountain Heights and rolled all the way down to the valley before it caught fire

There was no school next day it was the funeral we sang songs and scattered flowers on the graves

Nobody wanted to stand next to me

When it was over Miss Jones came along to see Libby I said good evening and she said it back but her eyes slipped away from me and she breathed kind of fast then Libby sent me out to play

Well when Miss Jones had gone Libby called me back she said didn't I tell you never never never to say goodbye to anyone again

She grabbed hold of me and her eyes were kind of burning she twisted my arm it hurt I screamed don't please don't but she went on twisting and twisting so I said if you don't let go I'll say goodbye to Max

It was the only way I could think of to make her stop

She did stop but she kept hanging on to my arm she said oh god you mean you can make it happen you can make them die

Well of course I can't but I wasn't going to tell her that in case she hurt me again so I said yes I can

She let go of me I fell hard on my back she said are you okay did I hurt you Karen honey I said yes and you better not do it again and she said I was only kidding I didn't mean it

So then I knew that she was scared of me I said I

want a bikini to wear on the beach a yellow one because yellow's my favorite color

She said well honey you know we have to be careful and I said do you want me to say goodbye to Max or not

She leaned against the wall and closed her eyes and stood quite still for a while and I said what are you doing and she said thinking

Then all of a sudden she opened her eyes and grinned she said hey I know we'll go to the beach tomorrow we'll take our lunch I said does that mean I get my new bikini and she said yes your bikini and anything else you want

So yesterday afternoon we bought the bikini and early this morning Lib went into the kitchen and fixed up the picnic fried chicken and orange salad and chocolate cake and the special doughnuts she makes for company she said Karen are you sure it's all the way you want it and I said sure everything looks just great and I won't be so scared of the waves now I have my bikini and Libby laughed she put the lunch basket into the car she has strong brown arms she said no I guess you won't

Then I went up to my room and put on my bikini it fitted just right I went to look in the glass I looked and looked then I clasped my hands in front I felt kind of funny I said slow and clear goodbye Karen goodbye Karen goodbye goodbye

Ramsey Campbell, winner of the British Fantasy Award and many-time finalist for the World Fantasy Award, relies less on oft-used mythologies for his foundations than those seemingly minor incidents in one's life that, for Ramsey, are never minor enough by the time he has finished developing his nightmares.

MIDNIGHT HOBO

by Ramsey Campbell

As he reached home, Roy saw the old man who lived down the road chasing children from under the railway bridge. "Go on, out with you," he was crying as though they were cats in his flowerbeds. He was brandishing his string bags, which were always full of books.

Perhaps the children had been climbing up beneath the arch; that was where he kept glancing. Roy wasn't interested, for his co-presenter on the radio show was getting on his nerves. At least Don Derrick was only temporary, until the regular man came out of hospital. As a train ticked away its carriages over the bridge, Roy stormed into his house in search of a soothing drink.

The following night he remembered to glance under the arch. It didn't seem likely that anyone could climb up there, nor that anyone would want to. Even in daylight you couldn't tell how much of the mass that clogged the corners was soot. Now the arch was a hovering block of darkness, relieved only by faint grayish sketches of girders. Roy heard birds fluttering.

Today Derrick had been almost tolerable, but he made up for that the next day. Halfway through *Our Town Tonight* Roy had to interview the female lead from *The*

191

Man on Top, a limp British sex comedy about a young man trying to seduce his way to fame. Most of the film's scrawny budget must have been spent on hiring a few guest comedians. Heaven only knew how the producers had been able to afford to send the girl touring to promote the film.

Though as an actress she was embarrassingly inexperienced, as an interviewee she was far worse. She sat like a girl even younger than she was, overawed by staying up so late. A man from the film distributors watched over her like a nanny.

Whatever Roy asked her, her answers were never more than five words long. Over by the studio turntables, Derrick was fiddling impatiently with the control panel, making everyone nervous. In future Roy wouldn't let him near the controls.

Ah, here was a question that ought to inspire her. "How did you find the experience of working with so many veterans of comedy?"

"Oh, it really helped." He smiled desperate encouragement. "It really really did," she said miserably, her eyes pleading with him.

"What do you remember best about working with them?" When she looked close to panic he could only say, "Are there any stories you can tell?"

"Oh—" At last she seemed nervously ready to speak, when Derrick interrupted: "Well, I'm sure you've lots more interesting things to tell us. We'll come back to them in a few minutes, but first here's some music."

When the record was over he broke into the interview. "What sort of music do you like? What are your favorite things?" He might have been chatting to a girl in one of the discotheques where he worked. There wasn't much that Roy could do to prevent him, since the program was being broadcast live: half-dead, more like.

Afterward he cornered Derrick, who was laden with old 78s, a plastic layer cake of adolescent memories. "I told you at the outset that was going to be my interview. We don't cut into each other's interviews unless invited."

"Well, I didn't know." Derrick's doughy face was growing pinkly mottled, burning from within. If you poked him, would the mark remain, as though in putty? He must look his best in the dim light of discos. "You know now," Roy said.

"I thought you needed some help," Derrick said with a kind of timid defiance; he looked ready to flinch. "You didn't seem to be doing very well."

"I wasn't, once you interfered. Next time, please remember who's running the show."

Half an hour later Roy was still fuming. As he strode beneath the bridge he felt on edge; his echoes seemed unpleasantly shrill, the fluttering among the girders sounded more like restless scuttling. Perhaps he could open a bottle of wine with dinner.

He had nearly finished dinner when he wondered when the brood would hatch. Last week he'd seen the male bird carrying food to his mate in the hidden nest. When he'd washed up, he strolled under the bridge but could see only the girders gathering darkness. The old man with the string bags was standing between his regimented flowerbeds, watching Roy or the bridge. Emerging, Roy glanced back. In the May twilight the archway resembled a block of mud set into the sullen bricks.

Was there something he ought to have noticed? Next morning, on waking, he thought so—but he didn't have much time to think that day, for Derrick was sulking. He hardly spoke to Roy except when they were on the air, and even then his face belied his synthetic cheerfulness. They were like an estranged couple who were putting on a show for visitors.

Roy had done nothing to apologize for. If Derrick let his animosity show while he was broadcasting, it would be Derrick who'd have to explain. That made Roy feel almost at ease, which was why he noticed belatedly that he hadn't heard the birds singing under the bridge for days.

Nor had he seen them for almost a week; all he had heard was fluttering, as though they were unable to call. Perhaps a cat had caught them, perhaps that was what the fluttering had been. If anything was moving up there now, it sounded larger than a bird—but perhaps that was only his echoes, which seemed very distorted.

He had a casserole waiting in the oven. After dinner he browsed among the wavelengths of his stereo radio, and found a Mozart quartet on an East European frequency. As the calm deft phrases intertwined, he watched twilight smoothing the pebble-dashed houses, the tidy windows and flowerbeds. A train crossed the bridge, providing a few bars of percussion, and prompted him to imagine how far the music was traveling.

In a pause between movements he heard the cat.

At first, even when he turned the radio down, he couldn't make out what was wrong. The cat was hissing and snarling, but what had happened to its voice? Of course—it was distorted by echoes. No doubt it was among the girders beneath the bridge. He was about to turn up the music when the cat screamed.

He ran to the window, appalled. He'd heard cats fighting, but never a sound like that. Above the bridge, two houses distant, a chain gang of telegraph poles looked embedded in the glassy sky. He could see nothing underneath except a rhomb of dimness, rounded at the top. Reluctantly he ventured onto the deserted street.

It was not quite deserted. A dozen houses further from the bridge, the old man was glaring dismayed at the arch. As soon as Roy glanced at him, he dodged back into his house.

Roy couldn't see anything framed by the arch. Grass and weeds, which looked pale as growths found under stones, glimmered in the spaces between bricks. Some of the bricks resembled moist fossilized sponges, cemented by glistening mud. Up among the girders, an irregular pale shape must be a larger patch of weeds. As he peered at it, it grew less clear, seemed to withdraw into the dark —but at least he couldn't see the cat.

He was walking slowly, peering up in an attempt to reassure himself, when he trod on the object. Though it felt soft, it snapped audibly. The walls, which were padded with dimness, seemed to swallow its echo. It took him a while to glance down.

At first he was reminded of one of the strings of dust that appeared in the spare room when, too often, he couldn't be bothered to clean. But when he stooped reluctantly, he saw fur and claws. It looked as it had felt: like a cat's foreleg.

He couldn't look up as he fled. Echoes sissified his

footsteps. Was a large, pale shape following him beneath the girders? Could he hear its scuttling, or was that himself? He didn't dare speculate until he'd slammed his door behind him.

Half an hour later a gang of girls wandered, yelling and shrieking, through the bridge. Wouldn't they have noticed the leg, or was there insufficient light? He slept badly and woke early, but could find no trace in the road under the bridge. Perhaps the evidence had been dragged away by a car. The unlucky cat might have been run over on the railway line—but in that case, why hadn't he heard a train? He couldn't make out any patch of vegetation among the girders, where it was impenetrably dark; there appeared to be nothing pale up there at all.

All things considered, he was glad to go to work, at least to begin with. Derrick stayed out of his way, except to mention that he'd invited a rock group to talk on tonight's show. "All right," Roy said, though he'd never heard of the group. "Ian's the producer. Arrange it with him."

"I've already done that," Derrick said smugly.

Perhaps his taste of power would make him less intolerable. Roy had no time to argue, for he had to interview an antipornography campaigner. Her glasses slithered down her nose, her face grew redder and redder, but her pharisaic expression never wavered. Not for the first time, he wished he were working for television.

That night he wished it even more, when Derrick led into the studio four figures who walked like a march of the condemned and who looked like inexpert caricatures of bands of the past five years. Roy had started a record and was sitting forward to chat with them, when Derrick said, "I want to ask the questions. This is *my* interview."

Roy would have found this too pathetic even to notice, except that Derrick's guests were grinning to themselves; they were clearly in on the secret. When Roy had suffered Derrick's questions and their grudging answers for ten minutes—"Which singers do you like? Have you written any songs? Are you going to?"—he cut them off and wished the band success, which they certainly still needed.

When they'd gone, and a record was playing, Derrick

turned on him. "I hadn't finished," he said petulantly. "I was still talking."

"You've every right to do so, but not on my program."

"It's my program too. You weren't the one who invited me. I'm going to tell Hugh Ward about you."

Roy hoped he would. The station manager would certainly have been listening to the banal interview. Roy was still cursing Derrick as he reached the bridge, where he balked momentarily. No, he'd had enough stupidity for one day; he wasn't about to let the bridge bother him.

Yet it did. The weeds looked even paler, and drained; if he touched them—which he had no intention of doing —they might snap. The walls glistened with a liquid that looked slower and thicker than water: mixed with grime, presumably. Overhead, among the encrusted girders, something large was following him.

He was sure of that now. Though it stopped when he did, it wasn't his echoes. When he fled beyond the mouth of the bridge, it scuttled to the edge of the dark arch. As he stood still he heard it again, roaming back and forth restlessly, high in the dark. It was too large for a bird or a cat. For a moment he was sure that it was about to scuttle down the drooling wall at him.

Despite the heat, he locked all the windows. He'd grown used to the sounds of trains, so much so that they often helped him sleep, yet now he wished he lived further away. Though the nights were growing lighter, the arch looked oppressively ominous, a lair. That night every train on the bridge jarred him awake.

In the morning he was in no mood to tolerate Derrick. He'd get the better of him one way or the other—to start with, by speaking to Ward. But Derrick had already seen the station manager, and now Ward wasn't especially sympathetic to Roy; perhaps he felt that his judgment in hiring Derrick was being questioned. "He says his interview went badly because you inhibited him," he said, and when Roy protested, "In any case, surely you can put up with him for a couple of weeks. After all, learning to get on with people is part of the job. We must be flexible."

Derrick was that all right, Roy thought furiously: flexible as putty, and as lacking in personality. During the whole of *Our Town Tonight* he and Derrick glared at or ignored each other. When they spoke on the air, it wasn't to each other. Derrick, Roy kept thinking: a tower over a bore—and the name contained "dreck," which seemed entirely appropriate. Most of all he resented being reduced to petulance himself. Thank God it was nearly the weekend—except that meant he would have to go home.

When he left the bus he walked home the long way, avoiding the bridge. From his gate he glanced at the arch, whose walls were already mossed with dimness, then looked quickly away. If he ignored it, put it out of his mind completely, perhaps nothing would happen. What could happen, for heaven's sake? Later, when an unlit train clanked over the bridge like the dragging of a giant chain in the dark, he realized why the trains had kept him awake: What might their vibrations disturb under the bridge?

Though the night made him uneasy, Saturday was worse. Children kept running through the bridge, screaming to wake the echoes. He watched anxiously until they emerged; the sunlight on the far side of the arch seemed a refuge.

He was growing obsessive, checking and rechecking the locks on all the windows, especially those nearest the bridge. That night he visited friends, and drank too much, and talked about everything that came into his head, except the bridge. It was waiting for him, mouth open, when he staggered home. Perhaps the racket of his clumsy footsteps had reached the arch, and was echoing faintly.

On Sunday his mouth was parched and rusty, his skull felt like a lump of lead that was being hammered out of shape. He could only sit at the bedroom window and be grateful that the sunlight was dull. Children were shrieking under the bridge. If anything happened there, he had no idea what he would do.

Eventually the street was quiet. The phrases of church bells drifted, interweaving, on the wind. Here came the old man, apparently taking his string bags to church. No: he halted at the bridge and peered up for a while; then, looking dissatisfied but unwilling to linger, he turned away.

Roy had to know. He ran downstairs, though his brain

felt as though it were slopping from side to side. "Excuse me—" (damn, he didn't know the old man's name) "—er, could I ask what you were looking for?"

"You've been watching me, have you?"

"I've been watching the bridge. I mean, I think something's up there too. I just don't know what it is."

The old man frowned at him, perhaps deciding whether to trust him. Eventually he said, "When you hear trains at night, do you ever wonder where they've been? They stop in all sorts of places miles from anywhere in the middle of the night. Suppose something decided to take a ride? Maybe it would get off again if it found somewhere like the place it came from. Sometimes trains stop on the bridge."

"But what is it?" He didn't realize he had raised his voice until he heard a faint echo. "Have you seen it? What does it want?"

"No, I haven't seen it." The old man seemed to resent the question, as though it was absurd or vindictive. "Maybe I've heard it, and that's too much as it is. I just hope it takes another ride. What does it want? Maybe it ran out of—" Surely his next word must have been "food," but it sounded more like "forms."

Without warning he seemed to remember Roy's job. "If you read a bit more you wouldn't need me to tell you," he said angrily, slapping his bagfuls of books. "You want to read instead of serving things up to people and taking them away from books."

Roy couldn't afford to appear resentful. "But since I haven't read them, can't you tell me—" He must be raising his voice, for the echo was growing clearer—and that must have been what made the old man flee. Roy was left gaping after him and wondering how his voice had managed to echo; when a train racketed over the bridge a few minutes later, it seemed to produce no echo at all.

The old man had been worse than useless. Suppose there was something under the bridge: It must be trapped in the arch. Otherwise, why hadn't it been able to follow Roy beyond the mouth? He stood at his bedroom window, daring a shape to appear. The thing was a coward, and stupid—almost as stupid as he was for believing that anything was there. He must lie down, for his thoughts were cracking apart, floating away. The lullaby of bells for evening mass made him feel relatively safe.

Sleep took him back to the bridge. In the dark he could just make out a halted goods train. Perhaps all the trucks were empty, except for the one from which something bloated and pale was rising. It clambered down, lolling from scrawny legs, and vanished under the bridge, where a bird was nesting. There was a sound less like the cry of a bird than the shriek of air being squeezed out of a body. Now something that looked almost like a bird sat in the nest—but its head was too large, its beak was lopsided, and it had no voice. Nevertheless the bird's returning mate ventured close enough to be seized. After a jump in the continuity, for which Roy was profoundly grateful, he glimpsed a shape that seemed to have lost the power to look like a bird, crawling into the darkest corners of the arch, among cobwebs laden with soot. Now a cat was caught beneath the arch, and screaming; but the shape that clung to the girder afterward didn't look much like a cat, even before it scuttled back into its corner. Perhaps it needed more substantial food. Roy needn't be afraid, he was awake now and watching the featureless dark of the arch from his bedroom window. Yet he was dreadfully afraid, for he knew that his fear was a beacon that would allow something to reach for him. All at once the walls of his room were bare brick, the corners were masses of sooty cobweb, and out of the darkest corner a top-heavy shape was scuttling.

When he managed to wake, he was intensely grateful to find that it wasn't dark. Though he had the impression that he'd slept for hours, it was still twilight. He wasn't at all refreshed: his body felt odd—feverish, unfamiliar, exhausted as though by a struggle he couldn't recall. No doubt the nightmare, which had grown out of the old man's ramblings, was to blame.

He switched on the radio to try to rouse himself. What was wrong? They'd mixed up the signature tunes, this ought to be— He stood and gaped, unable to believe what he was hearing. It was Monday, not Sunday at all.

No wonder he felt so odd. He had not time to brood over that, for he was on the air in less than an hour. He was glad to be leaving. The twilight made it appear that the dark of the bridge was seeping toward the house. His perceptions must be disordered, for his movements seemed to echo slightly in the rooms. Even the sound of a bird's claw on the rooftiles made him nervous.

Despite his lateness, he took the long way to the main road. From the top of the bus he watched furry ropes of cloud, orange and red, being drawn past the ends of side streets. Branches clawing at the roof made him start. A small branch must have snapped off, for even when the trees had passed, a restless scraping continued for a while above him.

He'd rarely seen the city streets so deserted. Night was climbing the walls. He was neurotically aware of sounds in the empty streets. Birds fluttered sleepily on pediments, though he couldn't always see them. His footsteps sounded effeminate, panicky, thinned by the emptiness. The builder's scaffolding that clung to the outside of the radio station seemed to turn his echoes even more shrill.

The third-floor studio seemed to be crowded with people, all waiting for him. Ian the producer looked harassed, perhaps imagining an entire show with Derrick alone. Derrick was smirking, bragging his punctuality. Tonight's interviewees—a woman who wrote novels about doctors and nurses in love, the leader of a group of striking undertakers—clearly sensed something was wrong. Well, now nothing was.

Roy was almost glad to see Derrick. Trivial chat might be just what he needed to stabilize his mind; certainly it was all he could manage. Still, the novelist proved to be easy: every question produced an anecdote—her Glasgow childhood, the novel she'd thrown out of the window because it was too like real life, the women who wrote to her asking to be introduced to the men on whom she based her characters. Roy was happy to listen, happy not to talk, for his voice through the microphone seemed to be echoing.

"—and Mugsy Moose, and Poo-Poo, and Trixie the Oomph." Reading the dedications, Derrick sounded unnervingly serious. "And here's a letter from one of our listeners," he said to Roy without warning, "who wants to know if we aren't speaking to each other."

Had Derrick invented that in a bid for sympathy? "Yes, of course we are," Roy said impatiently. As soon as he'd started the record—his hands on the controls felt unfamiliar and clumsy, he must try to be less irritable—he complained, "Something's wrong with the microphone. I'm getting an echo."

"I can't hear anything," Ian said.

"It isn't there now, only when I'm on the air."

Ian and one of the engineers stared through the glass at Roy for a while, then shook their heads. "There's nothing," Ian said through the headphones, though Roy could hear the echo growing worse, trapping his voice amid distortions of itself. When he removed the headphones, the echo was still audible. "If you people listening at home are wondering what's wrong with my voice,"—he was growing coldly furious, for Derrick was shaking his head too, looking smug—"we're working on it."

Ian ushered the striking undertaker into the studio. Maybe he would take Roy's mind off the technical problems. And maybe not, for as soon as Roy introduced him, something began to rattle the scaffolding outside the window and squeak its claws or its beak on the glass. "After this next record we'll be talking to him," he said as quickly as he could find his way through the echoes.

"What's wrong now?" Ian demanded.

"That." But the tubular framework was still, and the window was otherwise empty. It must have been a bird: No reason for them all to stare at him.

As soon as he came back on the air the sounds began again. Didn't Ian care that the listeners must be wondering what they were? Halfway through introducing the undertaker, Roy turned sharply. Though there wasn't time for anything to dodge out of sight, the window was blank.

That threw him. His words were stumbling among echoes, and he'd forgotten what he meant to say. Hadn't he said it already, before playing the record?

Suddenly, like an understudy seizing his great chance on the night when the star falls ill, Derrick took over. "Some listeners may wonder why we're digging this up, but other people may think that this strike is a grave undertaking . . ." Roy was too distracted to be appalled, even when Derrick pounced with an anecdote about an old lady whose husband was still awaiting burial. Why, the man was a human vacuum: No personality to be depended on at all.

For the rest of the show, Roy said as little as possible. Short answers echoed less. He suppressed some of the monosyllables he was tempted to use. At last the signature tune was reached. Mopping his forehead theatrically, Derrick opened the window.

Good God, he would let it in! The problems of the show had distracted Roy from thinking, but there was nothing to muffle his panic now. Ian caught his arm: "Roy, if there's anything—" Even if he wanted to help, he was keeping Roy near the open window. Shrugging him off, Roy ran toward the lift.

As he waited, he saw Ian and the engineer stalking away down the corridor, murmuring about him. If he'd offended Ian, that couldn't be helped; he needed to be alone, to think, perhaps to argue himself out of his panic. He dodged into the lift, which resembled a gray, windowless telephone box, featureless except for the dogged subtraction of lit numbers. He felt walled in by gray. Never mind, in a minute he would be out in the open, better able to think—

But was he fleeing toward the thing he meant to elude?

The lift gaped at the ground floor. Should he ride it back to the third? Ian and the engineer would have gone down to the car park by now; there would only be Derrick and the open window. The cramped lift made him feel trapped, and he stepped quickly into the deserted foyer.

Beyond the glass doors he could see a section of pavement, which looked oily with sodium light. Around it the tubes of the scaffolding blazed like orange neon. As far as he could judge, the framework was totally still —but what might be waiting silently for him to step beneath? Suddenly the pavement seemed a trap which needed only a footfall to trigger it. He couldn't go out that way.

He was about to press the button to call the lift when he saw that the lit numbers were already counting down.

For a moment—he didn't know why—he might have fled out of the building, had he been able. He was trapped between the lurid stage of pavement and the inexorable descent of the lift. By the time the lift doors squeaked open, his palms were stinging with sweat. But the figure that stumbled out of the lift, hindered a little by his ill-fitting clothes, was Derrick.

Roy could never have expected to be so glad to see him. Hastily, before he could lose his nerve, he pulled open the glass doors, only to find that he was still unable to step beneath the scaffolding. Derrick went first, his footsteps echoing in the deserted street. When nothing happened, Roy managed to follow. The glass doors snapped locked behind him.

Though the sodium glare was painfully bright, at least it showed that the scaffolding was empty. He could hear nothing overhead. Even his footsteps sounded less panicky now; it was Derrick's that were distorted, thinned and hasty. Never mind, Derrick's hurry was all to the good, whatever its cause; it would take them to the less deserted streets all the more quickly.

Shadows counted their paces. Five paces beyond each lamp their shadows drew ahead of them and grew as dark as they could, then pivoted around their feet and paled before the next lamp. He was still nervous, for he kept peering at the shadows—but how could he expect them not to be distorted? If the shadows were bothering him, he'd have some relief from them before long, for ahead there was a stretch of road where several lamps weren't working. He wished he were less alone with his fears. He wished Derrick would speak.

Perhaps that thought halted him where the shadows were clearest, to gaze at them in dismay.

His shadow wasn't unreasonably distorted. That was exactly the trouble. Without warning he was back in his nightmare, with no chance of awakening. He remembered that the thing in the nightmare had had no voice. No, Roy's shadow wasn't especially distorted—but beside it, produced by the same lamp, Derrick's shadow was.

Above all he mustn't panic; his nightmare had told him so. Perhaps he had a chance, for he'd halted several lamps short of the darkness. If he could just retreat toward the studio without breaking into a turn, perhaps he would be safe. If he could bang on the glass doors without losing control, mightn't the caretaker be in time?

The worst thing he could do was glance aside. He mustn't see what was casting the shadow, which showed how the scrawny limbs beneath the bloated stomach were struggling free of the ill-fitting clothes. Though his whole body was trembling—for the face of the shadow had puckered and was reaching sideways toward him, off the head—he began, slower than a nightmare, to turn away.

Jack C. Haldeman II, whose first novel, Vector Analysis, has been published this year, spends most of his writing time in the field of science fiction. His stories have appeared in virtually every major magazine and anthology, and now, for the first time, he moves into fantasy. A traditional myth. Not a traditional story.

SNAKES AND SNAILS
by Jack C. Haldeman II

The black water lapped quietly against the sides of the flat-bottomed boat as Mark pushed his way through the dark swamp like the ghost of some long forgotten gondolier. A lantern hung on a pole over his head, and in the shifting shadows Lisa, his young wife, was a still, unmoving figure. She stared absently at the baggage in the boat, focusing her attention anywhere but out into the dark unfamiliarity beyond the feeble circle of illumination. Something splashed in the darkness; a fish, a snake, an alligator. She shivered, and drew her jacket tightly to her chest.

"It won't be long now," Mark reassured his wife. "Just beyond this bend in the river."

"I don't see how you can remember all these things," Lisa replied. "It's been such a long time."

"When you're a child, you notice things like that. I often played in that tree."

Lisa looked up and saw a half-illuminated tree standing on the riverbank, its gnarled branches stretching out over the water toward the light. Spanish moss hung down like a thousand twisted fingers. She imagined it a haven for obscenely large frogs and all sorts of horrible snakes.

"What a perfectly dreadful place to play."

"We weren't supposed to be so far from home, but you know how kids are."

"Will we see your old house, what remains of it, that is?"

"Maybe tomorrow. I don't know, though, I really want to get started."

Lisa eased back in the boat. Though she couldn't see Mark's face clearly in the dark, she imagined his familiar features breaking into an excited grin. The thought comforted her. He was always happy when he was thinking about this summer, this trip, the old house, and his painting.

His painting, of course, was the key. Ever since he had graduated from the Rhode Island School of Design, it had been one job as a commercial artist after another. Each job had more rsesponsibility and pressure than the previous one. Each took more time away from his real love—painting. A month ago he had been making a great deal of money designing cigarette packages and labels for beer bottles and hating every minute of it. Then his family lawyer had called about some trivial matter of taxes or something and had mentioned casually that the old Esworthy estate was for rent ridiculously cheap.

They had talked it over, but from the very first she had seen how much this meant to him. Together they decided to rent the house for the summer. It was isolated, and he would be able to paint unencumbered by the demands of his job. Lisa felt she had never really had a chance to voice her concern about moving to such a remote location—in fact, she wasn't sure she would have said anything even if she had been given the opportunity. It was so obviously what Mark wanted. She could live with it, for a summer at least.

It was hard for her to realize that she, a New York City girl who thought a town the size of Baltimore was small, had cut loose from the civilized world and was now plunging through some dismal swamp in the wilds of southern Georgia. It would be worth it, she thought, if only Mark could regain some of the happiness they had shared when they first met.

"This is it. The Esworthy estate." Mark's sudden voice quieted the distant croaking frogs.

The house was a pale white shadow in the distance, set far back from the edge of the swamp and the small dock they were heading for. Mark threw a rope around one of the battered pillars and drew the boat alongside the dock.

"It doesn't look like much," she said, handing up suitcases and boxes of oil paints.

"It has lots of charm. Wait, you'll see."

Mark helped her out of the boat and together they looked with dismay at their large pile of belongings. It would take them several trips to the house.

"Evening, Mr. Mark." A large black man in ragged clothes stepped out of the darkness and, before they were able to say anything, he had bent over, picked up more than half of the suitcases, and started off toward the house. Recovering from the man's sudden appearance, Mark and Lisa picked up the rest and started after him.

"Who was that?" asked Lisa. "Scared the life out of me."

"I don't know. It may have been Charles, but I'm not sure. It's been a long time. A lot of people live back in the swamp. More now, I imagine, since the estates are no longer functioning. Somebody must have told him we were coming."

"I wish someone had told him not to sneak around like that," she said with a nervous laugh.

Their progress toward the house was slow because of their unfamiliarity with the overgrown path and the weight of the supplies they carried. By the time they reached the house, the man was nowhere to be seen and their suitcases sat in a neat pile on the front porch.

"It's so dark and gloomy here," said Lisa, looking around.

"No electricity, no modern conveniences, and best of all—no telephone. All an artist could ask for. Privacy."

Mark opened the creaking front door and in the illumination of the lantern, weird shadows danced rapidly across the faded wallpaper. They stood in a large entry foyer facing a wide, curving flight of stairs. A crystal chandelier hung what seemed to be miles above their heads. It caught the faint light and scattered it with sub- dued reflections.

"Bedrooms are upstairs," Mark said with a nod. "To the right is the living room and side porch. Around to the left is the dining room and kitchen."

"You really *do* know this house."

"Deirdre and I spent a lot of time together."

"Deirdre?"

"The Esworthys' daughter."

"A rival," said Lisa with a nervous smile. "I should have known."

"It was a long time ago. We were very young; children, really. I suppose she grew up and married an insurance salesman from Peoria."

"I can't imagine a girl staying very long around *here,* that's for sure."

"There are reasons," said Mark. "Wait until you see the place in the daylight."

Mark picked up the heaviest pair of suitcases and started up the stairs. Lisa followed behind him, carrying the lantern.

At the top of the stairs they entered a broad hallway with several closed doors going off at odd angles. Mark walked without hesitation to one of the doors and opened it.

"It's so big," exclaimed Lisa, stepping into the bed- room.

All her life Lisa had lived in just-barely-large-enough apartments in New York City, and she was totally un- prepared for the scandalous waste of space in the master bedroom. The twin beds sat on a level two steps up from the sitting area where they had entered. Overstuffed chairs and fragile-looking end tables were spaced around the room. A dainty writing table sat next to the double glass doors that opened out onto a second-floor balcony. The doors were slightly ajar and the white curtains waved quietly in the breeze. Mark walked over and shut them.

Bending over, Mark struck a match, igniting a gas fix- ture that had been built into a bricked-in fireplace. It glowed dully, giving off faint illumination and even less heat. Lisa shivered as if the feeble flame had actually made the room colder.

"It's the humidity," said Mark. "Everything is damp around here at night. Gets into your bones."

"Maybe it's just that I'm tired. I *am* hungry."

"Take the lantern down and see what you can find in the kitchen. The real estate agent said that he would have some food delivered. I'll start unpacking."

Lisa looked up in horror.

"Oh no," she exclaimed. "I couldn't."

"The kitchen is easy to find. Just go down the stairs and turn right."

"It's not that. It's just, well, I'd rather not go by myself."

"Damnit. You can't go through life being afraid of every little shadow." He grabbed the lantern. "I'll go down, you unpack."

Before she had a chance to say anything, he was gone, slamming the door behind him.

She hadn't realized how much light the lantern had given off until Mark took it with him. The only remaining illumination in the room was the flickering blue gas flame behind its metal grillwork. She turned and made her way up the landing toward the platform where the beds were.

Twin beds? They never had twin beds before, but she supposed there had been little choice. She opened the first suitcase and started to spread Mark's shirts out on one of the beds. She wasn't sure which of the many doors leading off the room were closets, and she didn't really feel like going around opening doors by herself. She draped one of her dresses over the back of a chair.

The noise was, at first, faint and far away—a background noise she wasn't *quite* sure she was hearing.

She moved around the room as vague uneasiness turned to nervousness. The floors creaked and there were noises in the trees outside. Her footfalls echoed, and yet—there was something else, something she couldn't quite separate from all the others. That rustling sound—was it the wind in the trees? Small animals? The faint, faraway bumps—was it Mark in the kitchen? Do 200-year-old houses *still* make all those settling groans? Voices? She stood by the bed with her back to the wall, facing the sitting room. She noticed that her hands were trembling, that her breath caught in her throat. Blood pounded in her ears. There were noises. Inside the house. Outside the door.

The latch on the door to the hall turned slowly with a faint, rusty, metallic sound. Her heart skipped and her legs went weak. She grabbed the ornate headboard for support and the door inched open. Whoever, or whatever, it was that entered in the darkness was not her husband.

All the small noises and quiet rumblings were driven into the background as she screamed, falling to her knees. The mysterious figure ran into the middle of the room, throwing the door wide open. Mark immediately stepped inside, dropping the lantern. He ran toward Lisa.

"Honey, honey—what happened?" He threw his arms around her shoulders and she sobbed and sobbed, tears flowing down her face.

She could see by the light of the deserted lantern that the mysterious figure standing in the middle of the room was simply a young woman, dressed in flowing black.

"I was so scared. The noises . . . and then the door. I didn't know what to think."

"It's all right now. It was just us."

"Who . . . ?"

The woman approached, carrying the lantern.

"Deirde. Deirdre Esworthy," she said in a dry, hollow voice.

"She came to the kitchen door while I was downstairs," explained Mark. "Can you imagine that? After all these years, she still lives around here."

Lisa tried to compose herself. "Sorry," she said, weakly. This was too much, really it was.

The girl moved closer, set the lantern down.

"Are you all right?" she asked in the same rasping monotone.

"Er, yes. I think so," Lisa replied, staring into Deirdre's angular-featured face, still holding Mark's arm tightly.

"You're bleeding," said Deirdre. "You must have bumped your head."

Lisa became aware of a warm stickiness that rolled down one temple. Deirdre reached out, seemingly in reflex, and touched Lisa's forehead. Deirdre's hand was cold against Lisa's own flushed face. Deirdre paused, held her hand there a bit longer than necessary. Lisa was drawn up into the extended moment, transfixed by Deirdre's gaze. The dark brown eyes, the deep brown eyes, the uneven teeth—so white through parted lips, hint of a concerned half-smile, long black hair falling over softly rounded shoulders, the rhythmic rising and falling of her breasts, the eyes, the teeth . . . Lisa tried to stand, stumbled, and four hands guided her toward the bed.

"You must be tired," said Deirdre. "It *is* difficult to get back in here."

"I'm sorry," said Lisa. "I don't know what came over me."

"This place takes some getting used to," said Mark. "Here, take this." He handed her some aspirin and a glass of water, drawn from a bathroom off the bedroom. Lisa propped herself up with a pillow.

Deirdre left the room and returned with a wet towel and a bottle of wine. Mark cleaned the blood from Lisa's forehead.

"It's not serious," said Lisa. "Thank you. I feel better now."

Mark stood up and found some candles, setting them in holders and lighting them. The room grew somewhat brighter.

"So where are you staying these days?" he asked, turning toward Deirdre.

"The old slave quarters."

"The one on the other side of the cemetery?"

Deirdre nodded, pouring the wine.

"Cemetery?" asked Lisa. "Sounds a little creepy."

"Not really," replied Deirdre. "Things are different down here. It's traditional in this area for people to be buried where they lived. Our family cemetery holds several generations of Esworthys. It was a comfort to my parents."

"I'm sorry. I didn't mean . . ."

"That's all right," said Deirdre with a chuckle that sounded like dry leaves crackling. "It's just a place where I live. This house had too many memories."

Lisa leaned back, dizzy. It had been a long day and the wine was warming her, numbing her. She felt sleepy.

She nodded and the last thing she remembered before she fell asleep was Deirdre and Mark sitting at a small table with a candle between them, talking in low voices. Were there other voices? She imagined she heard them, but she wasn't sure. Her sleep was fitful and her dreams were full of dark, unpleasant things.

When she woke, she found herself alone. Dull, gray light filtered through the curtains. It was cold, damp, musty, and when she went to the window she was greeted not by sunshine, but by a shifting, rolling fog. It was impossible to see beyond the trees that ringed the house and even they were indistinct in the fog. Somewhere in the distance a dog was barking.

She was in her nightgown, though she couldn't remember waking up and changing. Mark must have done it. Funny, she *never* slept that soundly. It must have been the tiredness, the wine, the blow on the head. Her hand went to her forehead and she felt a tender bump. She was a bit light-headed, unsteady.

The room looked different in what passed for daylight. It was still not a friendly room, yet it lacked the sinister foreboding she had felt in the night. Strange, Mark's bed didn't seem to have been slept in. It wasn't like him to take the trouble to make the bed. She thought of Deirdre's visit and shuddered. Maybe there was more to this "old friends" business than she was aware of.

A door off the bedroom was ajar and she could see it was the bathroom. She went inside to wash up and investigate the bump on her forehead.

It was a small, cramped bathroom with a low, slanted ceiling, no doubt built under one of the many sets of stairs that drifted through the house. A small, oval stained-glass window was set in the outside wall. Although she could wash up, there was no medicine cabinet and no mirror, so she had to go back into the bedroom and get a small pocket mirror from her pocketbook.

The bump didn't look serious.

Downstairs, she found Mark at work on the sun porch. In contrast to the darkness upstairs, this side room was fairly bright; small glass panes were from floor to ceiling. Mark had set up his easel and canvas in one corner and he looked up as Lisa entered.

"Good afternoon," he said.

"Is it that late? I had no idea."

"It's after two."

"I didn't mean to sleep so long," she said.

"No matter. I couldn't bring myself to wake you, you were sleeping so soundly. I finished unpacking and straightened up the bedroom as quietly as I could. I was down here working well before eight."

"Can I see what you've done so far?"

"It's rough. I've really only started."

She walked around Mark, stood behind him, and lightly touched his shoulder as she looked at the partially completed canvas. It was still in an early stage, but the background seemed almost complete. It was not what she had expected he would paint—it seemed so somber, so full of dark colors. Dead trees in the background, a small brick building set over to one side with an ugly, snarling dog tied outside straining at his rope, evidently trying to attack the unfinished female figure that stood in the foreground, half hidden by low bushes. A small bit of red in the woman's dress was the only bright color in the whole painting. Her face had not yet been filled in.

"I'm glad you've started," she said, giving his shoulder a squeeze.

He turned and grinned and a small smear of blue paint on his cheek gave him a young, boyish look. He was so obviously happy.

"I'm ready to take a break," he said. "Would you like to go for a walk?"

"I haven't had anything to eat yet."

"Easily taken care of," he said, rising. "I've already packed a picnic lunch."

"How romantic. A picnic in the fog."

"If you wait for a balmy, sunny day, we may be in our eighties before you get to see the place. This area isn't known for its resort qualitities."

"I am curious," she said. "Let's go."

Picking up a basket, they walked out the back door and away from the house. The path they followed started out as a broken flagstone walkway. It was apparent from the remains of various hedges and placement of the trees near the house that it had once been quite a gracious lawn. Years of neglect, however, had allowed the wilderness to creep in toward the house, giving it a wild, unkempt appearance.

Suddenly they were in the woods and the path degenerated into a faint dirt trail. Large trees hung over the path and they often had to duck under the low overhanging limbs. Conversation was held to a minimum as they concentrated on making their way through the overgrowth. Many of the trees seemed choked by large dead vines that wound like thick ropes around their trunks and often hung down, blocking their way. Just as Lisa was about to give up and suggest that they turn back, they came to the edge of a small clearing.

"We're about halfway there," said Mark. "Let's eat here."

"Halfway where? I didn't know we were going anywhere in particular."

Mark spread out the blanket they had brought from the house. He opened the wicker basket, removing some sandwiches and a bottle of wine.

"I thought we'd go by my old house. You wanted to, didn't you?"

"Yes, I'd like to see that," replied Lisa, sitting down and unwrapping a sandwich. "I'm curious as to how you ever grew up in a place like this."

"It wasn't altogether pleasant. I guess few of us have idyllic childhoods."

"You never talked much about it."

"There's not much to say. We were the last of several generations of wealthy families that settled here. I was born and grew up on the estate. We never went very far; I was even tutored by Mr. Esworthy. I didn't leave the area at all until my parents were killed and the house burned down."

"They were killed in the fire, weren't they?"

Mark stared at his glass of wine, swirling it around, watching it cling to the sides and slide down. For a moment he seemed lost.

"No," he replied. "You might as well know. They were murdered. Then the house was set ablaze."

"My God! Did they catch the murderer?"

"No. All traces were lost in the fire. It didn't seem to

matter who actually killed them. They weren't killed by individuals, they were killed by superstition."

"What?" Lisa stared back at Mark in horror; still he avoided her eyes.

"There were rumors. The swamp people are full of superstitious talk. Somehow they settled on my family for the explanation of several strange occurrences."

"What was that?"

"There was talk. There was talk of vampires."

"Mark! You can't be serious."

There was a quiet pause. The sun, wherever it was, went behind a cloud bank and it suddenly grew darker, colder and the fog seemed closer, heavier. Mark turned and locked onto Lisa's eyes with a hard, cold stare. The depths of feeling behind his eyes sent a cold shiver through her. She had never seen him this way; he seemed like a stranger.

"Of course I'm serious. They were killed. I saw it."

"Mark . . ."

"I was a child. Do you understand? *Just a child,* and I was the one who found them, lying there with stakes through their chests and then the fire . . ."

"Oh, Mark." She leaned forward and wrapped her arms around him, trying to absorb some of the pain and sorrow that overloaded him. She realized she was crying. Part of him gave in to her, she could feel that part relax, allowing the transference of pain. Yet another part of him, an un-obtainable part, remained cold and hard—a knot of pain and hatred she knew she could never touch, never soothe. They sat together quietly for several minutes until Mark broke the spell.

"I guess we ought to get moving if we want to get back before dark."

"Do you really want to go?" asked Lisa.

"I *have* to go."

They repacked the basket and walked across the field, back into the woods on the other side. They walked quietly, without speaking, and somehow Lisa felt closer to Mark than she had ever been before. Yet as they got deeper into the woods, closer to the house, Mark became more withdrawn. At last they arrived at an opening in the woods.

A crumbling brick chimney was all that could be seen from a distance, but as they approached, she could make out the pile of rubble that was all that remained of the house. Even though the scene was overgrown with weeds, Lisa could imagine the terror of that horrible night.

"Are they buried nearby?" she asked after a silent moment.

"There are no graves," he said evenly. "The fire was quite intense. The bodies were cremated."

"I'm sorry."

Mark seemed to be in another world. He walked around the remains, absently kicking small stones and occasionally stopping to pick up various objects. He was preoccupied with the past and Lisa sensed it. She sat on a large rock, perhaps once part of a wall, and quietly watched him. He continued walking for several minutes and then approached her.

"Even if their bodies had been recovered," he continued as if his train of thought had not be broken, "people would not have allowed *vampires* to be buried in the cemetery."

"Surely you don't think . . ."

"No. It was crazy for people even to suspect they were. But . . ."

"But what? What is it?"

"There was evidence. Something was happening."

"You *can't* believe in vampires."

"I don't know what to believe in. There were strange things happening, someone was doing them."

"Mark, I'm afraid. Can we go back now?"

"Just a minute. There is something I have to do."

Mark took two pieces of wood and tied them together with rope into a crude cross. He drove the cross into the ground by the chimney and turned to nod at Lisa. It was finished. They could return to the house now.

Although the sun wouldn't set for a while yet, it was growing dark in the deep woods, so Mark chose to take a shortcut back toward the house, skirting the edge of the swamp. Occasional small wooden houses, shanties, really, were scattered around the swamp. Often an old boat would be tied in front of one of the houses, but they never saw any people.

Eventually they passed by the Esworthy cemetery with its aboveground tombs and crypts. It was slightly overgrown with tall weeds, and Lisa wondered why, with relatives still living in the area, it was allowed to fall into such a state of disrepair. She was glad they didn't linger there or stop at the small brick building nearby where Deirdre was staying.

It was dark by the time the Esworthy mansion loomed ahead. Lisa could not believe she would have ever considered it a welcome sight, but after the events of the day, any object in the least bit familiar would be welcome. As they entered she found they were not alone in the huge house.

A figure was sitting in the darkness of the living room, half hidden in an overstuffed chair. As Mark lit the lantern, the figure rose. It was the man who had helped with their luggage the night before.

"Charles?" asked Mark.

"You have a good memory, Mr. Mark," slowly drawled the man. "It's been many years."

They shook hands and Lisa relaxed, only then realizing she had been holding her breath. Mark turned toward her in the flickering light.

"Charles was an old family friend. What can we do for you?"

"Nothing right now. I've cooked a hot dinner. You might relax a bit. It isn't wise to attempt too much on first arriving."

"Why, thank you Charles," said Lisa.

"It's Miss Deirdre that you should thank," replied Charles, starting to walk toward the dining room. "She's the one who provided the food and drink. I had only to prepare it."

"Thank you all the same."

"Dinner will be ready as soon as you have had a chance to wash up."

Taking the lantern, Lisa and Mark went upstairs. Evidently Charles had lit several candles that stood on small tables along the wall. The bedroom also had several candles burning and a kerosene lantern sitting on a table, smoke curling from its top. They took turns washing and, on impulse, Lisa put on the only fancy dress she had brought along. It was low cut, long and flowing. She slipped a thin silver necklace around her neck. Hanging from the necklace was a good-luck charm Mark had given her when they were married. Somehow, getting dressed up made her feel better, gave her some ties with the past. She was sure that everything would work out all right; Mark had done what he had to do in order to purge some of the bitterness of his childhood and now things might settle down. Given time to paint, who could tell where he might go.

Mark stepped out of the bedroom and whistled at his wife.

She turned, grinned, and gave a little curtsy.

"Do I look all right?"

"Like a million dollars."

"Let me check my hair." She started toward the bathroom and stopped, remembering that there was no mirror. Mark had second-guessed her and was digging her pocket mirror out of her purse. He handed it to her.

"I had to use it to shave this morning."

"This house *does* lack a few conveniences," she said, smiling.

"Just keep remembering—no annoying phone calls, no door-to-door salesmen."

"And no mirrors, no hot water, no lights."

"And no dinner if we don't get a move on," he added.

"I'm ready," she said.

Downstairs, the dining room was well lit. There was a candelabra on the table as well as sconces along the walls. Dinner was spread out on the large table.

"Where's Charles?" asked Lisa, sitting down at the place set at the side of the table.

"I don't know. Charles?" he called.

Mark sat at the head of the table. Wine had already been poured. They raised their glasses, touched them together.

"To happiness," said Lisa.

They drank in silence.

"It's not like him," said Mark.

"What's that?" asked Lisa.

"It's not like Charles to just leave. Not like him at all."

"Maybe he left a note somewhere."

"I don't think he can read or write. Besides, there's something else."

"What?"

"It's strange that he should be running errands for Deirdre, they never did get along."

"You've been away a long time. Things change."

Lisa stared at Mark. He appeared to be deeply absorbed in thought.

"When my parents were killed," Mark said evenly, "Charles was one of the few who stood up for them."

Lisa tried to figure out what Mark was trying to say. It became more difficult to follow his words. She was feeling dizzy, disoriented. It seemed to be too hot in the room. She reached for her glass of water and found that she couldn't control her hands very well—they moved with a jerk, knocking over her glass of wine. She stared at her clumsy, offending hands and they seemed to recede into the distance, then suddenly loom closer. The walls of the dining room canted at strange, shifting angles.

"Mark," she barely slurred, grabbing the edge of the table, pushing her chair back. Her stomach churned, the walls swam. Poisoned, or drugged, she thought but was unable to mouth the words. Mark was staring at her, but his features blurred and changed before her eyes.

Nausea swept in waves over her and she clumsily got up from the table and staggered toward the kitchen, sure that she was going to vomit. In the kitchen she slipped and half fell against a counter, horrified by what her disoriented senses were reporting to her. For it was blood she had slipped on—an incredible amount of blood—and it was splashed all over the kitchen and there was Charles lying in the middle of it, his throat slashed and all the faces at the window, torch-lit faces, all unfamiliar except for Deirdre, standing in the middle, smiling. She tried to scream but her mouth wouldn't work and she slowly slipped down onto the bloody floor as consciousness drifted away.

Lights, flames, and a sticky floor. Slowly the world came back into focus for Lisa. It was *too* focused, *too* sharp, and she closed her eyes to block out the sight of

Charles's still body, making her way toward the dining room with her eyes tightly shut.

The dining room was a mess. The table lay on its side, chairs were overturned. Mark was gone.

She stopped short, held her breath. The house was quiet—deadly quiet. She walked carefully to the door, listened to the darkness.

There were faint sounds, far-off sounds of chanting. They seemed to come from the general direction of the shanties in the swamp. Help, she would have to get help. She shuddered as she realized there was no one to help her, no way of summoning any aid. With sudden determination born from the depths of despair, she left the house in her blood-spattered evening gown and melted into the darkness.

She had thought the woods were frightening in the early evening; *now* they were filled with numbing terror. Every shadow threatened her as she slowly worked her way toward the chanting. Vampires, she thought, there's no such thing, and then she became aware of the sharp wooden tent peg in her hand. Without thinking, she must have grabbed it from their yet unpacked supplies on her way out of the house. She could see light ahead through the trees.

Crouching low, she made her way through the underbrush to the edge of the clearing. A large bonfire illuminated the eerie scene. Mark was an unmoving figure, lying on a large stone slab that had evidently been removed from one of the crypts. He was *so* still.

Deirdre stood over Mark, swaying hypnotically back and forth in rhythm to the chanting. She was wearing a long white dress and was covered with blood. *Oh please, oh please let that be Charles's blood.* Faceless, anonymous people moved slowly in and out of the darkness, chanting monotonously around the bonfire. Slowly Lisa made her way around the edge of the clearing until she was directly behind Deirdre, and, bending down, she picked up a large stone at her feet, waiting until there was no one near the pair.

Suddenly her chance came. She almost froze with fear, but somehow overcame it and leaped out of the darkness, striking Deirdre a glancing blow that sent them both tumbling onto the ground. Lisa was on top as they stopped rolling and Deirdre's eyes met hers with an expression of detached surprise. These eyes—they held hypnotic depths. Everything was held suspended for a long, drawn-out moment as Deirdre slowly grinned, a confident grin that exposed her unnaturally long canine teeth. Her grin spread and her eyes remained locked unblinkingly onto Lisa's. Blood trickled out of the corner of her mouth. Her teeth were stained red. Her arms went slowly around Lisa's neck, the eye contact was suddenly broken, and Lisa seemed to snap out of a hypnotic spell, all at once aware of the embrace she was locked into, the lips at the side of her neck, pressing down on her throbbing artery, so vulnerable just below the skin.

Without thinking, Lisa pressed back with both hands on Deirdre's chest, pushing her back against the ground, avoiding her eyes. The long tent peg was still in her hand and she reached down and picked up the discarded rock beside her. She balanced the stake on Deirdre's chest, it rose and fell with her rapid breath, then she struck the end with all her strength. There was initial resistance and then a sickening crunch as the girl beneath her was impaled. Blood frothed up through Deirdre's mouth as Lisa caught one last flash of awareness passing through her eyes; surprise and—release!

All this had taken only a few seconds. Mark was rising off the slab, supporting himself on one elbow. The people around the bonfire seemed dazed, unable to decide on a course of action. Lisa grabbed Mark, pulled him to his feet.

"Come on!" she shouted. Numbed and disoriented, he followed her into the woods. Soon they were running, crashing through the woods back toward the house. From the sounds behind them it was obvious that the remaining people had regrouped and were following them. At least they had a good head start.

As they approached the house, Lisa's heart sank. Flames were leaping from the roof and the house was completely involved in a roaring fire. Blindly, she stumbled closer, supporting the still dazed and exhausted Mark by one arm. She understood they would have to get to the boat if they were going to escape, but the fire captured her attention.

Mark held himself tightly against her, breathing heavily into her hair. She stared in through a broken window at the fire inside. The wind shifted, the flames changed position, and the remaining portion of the window opaqued.

Illuminated by the fire, she got a momentary reflection in the window, a reflection of herself, standing alone.

Mark's lips were on her neck; then his teeth.

Arthur L. Samuels is a professional violinist and currently concertmaster of the North Jersey Regional Orchestra. This short-short is more impressionistic than linear, but it contains a device no less suited to the world of horror than a story twice its length.

MASS WITHOUT VOICES
by Arthur L. Samuels

Craigus leaned over the bed of the dying violinist. On the walls were pictures of his friend in more hopeful days, Guarneri in hand, bow in position; higher up were a few pitiable mementos—honorable mention in the Queen Elizabeth competition, an autographed picture of Stokowski, but all irrelevant now. *Sic transit*, Craigus thought. "Please," the violinist said weakly, "you can't let them do this to me, it can't end this way. Remember our pact."

Craigus shrugged. "I remember," he said.

"Tell me you'll *do* it, please."

Craigus looked at the picture of the younger man, eyes full of hope, fingers arched nicely over a fingerboard that eventually they had not quite mastered. "I'll do it," he said.

The violinist died gratefully.

A deal was a deal. Late at night Craigus lit the oven. When the guage read 1,000 Celsius, he opened the heavy steel door and carefully slid the molds into the flaming hot recesses. He locked it securely. Ten minutes and a signal would let him know that the molds were ready. After that would come the small boxes and finally the large case. Big enough for a string section.

At the least the violinist should not have been turned down on audition for the Detroit Symphony. That was really unfair, Craigus thought. A judicious man, he added, it's merely restoring a balance. I promised. I'm no Detroit Symphony; I'll come through.

Craigus went to the long counter. He placed the suitcase on top and opened it, picked out a few samples, and laid them before the owner of Strad Music Company, Inc. "Beautiful," he whispered, "They should retail for three ninety-five each. You'd be foolish at this price not to take all of them."

"It's a good price," the old man said, "but I've got plenty of it I can't move."

"Not like this," Craigus said. He murmured something else.

The owner shrugged reluctantly and went to get a check.

Craigus passed through the doors with the rest of the crowd and sat in the last row, quietly. The Scala Chamber Orchestra, forty-five strong and true, drifted onto the stage. Each of the stands bore a fresh square of rosin; as Craigus watched, first the concertmaster and then the others absently rubbed it on their bows. Like children and mud, Craigus thought, string players could not keep their hands off fresh rosin. Like oboe players and their eternal reeds. They tuned deftly. The lights went down and the conductor entered. Craigus remembered him quite well. In his youth he had been a judge of the Queen Elizabeth competition. Of Brussels.

The Brandenburg Number Three. Craigus listened peacefully. The sounds began to go sharp and a cello squeaked. A violin made a rending sound, and the conductor suddenly let his instrument fall from his hand, a look of horror on his face that even at twenty-six rows Craigus could enjoy. Fine.

The odor began to waft through the hall. If it had already reached the last row of the orchestra, that meant it must be pretty bad down front. To say nothing of the stage. The La Scala players were trying to leave the stage, some of them holding mouths or stomachs. Not all made it. Craigus listened to the sounds of gagging.

Time to leave, he thought.

He stood and left.

"The pact," he said to the sky outside . . . while inside, the audience was beginning to scream.

The pact, he thought as he got into his car, the suitcase on the seat beside him. Perhaps a little more encompassing than the violinist wanted; but on the other hand, since it worked so well, why stop with Detroit? There were lots of orchestras that could use good resin.

William F. Nolan has peers, but no betters, in the field of horror fantasy. His stories and television/film adaptations are acknowledged as among the midcentury's best, and his sense of what frightened us all has been honed to razor-sharpness by material like that which follows.

Your editor used to like cats . . .

HE KILT IT WITH A STICK
by William F. Nolan

A summer night in Kansas City.

Ellen away, visiting her parents. The house on Forest empty, waiting.

Warm air.

A high, yellow moon.

Stars.

Crickets thrumming the dark.

Fireflies.

A summer night.

Fred goes to the Apollo on Troost to see a war film. It depresses him. All the killing. He leaves before it has ended, walking up the aisle and out of the deserted lobby and on past the empty glass ticket booth. Alone.

The sidewalk is bare of pedestrians.

It is late, near mdinight, and traffic is very sparse along Troost. The wide street is silent. A truck grinds heavily away in the distance.

Fred begins to walk home.

He shouldn't. It is only two blocks: a few steps to the corner of 33rd, then down the long hill to Forest, then right along Forest to his house at the end of the block,

226

near 34th. Not quite two blocks to walk. But too far for him. Too far.

Fred stops.

A gray cat is sleeping in the window of Rae's Drugstore. Fred presses the glass.

I could break the window—but that would be useless. The thing would be safe by then; it would leap away and I'd never find it in the store. The police would arrive and . . . No. Insane. Insane to think of killing it.

The gray cat, quite suddenly, opens its eyes to stare at Fred Baxter. Unblinking. Evil.

He shudders, moves quickly on.

The cat continues to stare.

Foul thing knows what I'd like to do to it.

The hill, sloping steeply toward Forest, is tinted with cool moonlight. Fred walks down this hill, filled with an angry sense of frustration: he would very much have enjoyed killing the gray cat in the drugstore window.

Hard against chest wall, his heart judders. Once, twice, three times. Thud thud thud. He slows, removes a tissue-wrapped capsule from an inside pocket. Swallows the capsule. Continues to walk.

Fred reaches the bottom of the hill, crosses over.

Trees now. Big fat-trunked oaks and maples, fanning their leaves softly over the concrete sidewalk. Much darker. Thick tree-shadow midnight dark, broken by three street lamps down the long block. Lamps haloed by green night insects.

Deeper.

Into the summer dark . . .

When Fred Baxter was seven, he wrote: "Today a kitty cat bit me at school and it sure hurt a lot. The kitty was bad, so I kilt it with a stick."

When he was ten, and living in St. Louis, a boy two houses up told Fred his parents wanted to get rid of a litter. "I'll take care of it," Fred assured him—and the next afternoon, in Miller Lake, he drowned all six of the kittens.

At fifteen, in high school, Fred trapped the janitor's Tabby in the gymnasium locker room, choked it to death, and carried it downstairs to the furnace. He was severely scratched in the process.

As a college freshman, in Kansas City, Fred distributed several pieces of poisoned fish over the Rockhurst campus. The grotesquely twisted bodies of seven cats were found the next morning.

Working in the sales department of Hall Brothers, Fred was invited to visit his supervisor at home one Saturday—and was seen in the yard playing with Frances, a pet Siamese. She was later found crushed to death, and it was assumed a car had run over the animal. Fred quit his job ten days later because his supervisor had cat hands.

Fred married Ellen Ferber when he was thirty, and she wanted to have children right away. Fred said no, that babies were small and furry in their blankets, and disturbed him. Ellen bought herself a small kitten for company while Fred was on the road. He didn't object—but a week after the purchase, he took a meat knife and dismembered the kitten, telling Ellen that it had "wandered away." Then he bought her a green parakeet.

ZZZZZZZ Click
This is Frederick Baxter speaking and I . . . wait, the sound level is wrong and I'll— There, it's all right now. I can't tell anyone about this—but today I found an old Tom in an alley downtown, and I got hold of the stinking, wretched animal and I . . .
ZZZZZZZ Click

The heart trouble started when Fred was thirty-five. "You have an unusual condition," the doctor told him. "You are, in effect, a medical oddity. Your chest houses a quivering-muscled heart—fibrillation. Your condition can easily prove fatal. Preventive measures must be taken. No severe exercise, no overeating, plenty of rest."

Fred obeyed the man's orders—although he did not really trust a doctor whose cat eyes reflected the moon.

ZZZZZZZ Click
. . . awful time with the heart. Really awful. The use of digitalis drives me to alcohol, which sends my heart into

massive flutters. Then the alcohol forces me into a need for more digitalis. It is a deadly circle and I . . .

I have black dreams. A nap at noon and I dream of smothering. This comes from the heart condition. And because of the cats. They all fear me now, avoid me on the street. They've *told* one another about me. This is fact. Killing them is becoming quite difficult . . . but I caught a big, evil one in the garden last Thursday and buried it. Alive. As I am buried alive in these black dreams of mine. I got excited, burying the cat—and this is bad for me. I must go on killing them, but I must *not* get excited. I must stay calm and not—here comes Ellen, so I'd better . . .

ZZZZZZZ *Click*

"What's wrong, Fred?"

It was 2 A.M. and Ellen had awakened to find him standing at the window.

"Something in the yard," he said.

The moon was flushing the grass with pale gold—and a dark shape scuttled over the lawn, breaking the pattern. A cat shape.

"Go to sleep," said his wife, settling into her pillow.

Fred Baxter stared at the cat, who stared back at him from the damp yard, its head raised, the yellow of the night moon now brimming the creature's eyes. The cat's mouth opened.

"It's sucking up the moonlight," Fred whispered.

Then he went back to bed.

But he did not sleep.

Later, thinking about this, Fred recalled what his mother had often said about cats. "They perch on the chest of a baby," she'd said, "place their red mouth over the soft mouth of the baby, and draw all the life from its body. I won't have one of the disgusting things in the house."

Alone in the summer night, walking down Forest Avenue in Kansas City, Fred passes a parked car, bulking black and silent in its gravel driveway. The closed car windows gleam deep yellow from the eyes inside.

Fred stops, looks back at the car.

How many? Ten . . . a dozen. More . . . twenty, maybe. All inside the car, staring out at me. Dozens of foul, slitted yellow eyes.

Fred can do nothing. He checks all four doors of the silent automobile, finds them locked. The cats stare at him.

Filthy creatures!

He moves on.

The street is oddly silent. Fred realizes why: the crickets have stopped. No breeze stirs the trees; they hang over him, heavy and motionless in the summer dark.

The houses along Forest are shuttered, lightless, closed against the night. Yet, on a porch, Fred detects movement.

Yellow eyes spark from porch blackness. A big, dark-furred cat is curled into a wooden swing. It regards Fred Baxter.

Kill it!

He moves with purposeful stealth, leans to grasp a stout tree limb which has fallen into the yard. He mounts the porch steps.

The dark-furred cat has not stirred.

Fred raises the heavy limb. The cat hisses, claws extended, fangs balefully revealed. It cries out like a wounded child and vanishes off the porch into the deep shadow between houses.

Missed. Missed the rotten thing.

Fred moves down the steps, crosses the yard toward the walk. His head is lowered in anger. When he looks up, the walk is thick with cats. He runs into them, kicking, flailing the tree club. They scatter, melting away from him like butter from a heated blade.

Thud thud thud. Fred drops the club. His heart is rapping, fisting his chest. He leans against a tree, sobbing for breath. The yellow-eyed cats watch him from the street, from bushes, from steps and porches and the tops of cars.

Didn't get a one of them. Not a damn one . . .

The fireflies have disappeared. The street lamps have dimmed to smoked circles above the heavy, cloaking trees. The clean summer sky is shut away from him—and Fred Baxter finds the air clogged with the sharp, suffocating smell of cat fur.

He walks on down the block.

The cats follow him.

He thinks of what fire could do to them—long blades of yellow crisping flame to flake them away into dark ash. But he cannot burn them; burning them would be impossible. There are *hundreds*. That many at least.

They fill driveways, cover porches, blanket yards, pad in lion-like silence along the street. The yellow moon is in their eyes, sucked from the sky. Fred, his terror rising, raises his head to look upward.

The trees are alive with them!

His throat closes. He cannot swallow. Cat fur cloaks his mouth.

Fred begins to run down the concrete sidewalk, stumbling, weaving, his chest filled with a terrible winged beating.

A sound.

The scream of the cats.

Fred claps both hands to his head to muffle the stab and thrust of sound.

The house . . . must reach the house.

Fred staggers forward. The cat masses surge in behind him as he runs up the stone walk to his house.

A cat lands on his neck. Mutely, he flings it loose—plunges up the wooden porch steps.

Key. Find your key and unlock the door. Get inside!

Too late.

Eyes blazing, the cats flow up and over him, a dark, furry, stifling weight. As he pulls back the screen, claws and needle teeth rip at his back, arms, face, legs . . . shred his clothing and skin. He twists wildly, beating at them. Blood runs into his eyes. . . .

The door is open. He falls forward, through the opening. The cats swarm after him in hot waves, covering his chest, sucking the breath from his body. Baxter's thin scream is lost in the sharp, rising, all-engulfing cry of the cats.

* * *

A delivery boy found him two days later, lying face down on the living room floor. His clothes were wrinkled, but untorn.

A cat was licking the cold, white, unmarked skin of Frederick Baxter's cheek.

THE GHOULS
by R. Chetwynd-Hayes

The doorbell rang. A nasty long shrill ring that suggested an impatient caller or a faulty bell-button. Mr. Goldsmith did not receive many visitors. He muttered angrily, removed the saucepan of baked beans from the gas ring, then trudged slowly from the tiny kitchen across the even smaller hall and opened the front door. The bell continued to ring.

A tall, lean man faced him. One rigid finger seemed glued to the bell-button. The gaunt face had an unwholesome greenish tinge. The black, strangely dull eyes stared into Mr. Goldsmith's own and the mouth opened.

"Oosed o love hore . . ."

The shrill clatter of the doorbell mingled with the hoarse gibberish and Mr. Goldsmith experienced a blend of fear and anger. He shouted at the unwelcome intruder.

"Stop ringing the bell."

"Oosed o love hore . . ." the stranger repeated.

"Stop ringing the bloody bell." Mr. Goldsmith reached around the door frame and pulled the dirt-grimed hand away. It fell limply down to its owner's side, where it swung slowly back and forth, four fingers clenched, the fifth—the index finger—rigid, as though still seeking a

233

bell-button to push. In the silence that followed, Mr. Goldsmith cleared his throat.

"Now, what is it you want?"

"Oosed o love hore," the stranger said again, unintelligibly, then pushed by Mr. Goldsmith and entered the flat.

"Look here . . ." The little man ran after the intruder and tried to get in front of him, but the tall, lean figure advanced remorselessly towards the living-room, where it flopped down in Mr. Goldsmith's favorite armchair and sat looking blankly at a cheap Gauguin print that hung over the fireplace.

"I don't know what your little game is," Mr. Goldsmith was trying hard not to appear afraid, "but if you're not out of here in two minutes flat, I'll have the law around. Do you hear me?"

The stranger had forgotten to close his mouth. The lower jaw hung down like a lid with a broken hinge. His threadbare, black overcoat was held in place by a solitary, chipped button. A frayed, filthy red scarf was wound tightly around his scrawny neck. He presented a horrible, loathsome appearance. He also smelled.

The head came around slowly and Mr. Goldsmith saw the eyes were now watery, almost as if they were about to spill over the puffy lids and go streaming down the green-tinted cheeks.

"Oosed o love hore."

The voice was a gurgle that began somewhere deep down in the constricted throat and the words seemed to bubble like stew seething in a saucepan.

"What? What are you talking about?"

The head twisted from side to side. The loose skin around the neck concertinaed and the hands beat a tattoo on the chair arms.

"O-o-sed t-o-o l-o-v-e h-o-r-e."

"Used to live here!" A blast of understanding lit Mr. Goldsmith's brain and he felt quite pleased with his interpretative powers. "Well, you don't live here now, so you'll oblige me by getting out."

The stranger stirred. The legs, clad in a pair of decrepit corduroy trousers, moved back. The hands pressed down on the chair arms, and the tall form rose. He shuffled towards Mr. Goldsmith and the stomach-heaving stench came with him. Mr. Goldsmith was too petrified to move and could only stare at the approaching horror with fear-glazed eyes.

"Keep away," he whispered. "Touch me and . . . I'll shout . . ."

The face was only a few inches from his own. The hands came up and gripped the lapels of his jacket and with surprising strength, he was gently rocked back and forth. He heard the gurgling rumble; it gradually emerged into speech.

"Oi . . . um . . . dud . . . Oi . . . um . . . dud . . ."

Mr. Goldsmith stared into the watery eyes and had there been a third person present he might have supposed they were exchanging some mutual confidence.

"You're . . .what?"

The bubbling words came again.

"Oi . . . um . . . dud."

"You're bloody mad," Mr. Goldsmith whispered.

"Oi . . . um . . . dud."

Mr. Goldsmith yelped like a startled puppy and pulling himself free, ran for the front door. He leaped down the stairs, his legs operating by reflex, for there was no room for thought in his fear-misted brain.

Shop fronts slid by; paving stones loomed up, their rectangular shapes painted yellow by lamplight; startled faces drifted into his blurred vision, then disappeared and all the while the bubbling, ill-formed words echoed along the dark corridors of his brain.

"Oi . . . um . . . dud."

"Just a moment, sir."

A powerful hand gripped his arm and he swung around as the impetus of his flight was checked. A burly policeman stared down at him, suspicion peeping out of the small, blue eyes.

"Now, what's all this, sir. You'll do yourself an injury, running like that."

Mr. Goldsmith fought to regain his breath, eager to impart the vital knowledge. To share the burden.

"He's . . . he's dead."

The grip on his arm tightened.

"Now, calm yourself. Start from the beginning. Who's dead?"

"He . . ." Mr. Goldsmith gasped . . . "he rang the bell, wouldn't take his finger off the button . . . used to live there . . . then he sat in my chair . . . then got up . . . and told me . . . he was dead . . ."

A heavy silence followed, broken only by the purr of a passing car. The driver cast an interested glance at the spectacle of a little man being held firmly by a large policeman. The arm of the law finally gave utterance.

"He told you he was dead?"

"Yes." Mr. Goldsmith nodded, relieved to have shared his terrible information with an agent of authority. "He pronounced it *dud.*"

"A northern corpse, no doubt," the policeman remarked with heavy irony.

"I don't think so," Mr. Goldsmith shook his head. "No, I think his vocal cords are decomposing. He sort of bubbles his words. They . . . well, ooze out."

"Ooze out," the constable repeated drily.

"Yes." Mr. Goldsmith remembered another important point. "And he smells."

"Booze?" inquired the policeman.

"No, a sort of sweet, sour smell. Rather like bad milk and dead roses."

The second silence lasted a little longer than the first, then the constable sighed deeply.

"I guess we'd better go along to your place of residence and investigate."

"Must we?" Mr. Goldsmith shuddered and the officer nodded.

"Yes, we must."

The front door was still open. The hall light dared Mr. Goldsmith to enter and fear lurked in dark corners.

"Would you," Mr. Goldsmith hesitated, for no coward likes to bare his face, "would you go in first?"

"Right." The constable nodded, squared his shoulders, and entered the flat. Mr. Goldsmith found enough courage to advance as far as the doormat.

"In the living-room," he called out. "I left him in the living-room. The door on the left."

The police officer walked ponderously into the room indicated and after a few minutes came out again.

"No one there," he stated simply.

"The bedroom." Mr. Goldsmith pointed to another door." He must have gone in there."

The policeman dutifully inspected the bedroom, the kitchen, then the bathroom before returning to the hall.

"I think it's quite safe for you to come in," he remarked caustically. "There's no one here—living or dead."

Mr. Goldsmith reoccupied his domain, much like an exiled king remounting his shaky throne.

"Now," the policeman produced a notebook and ballpoint pen, "let's have a description.

"Pardon?"

"What did the fellow look like?" the officer asked with heavy patience.

"Oh. Tall, thin—very thin, his eyes were sort of runny, looked as if they might melt at any time, his hair was black and matted and he was dressed in an overcoat with one button . . ."

"Hold on," the officer admonished. "You're going too fast. Button . . ."

"It was chipped." Mr. Goldsmith added importantly. "And he wore an awful pair of corduroy trousers. And he looked dead. Now I come to think of it, I can't remember him breathing. Yes, I'm certain, he didn't breathe."

The constable put his notebook away, and took up a stance on the hearthrug.

"Now, look, Mr. . . ."

"Goldsmith. Edward. J. Goldsmith."

"Well, Mr. Goldsmith . . ."

"The J is for Jeremiah but I never use it."

"As I was about to say, Mr. Goldsmith," the constable wore the expression of a man who was laboring under great strain, "I've seen a fair number of stiffs—I should say, dead bodies—in my time, and not one of them has ever talked. In fact, I'd say you can almost bank on it. They can burp, jerk, sit up, flop, bare their teeth, glare, even clutch when rigor mortis sets in, but never talk."

"But he said he was." Mr. Goldsmith was distressed that this nice, helpful policeman seemed unable to grasp the essential fact. "He said he was dud, and he looked and smelt dead."

"Ah, well now, that's another matter entirely." The constable looked like Sherlock Holmes, about to astound a dim-witted Watson. "This character you've described sounds to me like old Charlie. A proper old lay-about, sleeps rough and cadges what he can get from hotel kitchens and suchlike. A meths drinker no doubt and long ago lost whatever wits he ever had. I think he came up here for a hand-out. Probably stewed to the gills and lumbered by you when the door was open, intending to doss down in your living-room. I'll report this to the station sergeant and we'll get him picked up. No visible means of subsistence, you understand."

"Thank you." Mr. Goldsmith tried to feel relieved. "But . . ."

"Don't you worry anymore." The constable moved towards the door. "He won't bother you again. If you are all that worried, I'd have a chain put on your front door, then you can see who's there before you let them in."

Mr. Goldsmith said, "Yes," and it was with a somewhat lighter heart that he accompanied the policeman to the front-door and politely handed him his helmet.

"A talking dead man!" The constable shook his head and let out a series of explosive chuckles. "Strewth!"

Mr. Goldsmith shut the door with a little bang and stood with his back leaning against its mauve panels. By a very small circle of friends he was considered to be wildly artistic.

"He was." He spoke aloud. "He was dead. I know it."

He reheated the baked beans, prepared toast under the grill and opened a tin of mushrooms, then dined in the kitchen.

The evening passed. The television glared and told him things he did not wish to know; the newspaper shocked him and the gas fire went out. There were no more five-penny pieces so he had no option but to go to bed.

The bed was warm; it was safe, it was soft. If anything dreadful happened he could always hide under the sheets. His book was comforting. It told a story of a beautiful young girl who could have been a famous film star if only she would sleep with a nasty, fat producer, but instead she cut the aspiring mogul down to size, and married her childhood sweetheart who earned twenty pounds a week in the local bank. Mr. Goldsmith derived much satisfaction from this happy state of affairs and, placing the book under his pillow, turned out the light and prepared to enter the land of dreams.

He almost got there.

His heart slowed down its beat. His brain flashed messages along the intricate network of nerves and contented itself all was well, although the stomach put in a formal complaint regarding the baked beans. It then began to shut off his five senses, before opening the strong-room where the fantasy treasures were stored. Then his ears detected a sound and his brain instantly ordered all senses on the alert.

Mr. Goldsmith sat up and vainly fumbled for the light switch, while a series of futile denials tripped off his tongue.

"No . . . no . . . no . . ."

The wardrobe doors were opening. It was a nice, big wardrobe, fitted with two mirror doors, and Mr. Goldsmith watched the gleaming surfaces flash as they parted. A dark shape emerged from the bowels of the wardrobe; a tall, lean, slow-moving figure. Mr. Goldsmith would have screamed, had such a vocal action been possible, but his throat was dry and constricted and he could only manage a few croaking sounds. The dark figure shuffled towards the bed, poised for a moment like a tree about to fall, then twisted around and sat down. Mr. Goldsmith's afflicted throat permitted a whimpering sound as the long shape swung its legs up and lay down beside him. He could not see very well but he could smell and he could also hear. The strangled words bubbled up through the gloom.

"Oo . . . broot . . . cupper . . . Oi . . . hote . . . cuppers . . ."

They lay side by side for a little while, Mr. Goldsmith's whimpers merging with the bubbling lament.

"Oo . . . broot cupper . . . Oi . . . um . . . dud . . . hote . . . cuppers . . . oll . . . cuppers . . . stunk . . ."

Mr. Goldsmith dared to toy with the idea of movement. He longed to put distance between himself and whatever lay bubbling on the bed. His hand moved prior to pulling back the bedclothes. Instantly cold fingers gripped his wrist, then slid down to his palm to grasp his hand.

"Oi . . . um . .. dud . . ."

"Not again," Mr. Goldsmith pleaded. "Not again."

Minutes passed. Mr. Goldsmith tried to disengage his hand from the moist, cold grip, but it only tightened. Eventually, the form stirred and to Mr. Goldsmith's horror, sat up and began to grope around with its free hand. The light shattered the gloom, chasing the shadows into obscure corners and Mr. Goldsmith found himself looking at that which he did not wish to see.

The face had taken on a deeper tinge of green; the eyes were possibly more watery and seemed on the point of dribbling down the cheeks. The mouth was a gaping hole where the black tongue writhed like a flattened worm. The bubbling sound cascaded up the windpipe with the threatening roar of a worn out geyser.

"G-oot dr-oosed . . ."

The figure swung its legs off the bed and began to move towards the fireplace, still retaining its icy grip on Mr. Goldsmith's hand, and forcing him to wriggle through the bedclothes and go stumbling after it. Over the mantelpiece was an old brass-handled naval cutlass, picked up for thirty shillings, back in the days when Mr. Goldsmith had first read *The Three Musketeers*. This, the creature laboriously removed from its hooks and turning slowly, raised it high above the terrified little man's head. The bubbling sound built up and repeated the earlier order.

"G-oot dr-oosed . . ."

Mr. Goldsmith got dressed.

They walked down the empty street, hand-in-hand, looking at times like a father dragging his reluctant son to school. Mr. Goldsmith hungered for the merest glimpse of his friend the policeman, but the creature seemed to know all the back streets and alleys, pulling its victim through gaping holes in fences, taking advantage of every shadow, every dark corner. This, Mr. Goldsmith told himself in the brief periods when he was capable of coherent thought, was the instinct of an alley cat, the automatic reflexes of a fox. The creature was making for its hole and taking its prey with it.

They were in the dock area. Black, soot-grimed buildings reached up to a murky sky. Cobbled alleys ran under railway arches, skirted grim-faced warehouses, and terminated in litter-ridden wastelands cleared by Hitler's bombs, thirty years before. Mr. Goldsmith stumbled over uneven mounds crowned with sparse, rusty grass. He even fell down a hole, only to be promptly dragged out as the creature advanced with the ponderous, irresistible momentum of a Sherman tank.

The ground sloped towards a passage running between the remnants of brick walls. Presently there was a ceiling to which morsels of plaster still clung. Then the smell of burning wood—and a strange new stench of corruption.

They were in what had once been the cellar of a large warehouse. The main buildings had been gutted and their skeletons removed, but the roots, too far down to be affected by flame or bomb, still remained. The walls wept rivulets of moisture, the ceiling sagged, the floor was an uneven carpet of cracked cement, but to all intents, the cellar existed. An ancient bath stood on two spaced rows of bricks. Holes had been pierced in its rusty flanks, and it now held a pile of burning wood. Flame tinted smoke made the place look like some forgotten inferno; it drifted up to the ceiling and coiled lazily round the black beams like torpid snakes looking for darkness. A number of hurricane lamps hung from beams and walls, so that once again Mr. Goldsmith was forced to look at that which he would rather have not seen.

They were crouched in a large circle round the fire, dressed in an assortment of old clothes, with green-tinted faces and watery eyes, gaping mouths and rigid fingers. Mr. Goldsmith's companion quelled any lingering doubts he might have had with the simplicity of a sledgehammer cracking a walnut.

"Oll . . . dud . . . oll . . . dud . . ."

"What's all this then?"

Two men stood behind Mr. Goldsmith and his companion. One was a tall, hulking fellow and the other a little runt of a man with the face of a crafty weasel. It was he who had spoken. He surveyed Mr. Goldsmith with a look of profound astonishment, then glared at the creature.

"Where the hell did you find him?"

The bubbling voice tried to explain.

"Ooosed o love thore . . ."

"You bloody stupid git." The little man began to pummel the creature about the stomach and chest and it retreated, the bubbling voice rising to a scream, like a steam kettle under full pressure.

"Oosed o love thore . . . broot cupper . . ."

The little man ceased his punitive operations and turned an anxious face towards his companion.

" 'Ere what's all this, then? Did 'e say copper? His Nibs won't like that. Don't get the law worked up, 'e said."

The big man spoke slowly, his sole concern to calm his friend.

"Don't carry on, Maurice. Old Charlie's about 'ad it, ain't 'e? 'E'll be dropping apart soon if they don't get 'im mended and varnished up. The old brainbox must be in an 'ell of a state."

But Maurice would not be comforted. He turned to Mr. Goldsmith and gripped his coat front.

"Did you bring the law in? You call a copper?"

"I certainly summoned a police officer, when this," Mr. Goldsmith hesitated, "when this . . . person, refused to leave my flat."

"Cor strike a light." Maurice raised his eyes ceilingward. " 'E calls a copper a police officer! Respectable as Sunday dinner. Probably got a trouble and strife who'll scream to 'igh 'eavens when 'er little wandering boy don't come 'ome for his milk and bickies."

"You married?" the big man asked and Mr. Goldsmith, inspired by the wish to pacify his captors, shook his head.

"Live alone, aye?" The big man chuckled. "Thought so. Recognize the type. Keep yer 'air on, Maurice, he'll be just another missing person. The DP's will handle it."

"Yeah, Harry." Maurice nodded and released Mr. Goldsmith. "You're right. We'd better tie 'im up somewhere until His Nibs gets 'ere. He'll decide what to do with 'im."

Harry produced a length of rope and Mr. Goldsmith meekly allowed himself to be tied up, while "Charlie," for such it appeared was the creature's name, kept nudging Maurice's arm.

"Um . . . woont . . . meethy . . ."

"You don't deserve any methy." Maurice pushed the terrible figure to one side. "Making a bugger-up like this."

"Meethy . . ." Charlie repeated, "um . . . woont . . . meethy . . ."

"Bit of a waste of the blue stuff," Maurice remarked drily. " 'E's coming apart at the seams. Let me bash 'is 'ead in."

"Naw." Maurice shook his head. " 'Is Nibs don't like us taking liberties with units. Besides the new repairing and varnishing machine can do wonders with 'em. 'E'd better have 'is ration with the rest."

Mr. Goldsmith, suitably bound, was dumped into a corner where he soon witnessed a scene that surpassed all the horror that had ridden on his shoulders since Charlie had rung his doorbell.

Harry came out of a cubby hole bearing a large saucepan with no handle. Maurice followed with a chipped mug. At once there was a grotèsque stirring round the nightmare circle; legs moved, arms waved, mouths opened in the familiar bubbling speech and raucous cries. Placing the saucepan on a rickety table, Maurice began to call out in a high pitched voice.

"Methy . . . come on then . . . methy, methy, methy . . ."

There was a scrambling and scuffling, a united, bubbling, gurgling, raucous scream, and the entire pack came lumbering forward, pushing the feeble to one side, clawing in their determination to reach the enamel saucepan and the chipped mug. One scarecrow figure, clad in the remnants of an old army overcoat, fell or was pushed and landed with a resounding crash a few yards from Mr. Goldsmith. When he tried to rise, his left leg crumbled under him and the horrified spectator saw the jagged end of a thigh bone jutting out from a tear in threadbare trousers. There was no expression of pain on the green-tinted face but whatever spark of intelligence that still flickered in the brain finally prompted the creature to crawl over the uneven ground until it reached the table. Maurice looked down and kicked the writhing figure over on to its back. It lay howling in protest, like an upturned beetle, legs and arms flailing helplessly.

The chipped mug was dipped into the saucepan, a quarter filled with some blue liquid, then presented to the nearest gaping mouth. A green-tinted, wrinkled neck convulsed, then the mug was snatched away to be filled for the next consumer. Harry pulled the "fed one" to one side, then gave it a shove that sent the bundle of skin-wrapped bones lurching across the floor. Whatever the liquid was that came out of the saucepan, its effect on the receiver was little short of miraculous. All straightened up; some danced in a revolting, flopping, jumping movement. One creature did six knee-bends before its right knee made an ominous cracking sound. Another began clapping its hands and Maurice called out, "Cut that out," but his warning came too late. One hand fell off and landed on the floor with a nasty, soft thud. Mr. Goldsmith's stomach was considering violent action when Harry sauntered over and pointed to the offending item.

"Pick that up," he ordered.

The creature, still trying to clap with one hand, gazed at the big man with blank, watery eyes.

"Glop . . . glop," it bubbled.

"Never mind the glop-glop business. Pick the bloody thing up. I'm not 'aving you leave yer bits and pieces about. I'm telling yer for the last time—pick it up."

He raised a clenched fist and the creature bent down and took hold of its late appendage.

"Now put it in the bin," Harry instructed, pointing to an empty oil drum by the far wall. "You lot might be bone idle, but yer not going to be dead lazy."

Harry then turned to Maurice, who was completing his culinary duties.

"This lot's dead useless, Maurice. They're falling to bits. If this goes on, all we'll 'ave is a load of wriggling torsos. You've put too much EH471 in that stuff."

"Balls." Maurice cuffed a too eager consumer, who promptly retreated with one ear suspended by a strand of skin. "We can do some running repairs, can't we? A bit of tape, a few slats of wood, a few brooms. You carry on like a nun in a brothel."

"Well, so long as you explain the breakages to 'Is Nibs,

it's all right with me," Harry stated, kicking a wizened little horror that was trying to turn a somersault on one hand and half an arm. "What's 'e hope to do with this lot?"

"Search me," Maurice shrugged. "Probably carve 'em up. 'E could take a leg from one, an arm from another, swop a few spare parts, and get 'imself a few working models."

Mr. Goldsmith had for some time been aware that some of the more antiquated models were displaying an unhealthy interest in his person. One, who appeared to have a faulty leg, shuffled over and examined the little man's lower members with a certain air of deliberation. A rigid forefinger poked his trouser leg, then the creature, whose vocal cords seemed to be in better working order than Charlie's, croaked: "Good . . . good."

"Go away," Mr. Goldsmith ordered, wriggling his legs frantically. "Shush, push off."

The creature pulled his trouser leg up and stared at the plump white flesh, like a cannibal viewing the week-end joint. He dribbled.

"Maurice—Harry." A sharp voice rang out. "What is the meaning of this? Get the units lined up at once."

It could have been the voice of a sergeant-major admonishing two slack NCOs; or a managing-director who has walked in on an office love-in. Maurice and Harry began to shout, pulling their charges into a rough file, pushing, swearing, punching, occasionally kicking the fragile units. His own particular tormentor was seized by the scruff of the neck and sent hurling toward the ragged line that drooped, reeled, gurgled and bubbled in turn.

"Careful, man," the voice barked, "units cost money. Repairs take time."

"Sir." Maurice froze to a momentary attitude of attention, then went on with his marshaling activity with renewed, if somewhat subdued, energy.

"Get into line, you dozy lot. Chests out, chins in, those who 'ave 'ands, down to yer flipping sides. Harry, a couple of brooms for that basket, three from the end. If 'e falls down, 'is bleeding 'ead will come off."

For the first time Mr. Goldsmith had the opportunity to

examine the newcomer. He saw a mild-looking, middle-aged man, in a black jacket and pin-striped trousers. Glossy bowler hat, horn-rimmed spectacles and a brief-case completed the cartoonist conception of a civil servant. Maurice marched up to this personage and swung up a rather ragged salute.

"Units lined up and ready for your inspection, sir."

"Very well." His Nibs, for such Mr. Goldsmith assumed him to be, handed his briefcase to Harry, then began to walk slowly along the file, scrutinizing each unit in turn.

"Maurice, why has this man got a hand missing?"

"Clapping, sir. The bleeder . . . beg pardon, the unit got carried away after methy, sir. Sort of came off in his 'and, sir."

His Nibs frowned.

"This is rank carelessness, Maurice. I have stressed time and time again, special attention must be paid to component parts at all times. Spare hands are hard to come by and it may become necessary to scrap this unit altogether. Don't let me have to mention this matter again."

"Sir."

His Nibs passed a few more units without comment, then stopped at the man whose ear still dangled by a single thread. He made a tut-tutting sound.

"Look at this, Maurice. This unit is a disgrace. For heaven's sake get him patched up. What HQ would say if they saw this sort of thing, I dare not think."

"Sir." Maurice turned his head and barked at Harry over one shoulder. "Take this unit and put his lughole back on with a strip of tape."

When His Nibs reached the unit propped up on two brooms, he fairly exploded.

"This is outrageous. Really, Maurice, words fail me. How you could allow a unit to come on parade in this condition, is beyond my comprehension."

"Beg pardon, sir, it fell over, sir."

"Look at it," His Nibs went on, ignoring the interruption. "The neck's broken." He touched the head and it wobbled most alarmingly. "The eyeballs are a disgrace, half an arm is missing, one leg is about as useful as a woollen vest at a nudist picnic, and one foot is back to front."

Maurice glared at the unfortunate unit, who was doing his best to bubble-talk. His Nibs sighed deeply.

"There is little point in berating the unit now, Maurice. The damage is done. We'll have to salvage what we can and the rest had better go into the scrap-bin."

Having completed his inspection, His Nibs turned and almost by chance his gaze alighted on Mr. Goldsmith.

"Maurice, what is this unit doing tied up?"

"Beg pardon, sir, but this ain't no unit, sir. It's a consumer that Charlie Unit brought in by error, sir."

His Nibs took off his spectacles, wiped them carefully on a black-edged handkerchief, then replaced them.

"Let me get this clear. Maurice. Am I to understand that this is a live consumer? An actual, Mark one, flesh and blood citizen? In fact, not to mince words—a voter?"

"Yes, sir. A proper old Sunday-dinner-eater, go-to-Churcher, and take-a-bath-every-dayer, sir."

"And how, may I ask, did this unfortunate mistake occur?"

"Sent Charlie Unit out with a resurrection party, sir. Wandered off on his own; sort of remembered a place where 'e used to live, found this geezer—beg pardon, sir —this consumer, and brought 'im back 'ere, sir."

"Amazing!" His Nibs examined Mr. Goldsmith with great care. "A bit of luck, really. I mean, he'll need no repairs and with care he'll be ready for a Mark IV MB in no time at all."

"That's what I thought, sir." Maurice smirked and looked at Mr. Goldsmith with great satisfaction. "Might start a new line, sir. Bring 'em back alive."

"That's the next stage." His Nibs took his briefcase from Harry. "In the meanwhile you had better untie him and I'll take him down to the office."

The office was situated through the cubby hole and down twelve steps. It was surprisingly comfortable. A thick carpet covered the floor, orange wallpaper hid the walls and His Nibs seated himself behind a large, mahogany desk.

"Take a seat, my dear fellow," he invited, "I expect you'd like a cup of tea after your ordeal."

Mr. Goldsmith collapsed into a chair and nodded. The power of speech would return later, of that he felt certain. His Nibs picked up a telephone receiver.

"Tea for two," he ordered, "and not too strong. Yes, and some digestive biscuits. You'll find them filed under pending."

He replaced the receiver and beamed at Mr. Goldsmith."

"Now, I expect you're wondering what this is all about. Probably got ideas that something nasty is taking place, eh?"

Mr. Goldsmith could only nod.

"Then I am delighted to put your mind at rest. Nothing illegal is taking place here. This, my dear chap, is a government department."

Mr. Goldsmith gurgled.

"Yes," His Nibs went on, "a properly constituted government department, sired by the Ministry of Health, and complete with staff, filing cabinets and teacups. When I tell you this project sprang from the brain of a certain occupier of a certain house, situated in a certain street, not far from the gasworks at Westminister, I am certain that whatever doubts you may have entertained will be instantly dispelled."

Mr. Goldsmith made a sound that resembled an expiring bicycle tire.

"I expect," His Nibs enquired, "you are asking yourself—why?"

Mr. Goldsmith groaned.

"The answer to your intelligent question can be summed up in two words. Industrial strife. Until recently there was a dire labor shortage, and the great man to whom I referred was bedeviled by wage claims, strikes and rude men in cloth caps who would never take no for an answer. Then one night over his bedtime cup of cocoa, the idea came to him. The idea! Nay, the mental earthquake."

The door opened and a blonde vision came in, carrying a tea tray. The vision had long blond hair and wore a neat tailored suit with brass buttons. Mr. Goldsmith said: "Cor."

"Ah, Myna and the cup that cheers," announced His Nibs with heavy joviality. "Put it down on the desk, my dear. Did you warm the pot?"

"Yes, sir." Myna smiled and put her tray down.

"Have the national intake figures come through yet?" His Nibs inquired.

"Yes, sir."

"And?"

"Three thousand, nine hundred and thirty-four."

"Capital, capital." His Nibs rubbed his hands together in satisfaction, then aimed a slap at Myna's bottom, which happened to be conveniently to hand. The after-effect was alarming.

Myna jerked, stiffened her fingers, opened her mouth and bubbled three words.

"Oi . . . um . . . dud . . ."

"Excuse me," His Nibs apologized to Mr. Goldsmith, "Merely a technical hitch."

Rising quickly, he hurried round to Myna's front and twisted two brass buttons. The fingers relaxed, the eyes lit up and the mouth closed.

"Anything else, sir?" she inquired.

"No thank you, my dear," His Nibs smiled genially, "not for the time being."

Myna went out and His Nibs returned to his desk.

"Latest streamlined model," he confided, "fitted with the Mark IV computer brain, but one has to be jolly careful. Slightest pat in the wrong place and puff—the damn thing goes haywire. Now where was I? Oh, yes. The great idea."

He leaned forward and pointed a finger at Mr. Goldsmith.

"Do you know how many living people there are in Britain today?"

"Ah—ah . . ." Mr. Goldsmith began.

"Precisely." His Nibs sat back. "Sixty-two million, take or lose a million. Sixty-two million actual or potential voters. Sixty-two million consumers, government destroyers and trade unionists. Now, what about the others?"

"Others," echoed Mr. Goldsmith.

"Ah, you've got the point. The dead. The wastage, the unused. One person in two thousand dies every twenty-four hours. That makes 30,000 bucket-kickers a day, 3,000,000 a year. One man, and one man only, saw the potential. Sitting there in his terrace house, drinking his cocoa and watching television, it came to him in a flash. Why not use the dead?"

"Use the dead," Mr. Goldsmith agreed.

"Taking up valuable building space." His Nibs was becoming quite heated, "Rotting away at the state's expense, using up marble and stonemason's time, and not paying a penny in taxes. He knew what had to be done. How to get down to the 'bones' of the matter."

For a while His Nibs appeared to be lost in thought. Mr. Goldsmith stared at a slogan that had been painted in black letters on the opposite wall

WASTE NOT—WANT NOT

Presently the precise voice went on.

"First we imported a few voodoo experts from the West Indies. After all, they had been turning out zombies for centuries. But we had to improve on their technique, of course. I mean to say, we couldn't have them dancing round a fire, dressed up in loincloths and slitting cockerels' throats. So our chaps finally came up with METHY. *Ministry Everlasting Topside Hardened Youth.* No one knows what it means, of course, but that is all to the good. If some of Them from the other side got hold of the formula, I shudder to think what might happen. The basis is methylated spirit—we found that pickled fairly well—then there's R245 and a small amount of E294 and most important, 25% EH471 with 20% HW741 to cancel it out. You do follow me?"

Mr. Goldsmith shook his head, then fearful of giving offense, nodded violently.

"You have keen perception," His Nibs smiled. "It makes a nice change to talk to a consumer of the lower-middle class who does not confuse the issue by asking embarrassing questions. The latest stage is the Mark IV Mechanical Brain. After the unit has been repaired, de-coked, and sealed with our all-purpose invisible varnish the nasty old, meddling brain is removed and Dr. You-Know-Who inserts his M. IV M.B., which does what it's told and no nonsense. No trade unions, no wage claims— no wages, in fact—no holidays, no food. Give 'em a couple of cups of METHY a day and they're good for years. Get the idea?"

Mr. Goldsmith found his voice.

"Who employs them?"

"Who doesn't?" His Nibs chuckled, then lowered his voice to a confidential whisper.

"Keep this under your hat, but you may remember a certain very large house situated at the end of the Mall, which had rather a lot of problems over the housekeeping bills.".

Mr. Goldsmith turned pale.

"Not any more. All the lower servants were elevated from the churchyard, and some of the senior go out through one door and come back in through another, if you get my meaning. In fact there has been a suggestion . . . Well, never mind, that is still but a thought running round in a cabinet.

"Now, what are we going to do about you?"

Mr. Goldsmith stared hopefully at his questioner. He dared to put forward a suggestion.

"I could go home."

His Nibs smilingly shook his head.

"I fear not. You've seen too much and thanks to my flapping tongue, heard too much. No, I think we'd better give you the treatment. A nice little street accident should fill the bill. You wouldn't fancy walking under a moving bus, I suppose?"

Mr. Goldsmith displayed all the symptoms of extreme reluctance.

"You're sure? Pity. Never mind, Harry can simulate these things rather well. A broken neck, compound fracture of both legs; nothing we can't fix later on, then a tip-top funeral at government expense and the certainty of life after death. How's that sound?"

Mr. Goldsmith gulped and started a passionate love affair with the door.

"I can see you are moved," His Nibs chuckled. "You've gone quite pale with joy. I envy you, you know. It's not all of us who can serve our country. Remember: 'They also serve who only lie and rotticate.' Ha . . . ha . . . ha . . ."

His Nibs roared with uncontrollable merriment and lifted the receiver of his desk telephone.

"Myna, be a good girl and get Harry on the intercom. What! Tea break! We'll have none of that nonsense here. Tell him to get down here in two minutes flat, or I'll have him fitted with an M. IV MB before he can put water to teabag."

He slammed the receiver down and glared at Mr. Goldsmith.

"Tea break! I promise you, in five years' time there'll be no more tea breaks or dinner breaks, or three weeks' holiday with pay. We'll teach 'em."

The door opened and Harry all but ran into the office. He stamped his feet, stood rigidly to attention and swung up a salute.

"Resurrection Operator Harry Briggs reporting, sir."

His Nibs calmed down, wiped his brow on the black-edged handkerchief and reverted to his normal, precise manner of speech.

"Right, Harry, stand easy. This consumer is to be converted into a unit. I thought something in the line of a nice, tidy street accident. He won't be a missing person then, see. What are your suggestions?"

"Permission to examine the consumer, sir?"

His Nibs waved a languid hand.

"Help yourself, Harry."

Harry came over to Mr. Goldsmith and tilted his head forward so that his neck was bared.

"A couple of nifty chops should break his neck, sir, and I could rough his face up a bit—bash it against the wall. Then, with your permission, sir, run a ten-ton truck over his stomach—won't do 'is guts much good but 'e won't be needing 'em."

"Methy," His Nibs explained to Mr. Goldsmith, "works through the nervous system. The stomach is surplus to requirements."

"Then I thought a couple of swipes with an iron bar about 'ere." Harry pointed to Mr. Goldsmith's trembling thighs. "And 'ere." He indicated a spot above the ankles.

"Won't do to touch the knee caps, seeing as 'ow they're 'ard to replace."

"You'll have no trouble with repairs afterwards?" His Nibs inquired.

"Gawd bless us, no, sir. A couple of rivets in the neck, a bit of patching up here and there. We'll have to replace the eyes. They gets a bit runny after a bit. Otherwise, 'e'll make a first class unit, such as you can be proud of, sir."

"Very creditable." His nibs beamed his approval. "You'd better fill in an LD142 and lay on transport to transfer the eh . . . unit to the accident point. Let me see . . ." He consulted a desk diary. "Today's Wednesday—coroner's inquest on Friday—yes, we can fit the funeral in next Tuesday."

"Tuesday, sir," Harry nodded.

"Then your resurrection units can get cracking Tuesday night. No point in letting things rot, eh?"

His Nibs roared again and Harry permitted himself a respectful titter.

"Well, my dear chap," His Nibs said to Mr. Goldsmith. "This time next week you should be doing something useful."

"Where were you thinking of fitting 'im in, sir?" Harry inquired.

"We'll start him off as a porter at Waterloo Station. The railway union have a wage claim in the pipeline and one more nonindustrial action vote will do no harm. Right, Harry, take him away."

Fear may make cowards; it can also transform a coward into a man of action. The sight of Harry's large hand descending on to his neck triggered off a series of reflexes in Mr. Goldsmith which culmintated in his leaping from his chair and racing for the door. His behavior up to that moment had been cooperative, so both His Nibs and Harry were taken by surprise and for three precious moments could only stare after him with speechless astonishment. Meanwhile, Mr. Goldsmith was through the door and passing Myna, who presumably had not been programmed for such an emergency, for she sat behind her desk, typing away serenely, ignoring Harry's bellows of rage. But they spurred the little man to greater efforts and he mounted the stairs with the determination of an Olympic hurdler chasing a gold medal. He burst into the cellar, by-passing the recumbent units, and was on his way to the exit before a startled Maurice had been galvanized into action.

He was like a rabbit chased by two blood-thirsty hounds, when he pounded up the ramp and came to the waste ground. A sickly moon played hide and seek from behind scudding clouds and a black cat screamed its fear and rage, as he went stumbling over mounds and potholes, discarded tins clattering before his blundering feet. They were about twenty feet behind, silent now, for the unmentionable was heading for the domain of the commonplace and their business must be done in shadows without sound or word.

Mr. Goldsmith crossed a cobbled road, galloped under a railway arch and stumbled into a narrow alley. A convenient hole in a fence presented itself; he squeezed through just before running footsteps rounded the nearest corner. They came to a halt only a few paces from his hiding place. Maurice's voice was that of a weasel deprived of a supper.

"The little bleeder's got away."

"Won't get far," Harry comforted.

"Better get back," Maurice admitted reluctantly. "His Nibs will have to notify a DPC."

The footsteps shuffled, then retreated and Mr. Goldsmith dared to breathe again. He emerged from his hole and began to trudge wearily down the alley. He wandered for a long time, completely lost, shying from shadows, running before a barking dog, adrift in a nightmare. He came out into a small square and there on the far side, its steeple reaching up towards the moon, was a church. The doors were tight shut, but the building evoked childhood memories, and he knelt on the steps, crying softly, like a child locked out by thoughtless parents.

Heavy footsteps made him start and he rose quickly, before casting a terrified glance along the moonlit pavement. A tall, burly figure was moving towards him with all the majesty of a frigate under full sail. His silver buttons gleamed like stars in a velvet sky. His badge shone like a beacon of hope. Mr. Goldsmith gave a cry of joy and ran towards his protector. He gripped the great coarse hands; he thrust his face against the blue tunic and sobbed with pure relief.

"Now, what's all this?" the officer inquired. "Not more dead men that talk?"

"Hundreds of them." Mr. Goldsmith stammered in his effort to be believed. "They are emptying the churchyards. You've got to stop them."

"There, there. You leave it all to me, sir. Just come along to the station and we'll get it all down in a statement."

"Yes . . . yes." Mr. Goldsmith perceived the sanity in such an arrangement. "Yes, I . . . I will make a statement. Then you'll lock me up, won't you? So they can't reach me?"

"Anything you say," the constable agreed. "We'll lock you up so well, no one will ever be able to reach you again. Come along now."

They moved away from the locked church with Mr. Goldsmith pouring out a torrent of words. The policeman was a good listener and encouraged him with an occasional: "Beyond belief, sir . . . You don't say so, sir . . . It only goes to show . . . Truth is stranger than fiction."

Mr. Goldsmith agreed that it was, but a disturbing factor had caused a cold shiver to mar his newly acquired sense of well-being.

"Why are we going down this alley?"

"A short cut, sir," the constable replied. "No sense in tiring ourselves with a long walk."

"Oh." Mr. Goldsmith snatched at this piece of logic like a condemned man at the rope which is to hang him. "Is the station far?"

"A mere stone's throw, sir. A last, few steps, you might say."

They progressed the length of the passage, then turned a corner. The officer trod on an upturned dustbin lid and promptly swore. "Damned careless of someone. You might have broken your neck, sir."

"This is the way I came," Mr. Goldsmith stated and the policeman's grip tightened.

"Is it now, sir? Sort of retracing your footsteps."

Hope was sliding down a steep ramp as Mr. Goldsmith started to struggle. "You . . . ." But the grip on his arm was a band of steel. He clawed at the blue tunic and twisted a silver button. The bubbling words came from a long way off.

"Oi . . .um . . . dud . . ."

The moon peeped coyly from behind a cloud and watched a burly but dead policeman drag a struggling little man towards eternity.